Also by Patrice Lawrence:

Orangeboy
Indigo Donut
Rose, Interrupted
Eight Pieces of Silva

SPLINTERS OF SUNSHINE

PATRICE LAWRENCE

Hodder
Children's
Books

HODDER CHILDREN'S BOOKS

First published in Great Britain in 2021 by Hodder & Stoughton

1 3 5 7 9 10 8 6 4 2

Text copyright © Patrice Lawrence, 2021

The moral rights of the author have been asserted.

Images used under license from Shutterstock.com

A CIP catalogue record for this book is available from the British Library.

Trade ISBN 978 1 444 95477 7
Waterstones Exclusive ISBN 978 1 444 96596 4

Typeset by Avon DataSet Ltd, Arden Court, Alcester, Warwickshire

Printed and bound in Great Britain by Clays Ltd, Elcograf S.p.A

The paper and board used in this book
are made from wood from responsible sources.

Hodder Children's Books
An imprint of Hachette Children's Group
Part of Hodder & Stoughton
Carmelite House
50 Victoria Embankment
London EC4Y 0DZ

An Hachette UK Company
www.hachette.co.uk

www.hachettechildrens.co.uk

Librarians and booksellers, we've needed you
more than ever to guide us to new worlds.
Thank you.

Benni

Dear Spey,

There are so many things I want to say to you. But words aren't my speciality. I don't know how much time I should spend hunting for the right ones.

There's a bit of me that hopes for a happy ending, but, man, I never did like fairy tales. I never wanted to rescue no one nor be rescued by no one. Seriously, Spey, even as a kid, I didn't want to be that prince scratching myself up on thorn bushes just to kiss a girl I've never seen before. And if I was Aladdin, that lamp was gonna stay right where it was because, one thing I do know, Spey, nothing comes for free. There's always gonna be a debt that needs paying.

Maybe you were different when you were a small kid. I wish I'd been around to know. Sorry. Maybe you *were* the hero in your stories. I stayed in a kids' home once and there was a girl called Beatrice. She swore that her mum was a big-time movie star and was too busy racking up blockbusters to look after her. Just one more film and her mum would be on her way back to England to pick up our girl in her limousine. Of course none of us believed her, but it was only when I was way older and saw it on telly that I realised she'd taken it all from *Tracy Beaker*. I still hope everything turned out all right for Beatrice, though.

Back to us, Spey, because this is what it's all about – you and me. The Better Dads guy told me to write down everything I want to say in a letter then cut out the bits that it's best I hold back.

Is it still a letter if I'm talking into a phone recorder? I'm gonna say 'yes'. If I write a letter, I'm gonna worry too much if I'm getting my spelling right. That's never been my strong point. I missed too much school when I was a kid. These *are* the words I want to send you. Though, man, I'm gonna sound old now. I'm trapped in those days when the only reason you speak into a phone is to hear someone speak back. It seems long ago, but close too. Prison time messes with your head. The days you remember are the ones when something happens and most times, that something isn't good.

Okay. I'm definitely gonna cut that bit out if I ever pass this on to you. I might even just dump it all if it ends up sounding like a load of whinge. You don't wanna hear me groaning on about prison when I'm the one that put me here. I haven't come back into your life to make excuses. I want to give you something positive, not string you a load of excuses. So this is what I want to say, Spey. The Better Dads guy told us that we have to take steps to rebuild ourselves and our relationships, like with Alcoholics

Anonymous. The step I've reached is about making amends, with you and all my kids.

So this is it, Spey. It's time for me to be the dad you deserve.

Love, Benni

Spey

Mum says it's a Christmas snowball. It's her family tradition and the time has come for it to be ours too. It's supposed to be a drink but it looks like an omelette in a glass with a cherry on top. I don't want my mouth anywhere near it, but Mum's happy and it's making her talk about being a kid. That doesn't happen often and usually if she starts to say something she'll stop, like she's been poked. Now she's smiling.

'Christmas wasn't Christmas until Aunty Miranda cracked open the Advocaat,' Mum says. 'She was in charge of pouring.'

Mum wiggles her glass so the yellow gloop wobbles. The cherry she's been trying to float makes its last dive to the bottom and stays there.

'How old were you?' I ask.

'What?' She's staring at the cherry like her mood's getting ready to follow it down.

'How old were you when Christmas was Christmas?'

'Eight or nine.' She smiles at me. 'They started us young, our lot. See what a good parent I am, Spey? I saved your snowball induction until you were fifteen.'

She points to my glass on the table. Custard or frothy

banana yoghurt or . . . Yeah, an omelette in a glass with a neon cherry spiked on a cocktail stick and balanced across the rim.

Mum tips back her glass. The drink's so thick it should bounce off her lips and down again. I lean over and pick up my snowball. Even calling it a snowball . . . Because everyone wants to drink yellow snow. I sniff it. Sweet, but not creamy. I take the cocktail stick and ease off the cherry. It plops into the drink.

'Stop delaying,' Mum kind of sings at me.

I could joke about reporting her to social services for child cruelty, but Mum doesn't like those jokes. She reckons that if someone had done that for my dad, he would have turned out differently.

I gulp some back. It's actually okay. Sort of fizzy milkshake with alcohol. I take another gulp. Half of it's gone. That's way too quick. I put my glass down and realise Mum's is virtually empty. It's only the froth that makes it appear she still has loads to drink. I watch her refill her glass; a side-eye look so she won't notice. It's half-yellow-stuff and half-lemonade. She drops in another cherry that bumps fists with the sunk one in the bottom of the glass. At least they'll displace some of the alcohol.

'Shall we get on with Christmas Eve, then?' she says.

'Yeah!' Maybe it was the snowball, but my 'yeah' was properly cheerful.

'Well, sort out the music, Spey!'

I scroll through my playlist. There's nothing on here to power a Christmas Eve tree-decorating session. We were supposed to do it a couple of weeks ago, but somehow we just never got round to it. I think Mum puts it off because it reminds her that we're heading for another Christmas without Fi.

'Oh, look! They still work!'

Mum's dragged a string of lights out of the Christmas box and plugged them in. They're bright orange and shaped like chilli peppers. They must have been Fi's. She took almost nothing when she went off to uni eight years ago. Mum thought it was because she was always planning to come back. I knew it was because she wanted to start again. She's already phoned to wish us a happy Christmas. It's nine hours ahead in Japan.

I plug the speakers into my phone and press play, turning the volume right up. For a moment, Mum goes still and then she grins.

'Most excellent choice!' She starts singing along.

I used to think that I was the only Black boy in my school who knows all the words to 'Bohemian Rhapsody'. Though that couldn't be too hard, as I'm one of the only Black boys in my school, full stop. There's five scattered through Years Seven and Eight, and me and Michael in Year Ten. He's the one who knows all the words too, or I assume he does. He played the whole thing on his cello at the Christmas assembly. Even the Galileo bits. Mum said afterwards that she

6

didn't know a cello could make a sound like that.

The sound Mum makes when she's singing is good, though. She hits all the right notes, which is more than I've ever done, even when I was a little kid. We rummage through the Christmas box doing alternate *mamma mias*. Mum's the low *mammas* and I'm up high. Maybe the snowball helped with that too. Then we're on to 'We Will Rock You' as we try to untangle tinsel. The piece I'm struggling with is so long it could zipwire Santa in from Lapland.

'You're making it worse,' Mum says. 'I'll do it.'

As she untwists tinsel from the last of the fairy lights, I dig through the box to pick out some baubles. Loads are cracked, probably because Mum chucked them back in like grenades when she split up with Pete last year. I find seven decent ones then realise that two of them are missing the little wire hoop to thread cotton through. We're down to five: a small and silver one, two gold ones, a giant knobbly green one and a wooden one painted to look like Jiji, the sarcastic black cat from *Kiki's Delivery Service*.

I look at the baubles, then back at the tree. I don't think we screwed in the base properly because it's leaning off the coffee table like it wants to take a bow. Mum tries to straighten it.

'You better put those windowside,' she says.

'You sure?'

We both glance out. Most of our neighbours look like they went to John Lewis in a sleigh and brought the whole of the Christmas hall back with them.

Mum shakes her head. 'Those new people opposite must have kidnapped Rudolph. No one sells fake reindeer that big.'

'Maybe it *is* a real one. They killed it and stuffed it.'

'Or sedated it.'

'Or hypnotised it.'

We look down at our decorations and Mum sighs. 'Yes, hypnotised.'

'This is for us,' I say. 'Not them.'

'Yeah.' Mum draws the curtains. 'Of course it is. Hand me a bauble.'

I go for the big green one.

'Blimey,' she says. 'This is the only one left over from a set I bought for Fi's first Christmas. Because you know what's good for a toddler? A load of shiny baubles that shatter into deadly shards if you so much as breathe on them.'

'Did she like them?' I ask.

Mum half-smiles. It's hard to imagine Fi liking much, or at least showing it, though she seems to like being far, far away from us. As she's eleven years older than me, all I can really remember are the blow-up rows with Mum.

'She completely ignored them,' Mum says. 'My mother bought her a shed-load of plastic crap and she was happily distracted with that. Never before have I been so happy for plastic crap.'

'She seems to be enjoying Christmas in Japan,' I say.

'Yeah,' Mum says. 'In KFC.'

I don't know why, but that makes me laugh. According to Fi, Christmas lunch in KFC is a big thing in Tokyo. 'I Was Born to Love You' comes on. How do I even know this song? It's not one of Freddie Mercury's most famous.

'If I was ever stupid enough to get married,' Mum says, 'I'd dance down the aisle to this!'

She tugs some untangled tinsel out of the Christmas box and flings it around her neck. Then she grabs the Advocaat bottle. I think she's going to swig it back neat, but, no, it's a microphone and my mother knows every single word. What else can I do but film it? That will definitely go to Fi.

'Ah!' Mum slumps on to the sofa. 'Freddie could be really romantic when he wanted to. Though the video had him chasing a posh white girl through some swish apartment. What's the point?' She waves the bottle. 'Everyone knew he was gay!'

I give Mum another one of my side-eyes, but this time she catches it. She raises her eyebrows.

'I'm not being homophobic, Spey. I just don't like being lied to.' She sits forward. 'Put Jiji at the top. We need good luck to watch over us.'

I have to stretch up on to tiptoes to reach anywhere near the top of the tree. My calf tendons ping. I'm not sure if I hear it or just feel it because Freddie and the rest of Queen have headed over to the Seven Seas of Rhye and no one can hear anything above that chorus. I manage to loop the thread from the bauble around a highish branch and slowly let my calves relax. I imagine my tendons whipping back into position like the plug flex in a vacuum cleaner. (Mum says that was one of my favourite games when I was three – pushing the button on the vacuum cleaner for the plug to shoot in. I was always a cheap kid.)

'A couple of inches more and you'll be as tall as your father,' Mum says.

'Not very tall, then,' I say.

'Nope. I'm good like that. I don't mind short arses.'

'Thanks, Mum.'

I look at the last three baubles. Maybe I can manage a sort of triangle design.

Mum comes up behind me. 'Sorry, Spey. That wasn't the best thing to say. It's the snowballs. All quiet and then they thwack you round the head with alcohol and your mouth goes off.'

I hang one of the gold baubles. The thread barely stretches over the branch and it's balancing on the tip. It'll just take someone to sneeze across the road for it to drop off. Maybe I should leave a cushion underneath, just in case. Mum tries to push the other gold bauble up another branch. She's not having much more luck than me.

'Your dad wanted to call you Frederick,' she says.

I double take. 'As in Mercury?'

Mum's laugh is even louder than 'Seven Seas'. 'I don't think he's into seventies rock. Not unless he's changed a lot since we were together. No, after Frederick Douglass.'

A Black guy who fought injustice. (Mum's made sure I'm up on my Black history.) That makes sense. Mum once told me that my father became a conscious man in prison. I had to look up what that means. Apparently, a conscious man takes responsibility for his own actions and blames no one else. There's also a pretty good reggae song called 'Conscious Man' but Mum heard me playing it and gave me the bad-eye because she says it's sexist. If my father came over all conscious, it didn't stop him having two women pregnant at the same time. Oh, and going back to prison again. And again.

'What did he think of "Spey"?' I ask, though it's more out of politeness. I'm not interested in knowing what he thinks about anything.

Another loud laugh. 'He absolutely bloody hated it. "What? You think he's some posh boy or something? Sticking him with that Latin crap! The boy's going to be bullied for the rest of his days!"'

Mum always does a slightly weird accent when she's pretending to be my father. It makes him sound like Hagrid. Pity he isn't Hagrid. I'd be a bit taller.

'That's when I decided you were going to have every opportunity,' Mum says. 'You were not going to be some stupid stereotype like your—' She takes a gulp of snowball. 'You don't get bullied at school, do you?'

I shake my head, but then I haven't told anyone that

11

Spey's taken from Latin for 'to hope'. They probably think it's just some weird Black-boy name. Grandma says I sound like a neutered cat. Fi never tells anyone her full name's Fiducia, neither. That's 'faith' in Latin. It's probably another reason why she's permanently vexed at Mum.

'I'm so proud of you,' she says. 'You've dealt with all the crap and come through it so . . . so fine.'

'I have an excellent mother, remember?'

Her eyes narrow. 'Are you expecting big presents?'

I smile mysteriously even though we both know that all the money's gone into getting me a new laptop. Mum must have worked out my present to her too. Fi can probably smell those Lush bath bombs from Japan.

'Let's get this done!' She bounces off the sofa, trailing pink tinsel behind her.

I hang the silver bauble. The tinsel gets draped in that droopy uneven way that you never see on Christmas cards. We finish up with the chilli lights just as Freddie and the gang are about to explode like an atom bomb that's out of control.

'I wonder if Michael ever tried this one on his cello,' Mum says.

I try and make cello sounds playing 'Don't Stop Me Now'. That makes us both laugh again. We stand back and admire our Christmas tree effort and high-five.

'Are you going to help sort out that duck for dinner tomorrow?' Mum asks.

'Yeah. Of course.'

I've no idea what 'sorting out a duck' means, but I know Mum's bought a whole load of luxury ham and olives for starters. There's panettone for pudding as well as mince pies, the deep ones, so you're not just chewing pastry, and cream. I've spotted freshly squeezed orange juice too, though Mum reckons it was freshly squeezed in a factory a couple of weeks ago. We have an old-school tin of chocolates and random biscuits with ginger pieces in them. Mum's bought crackers and even some special Christmas paper serviettes decorated with blue angels. *And* there's some of those half-baked croissants you warm up in the oven for breakfast.

I turn off the overhead light and Mum flicks on the chillies. There's a warm glow.

'Something's still missing,' Mum says.

She reaches behind an armchair and pulls out a plastic bag full of presents. She empties it out under the tree. I think it's just wrapped up boxes for show, maybe left over from Mum's work decorations, but I see a label with my name on it. I raise my eyebrows and reach over to look.

Mum lunges in front of me. 'No cheating!'

'Who are these from?'

'Your nan and stuff.'

'And stuff?'

'Fi sent something from Tokyo.'

'Did she?'

'She sent it in October. Just in case.'

'And the rest?'

'Some little things from me.'

'Mum!'

'Sorry, Spey. I can't resist.'

I kiss her on her forehead. 'Thank you, but you don't have to. The laptop's enough.'

'I know, but you're getting older. And soon you'll be like Fi.'

'I'm not planning to move to Japan, Mum.'

'Maybe not. But you'll spread your wings. That's what I brought you both up to do.' She smiles. 'Shall we watch a film?'

'Sure.' It's been a long time since we've done that. Probably only a couple of times this year.

'Do you mind if I choose?'

'I trust you.' Though only now that she's stopped trying to make me watch the stuff she liked as a kid. I didn't mind *The Bionic Woman* but that bald American kid with the big head and the dog that sleeps on the roof of its kennel? Nah.

Mum checks the DVD cabinet. She reckons our Wi-Fi is too dodgy to risk streaming but I think she just likes the feeling of clicking the box open and sliding the disc into the slot. I check my phone. There's a whole list of messages. Vinny and Drew went into central and got thrown out of Leicester Square McDonald's. They're on their way home now. I don't need to see the picture of puke, though. Marta's hanging with her sisters, cooking up something special for

14

tomorrow. Paul's a Jehovah's Witness and they don't celebrate, but he's wished me Happy Christmas anyway. Oli's mum's French so they're having their big night tonight.

I take a picture of our tree. Chilli lights, five baubles with a cartoon cat instead of a star. Two years ago, I'd have posted it with a stupid caption on my private account, the one Mum doesn't know about. But now . . . it's just a picture.

Mum sees me. 'Are you sending it to Fi?'

'Maybe.'

I won't, though. It'll be like telling her how much fun we have without her. And she'll prefer the one of Mum singing along with Freddie, anyway.

'This one!' Mum's waving *The Blues Brothers*. 'Car crashes and nuns and singing. It's proper Christmas fare.'

'Good choice.'

We settle down. The film goes on for ages. I always forget that, but the music's good.

'Most of them are dead now,' Mum says. 'Ray Charles, Aretha Franklin, John Belushi. Even Carrie Fisher.'

I don't know what I'm supposed to say to that. We watch in silence as Carrie Fisher stalks John Belushi through a sewer. She's carrying a gun the size of a small tree. Mum nudges me.

'Life's short,' she says. 'We have to make the most of it.'

When the film finishes, we say Merry Christmas to each other and I go upstairs. She's digging around in the DVD drawer, like she's planning to keep on until morning.

Technically, I could open my presents now as it is Christmas Day. Mum says that when I was little, I never used to wake up early on Christmas like other kids. She used to prod me awake at about ten in the morning because she was getting bored of waiting for me.

In my room, I sit on the bed and go through my friends' stories. Some are having a good time and I flick past those. It's the other ones that make me stop. Shauna's stuck with her dad and her step-mum, who's nearer Shauna's age than her dad's. She's videoed her baby sister snoring and is complaining that she's got to share a room with her. Marta had a row with her sister and she's sitting outside her flat filming the drunk people coming out of the pub opposite.

I lie down and turn off the light. I wonder what Mum's watching now and turn down my music to see if I can work it out. It's got a woman in it . . . That's all I can hear. It's probably *Love, Actually* again. No wonder she didn't mind me going to bed. She always forgets the porn bit with Martin Freeman and stares at her feet until it's over.

I'm glad she didn't realise how much I was dreading tonight. I didn't even want school to end because it meant Christmas was closer. I just wanted to stand still and close my eyes and let the days stream past me. But it was all right. Mum wasn't so upset this year about Fi not coming home. I don't feel that I have to try and be extra-special because it's just me and Mum with no sister and no dads. I'm glad we're not going to Grandma's tomorrow. I've got a day's delay until

I have to sit through Uncle and the aunties bigging up my cousins. All of them are going to be top lawyers, or accountants or heart consultants, or ready to score thirteen GCSE grade 9s as soon as they hit Year Seven.

Instead, me and Mum are going to eat the duck and open our presents and watch *Up* and have the most chilled Christmas Day ever.

I pull on my headphones and carry on scrolling through my phone. I don't want music. When I close my eyes, songs take me to different places, and I can't control it. I find a Sherlock Holmes story. Mum read me a load of them when I was eight. She tells me now that she handpicked them to avoid the dodgy ones. I choose one where I know who the killer is. It's the first Christmas Eve in ages I've gone to bed without a stress lump in my stomach. I'm not in the mood for surprises.

Dee

Rosa 'Deep Secret'
SUPERHERO
RED DOUBLE KNOCKOUT
DEEP SECRET

In my bedroom at Nan's, I had a bed, a wardrobe, a desk, drawers and a table next to my bed. Nan bought me a rug shaped like a white rose. I told Nan I didn't think I wanted it because the names of red roses are better. Superhero, Red Double Knockout, Deep Secret. There's even one called Amalia. I'm never gonna have kids, but if I did, I'd call the first one Amalia, no matter if it was a boy or girl. Nan couldn't change the rug because it was a bargain at Dalston Waste. It was the only one they had, but she thought we could work out how to dye it. She forgot, so I tried to do it with some strawberry Ribena, though it didn't work.

In my room at Chalkleighs, I had a bed, a wardrobe, drawers and a table next to my bed. The bed had drawers underneath it for my clothes. The table next to my bed had a drawer with a key where I could put my special things. My special thing was my flower book, but that got torn up.

My room here has a window and a mattress and some

cardboard boxes and a ceiling. The duvet and pillows smell like mud. The mattress smells like puddles. The floor's made from plastic tiles and there's a rug that isn't a white rose or a red rose. It's square and made from wool in different colours like scribbles. There's dark patches from stuff that was spilled on it. It's not Ribena. Tomorrow's Christmas, but we haven't got no decorations. Ingram's gone out. I asked him if maybe he could get some, because maybe he wants his flat to look nice. He just laughed. He said the flat's not really his no more and, anyway, we're running low on electricity, so he's got to use his money for that.

Nan used to love programmes that showed you inside other people's houses. After she picked me up from school, she'd make herself a cup of tea and we'd sit on the sofa and watch them together. She complained that some people's houses were too shiny and you'd need sunglasses every time you went in the kitchen. She said saucepans don't shine like that if you use them to cook with, nor does a cooker, even if you clean it twice a week. *What do you want a posh steel kettle for, Dee, when you can get a Russell Hobbs for a tenner at Dalston Waste? It's gonna boil water just as well.* She said a home should be lived in and one or two little smudges or stains made it real.

Not these stains, though. I think about what Nan would say if she came to this place.

Dee, why are you bringing me down these steps? You know I hate steps. They make me dizzy.

19

Dee, why's there a mattress against that window instead of glass?

Dee, was that fridge on fire? It's all burnt and the door's open.

Dee, what are you supposed to sit on? Those dirty old boxes?

Dee, walk right back up those stairs and find your way home.

I haven't got no home, Nan. This is it.

Spey

Screaming. It's head back, big-throat screaming. It's last girl in the cabin in the forest who's just caught sight of the Babadook screaming. I open my eyes. The screaming doesn't stop. The screamer must have a couple of extra lungs because normal people need to draw breath.

I reach out of my bed and touch the window. It's not shaking but it should be. Any second now, there's going to be a crack. I shift myself and lift the blind. The kids next door have opened their presents and they must have had Smarties for breakfast because they're fuelled. The girl's on a wooden tricycle going so fast she looks like she's going to smash through the fence at the end of the garden and into Tesco's car park. The boy is setting up a marble chute. I actually want to go down and help him, but when his dad tries to lend a hand, the boy screams. So that's where it's coming from. The dad steps back, but you know he's going to dive in again any second soon. I let the blind flop down.

I check the time. It's eight-thirty, way too early to get up. I close my eyes again, but the boy's scream button's jammed and the noise is burning a straight line up through my brain. If I sniff too hard, I'll smell scorching. I sit up. I wonder if Mum's been disturbed too. I know she wasn't planning any early morning preparations. She wanted to enjoy the lie-in. I listen but can't hear Mum about yet, not unless her eardrums have already exploded and she's collapsed in the kitchen, crying for help.

I pull on some trackie bottoms. That's another good thing about staying home on Christmas Day. I don't have to check the back of my wardrobe for the smart stuff. I throw on yesterday's T-shirt too. I go out into the hallway and into the bathroom and do what I need to do, pleased that the snowball doesn't leave my body the same way it looked when it went in. I come out and I still can't hear Mum. Maybe she fell asleep on the sofa watching another film to clear Martin Freeman's butt cheeks out of her head. Something like *Shaun of the Dead*. Though Martin Freeman's in that too. Maybe *Saw III*. That could work.

I plod down the stairs. I can smell that Lush gift box from here. I can almost taste it. I suppose I could make Mum a cup of coffee and take it up to her. I forgot her birthday this year and we had to go to Grandma's for Mother's Day. So, yeah, I owe her. And Fi would never do that. I'm not trying to be Best Child or anything. Well, actually, I am. I'm always with Mum over Christmas so Fi doesn't have to feel guilty about not returning. That gives me automatic Best Child status.

I open the sitting room door. There's a man on the sofa, fast asleep.

Okay, I'll be even clearer. There's a man on the sofa that I've never seen before in my life. And, no, he hasn't got a white beard and matching red trousers and jacket. I stare at him. He's . . . I don't know, in his forties? He's wearing jeans, a green jumper and I can see the edge of a red tee beneath it. Christmas colours but still not Santa. His hair's razed short, with a couple of nicks from where the clippers caught his scalp. His toe's poking through one of his socks.

Reverse back a minute, Spey. There's a man you've never seen before fast asleep on the sofa and you're just standing here checking out his fashion. You have to wake him up! But what if he's on some weird trigger and jumps up and grabs me by the throat?

How the hell did he get in? I check the window behind the Christmas tree. It's closed, but that means nothing. He could have broken in and shut it afterwards. The tree's in the way, though, and none of our baubles have shifted. They still look as if a big yawn would make them fall off.

I should call the police. That's the safest option. They'd even get here quickly because full-on Christmas Day stress hasn't got going yet. A door opens upstairs. My heart starts banging. Mum! The cold water tank rumbles. She's in the bathroom. Okay. I have a little bit of time to get him out before she comes down.

'Oi!' It's a shouty whisper. 'Get up!'

The man opens one eye slowly, than the other one, like he's been overproducing the eye gum. He pushes himself up slowly and groans.

'You can't stay here!'

I'm pretty sure that's the bathroom door opening upstairs. *Please, Mum. Don't come down yet.*

He rubs his eyes. 'Spey?'

He knows my name? Well, that's not tough to work out. It's written on most of the presents under the tree.

'I'm going to call the police,' I say. 'Right now.'

'No.' He frowns. 'Please don't do that.'

I can't really do it because I've left my phone on my bed. But I can run upstairs and stop Mum from coming down. We can lock ourselves in the bathroom until the police do come.

Mum hasn't returned to her bedroom though. She's coming down the stairs. Her footsteps are quick, like her Mum-psychic powers know there's something wrong.

'No, Mum!' I dive towards the door. It slams shut, but she pushes the door hard and I stumble back. She stands in the doorway, looking from me to the stranger on our sofa. I try and pull her back towards the hall.

'I've got this, Mum! I'll stay here and make sure he doesn't take anything. You go and call the police.'

Mum takes my hand and gently prises me off her.

'Morning, Gilda,' the intruder says.

'Mum?' I turn to her. 'He knows your name.'

Then I realise that she's wearing lipstick. I only notice because it's the very red Christmas lipstick.

'Mum?' I say again.

'Yes, Spey,' she says. 'I wanted to catch you before you came down. You're never usually up this early unless you

24

have to be. It's going to be three of us for lunch today. This is Benni, your dad.'

If my mouth had been open, it would have snapped shut.

'Happy Christmas, Spey,' the intruder says, holding out a shoe box wrapped in penguin paper.

I turn round and go back upstairs.

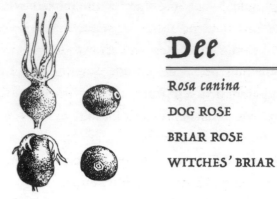

Dee

Rosa canina

DOG ROSE

BRIAR ROSE

WITCHES' BRIAR

Ingram hasn't come back, so I haven't got no decorations. We haven't got much electricity, neither. I'm gonna keep the lights off. Ingram keeps food in his room, so I'm gonna have a look if he doesn't come back. He doesn't lock it. He says there's nothing worth taking.

I always used to get Christmas presents from Nan and Aunty Janet. Sometimes my mum would send something but usually Nan bought something for her to give to me.

One year, Aunty Janet bought me some manga books. She said there weren't so many words because the pictures said more. She knew I liked to make up places and the made-up places in manga were really good. She knew my imagination could do things like that too. Aunty Janet also gave me a sketchbook and pencils and told me to make my own book. She said I didn't have to show no one unless I wanted to because my stories were for me.

I made a world out of dog roses. I'd read about them

in my flower book. I had rose dogs with waistcoats and grey faces and one pink petal like a tongue and whiskers that looked like ragged robins and thorns going down their legs. Their tails had been cut off. Amandalions were mixed-up dandelions and yellow roses called Amanda roses. They had fluffy white tails and teeth like fangs. They only showed their teeth when they were mad. The rose dogs and Amandalions were mates until the Green Army made friends with The Garden Lady. Then it was war.

Aunty Janet was right. My world was as good as the manga ones and I was going to show it to Aunty Janet, but I showed it to Mum when she came to see me at Nan's. She said she'd bring it to Aunty for me. She took my pencils too and Nan's purse.

The window sill's mucky here and the light's got a shade with marching soldiers on it. All the other rooms have only got plain bulbs. I think Ingram used to have a son but he's gone now. Maybe he's gone to see him for Christmas. I wish he hadn't locked the front door.

Spey

I go and lie down on my bed. How the hell could they pull this stunt on Christmas Day? Am I supposed to feel kind and generous and think that Benni's just an extra-big present? I'm surprised he didn't wrap himself up in the penguin paper and wait for me under the tree. I'm really going to enjoy the registration-group chat when school's back.

What did you get for Christmas, Spey?

Me, Michael? A refurbished Mac and a spare father. What about you?

I suppose it makes a difference from half the kids in my year, who'll be handed £500 and their own hologram Steve Jobs.

I pick up my phone. I want to tell someone about this. I *need* to tell someone about this. Michael? I drop him a quick message.

Woke up this morning and my dad was on the sofa.

Man, I sound like Bleeding Gums Murphy in *The Simpsons*. I delete the message before sending it. I don't want to mash up his Christmas Day before it gets going. I could always message Paul. Nuh, he shouldn't be punished just because he doesn't celebrate. There's always Fi . . .

There's a knock on my door. I drop my phone on my bed.

28

It better not be him. He will not come into my room. *This is Benni, your dad.* Seriously, what did Mum expect me to do? Run up and kiss him? There's another knock. I stay where I am. Mum calls my name. The knock is now a thump. The door wood isn't thick and any second now, her fist's going to come right through.

'Please open up, Spey.'

Thump!

'If you don't open this door, I'm coming straight in. You're not too old to be told!'

Too old, Mum? I'm old enough to be responsible and mature and focus on my grades and plan for the future, but not old enough to decide if I want to meet the unknown father on Christmas Day. I shout this in my head, of course.

She knocks again. A knock, not a thump.

'Spey? I just want to explain.' She sounds tired.

I roll off my bed and go and open the door.

Mum's been crying. Her eyes are red and there's a black streak of eyeliner heading towards her ear. She steps into my bedroom and her foot slips on my school shirt. She looks down but doesn't say anything.

I don't know what to do when Mum's crying. It doesn't happen much now, except during films. She actually sobbed out loud in the middle of Picturehouse when Tony Stark died in *Endgame*. Luckily, no one noticed. She did cry a bit when she finished with Pete, but she said that was plain fury.

We stand there. Maybe we're both thinking the same thing. Four years ago, I would have flung my arms round her. It would just feel weird now that we're the same height.

'Benni called me last night,' Mum says. 'After you'd gone up. He's been writing to me from prison on and off over the last few months. To be honest, I wasn't going to reply. I hadn't heard from him for so long. But he was in a bad way, Spey, worried about coming out of prison and trying to make a new life. He didn't have much hope and sometimes Christmas makes things worse.'

'So he invited himself over?'

'No, Spey. I invited him. He'd already bought a present for you. I thought he might like to give it to you in person.'

'I don't need his presents.'

Mum takes a step back. 'Please don't use that tone about him, Spey.'

'Mum! This bloke treated you like crap. Why do you expect me to be all right with it? Why are you all right with it?'

She comes into my bedroom and closes the door. She glances around at my chaos, but still says nothing.

'Because I couldn't sit down with you and eat that bloody duck knowing that he was by himself in a hostel. It felt like a kind thing to do. And that's what I want you to do, Spey. Be kind. Just for today. And don't worry, Benni and me aren't planning to start up where we left off.'

God. I wasn't worrying about that, but I am now. 'He's just

here for a free lunch, then.'

'No. He wants to see you. And Fi met her dad, didn't she? So maybe you should too.'

Mum wasn't exactly happy about Fi meeting up with her father, but it's probably best not to bring that up now.

I say, 'What's stopped him before?'

'He was in prison, Spey. You know that. And then he came out on licence and was helping—'

'A security guard with his cashbox?'

Mum's jaws move. She is actually gritting her teeth. 'Your sister,' she says. 'He was helping your sister.'

'Fi?'

Another time, she would have laughed at the look on my face. But she's still angry. 'Of course not Fi. I've told you about your other sister, Becks.'

Yes, there's a few of us. I don't know a single one of them and as far as I care, I've only got one sister and that's Fi. She's more than enough.

Mum says, 'He was helping Becks and ended up missing a probation appointment. He got recalled to prison. That's when he reached out to me.'

'You shouldn't have invited him! Not without asking me first!'

'You'd gone to bed!' Mum tries to make her face go back to neutral, her voice too. 'And what with the snowballs and stuff, maybe I wasn't thinking. If you must know, Spey, it felt like a film. You and your dad, reunited on Christmas Day.'

'And we'll all live happily ever after.'

She wipes her eyes. The back of her hand is smudged with make-up.

'I'd really like you to join us,' she says.

She leaves, closing the door quietly behind her.

The kids start up in their garden again. There's more shrieking coming from up the street. It's pretty sunny outside, not real Christmas weather, though by the time I'm thirty we'll probably be serving our turkey under palm trees growing wild on Stoke Newington Common. I check my phone. Phoebe and Jade have sneaked out to go for a skate round the park. Phoebe's got a new board, though she's had to transfer her old wheels. There's a close-up of the wheels. Nice. Michael's helping his mum make a trifle. He focuses on a jug of cold custard. Why would you want to eat that? Maybe he deserves to hear about my jail-time dad, after all.

Oh, and here's my cousin, January, in Bali, sipping cocktails with her girlfriend. (And, yes, I really do have a cousin called January.) It's just as well my grandma isn't on Insta. The official line is that January's too busy hunched over her medical books to make family Christmas. Marta's called a truce with her sister but Shauna hasn't posted anything. I want to DM:

You got a snoring sister? This morning I found a snoring dad.

If I'd had my phone on me, I could have taken a picture of him flat out on our sofa. But maybe it's just as well I didn't. When he's gone, I don't want a keepsake.

32

I throw my phone across my bed, then I go and pick it up again. There's only one person who is going to understand this crap. And, yeah, she's going to choke on her Tokyo KFC nuggets because she's laughing so hard.

Fi and I always knew that we had different fathers but never really talked about it much. It's Mum that held us together. Neither of us had any early dad-memories at all. Fi told me she wasn't bothered about looking for hers. I found out later that she was already seeing him behind Mum's back.

I suppose it matters more to me because I'm the only brown one in our family. It's like a whole piece of me is missing. It didn't really matter so much being dadless at primary school. It was the mums and grandmas and big sisters and childminders that did the school stuff, coming to assemblies and parents' evenings and music nights. But when I moved to secondary school, it was suddenly, 'What do your parents do?' I mean, who asks that? At Beckford Academy they do. Whether I want to or not, I know that Sophie's mum runs a travelling theatre. Her dad's an architect and designed their new house from scratch. Mo Number One's dad designs equipment for microsurgery and Mo Number Two's mum's an MP.

And me? Mum runs the local doctor's surgery. Six doctors and four nurses and some interpreters and thousands of patients. If the cleaning's crap or the phones are engaged or the touch-screen appointment check-in randomly reboots, it's Mum's fault. I know this, because she's been telling me her stress stories for as long as I can remember. It doesn't bother me to tell anyone what she does. It's a distraction from when they try to work out what I am. The mixed-race kids get it straight away. The white kids are confused. Folks sometimes think I'm white, especially when my hair's cut low. But I've been asked if I'm Turkish or Colombian and once if I was North Korean. (Of course I said, 'Yes.' So the girl asked me to say something in Korean to her. I said, 'Welcome,' in Arabic because we'd learned it in playgroup.) The Black kids just raise their eyebrows, probably waiting to see what side I'm going to take.

And . . . it's the clichéd side. The absent-Black-dad side. The Black-dad-that-abandoned-my-mum side. The absent-Black-dad-that's-in-prison side. I'm sure there's a few stereotypes I've left out. I can probably top them up if I go downstairs and get to know him better.

And that's the thing. Mum should know that I don't need to know him better. It's not like he hasn't got kids to spare. The man offers out his DNA like it's McDonald's vouchers. Yeah, another damn stereotype to add to the pile.

But – what *am* I going to do? Lie in here all day? I've got no problem with that.

No problem except for the guilt (and marble-run boy screaming his head off). The guilt feels like Fi's chilli lights are stuck in my head, glowing hot, with the pointy bits poking into my brain. And the off switch has snapped. The guilt isn't about Benni, it's about Mum. Why was she really crying?

What if she wanted to say more, but I wouldn't let her? Did she close the door, so he couldn't hear what she was saying? I didn't give her a chance. He could be dangerous. Eight and a half years in prison is a long time. It changes people. He could have bullied her and made her feel so crap she agreed he could come over. She might need me downstairs to get him out. He's probably relying on me *not* going down.

I open my bedroom door and listen. Nothing.

What if he's . . . he's . . . hurt her? I run downstairs.

Mum's by herself in the kitchen. The raw duck's laid out on a chopping board.

She gives me a big smile, but doesn't say anything.

'Is everything okay, Mum?'

'Fine, apart from the fact that I went to chop some onions and they've all gone manky. I've sent Benni out for more.'

She doesn't look like she's been bullied. She looks quite happy standing there, peeling potatoes.

'Can you do the carrots for me, Spey?'

I hesitate and just stop myself from saying, 'So we're going to carry on like him coming here is normal, are we?' Mum looks at me like she's expecting it. But I don't want to do it. Muck up her Christmas, I mean. Not prepare the carrots, though that's not exactly calling to me, neither.

I say, 'Have we got another peeler?'

'You don't need to peel them. Just give them a scrub and cut them lengthways.'

I take a clean scrubbing pad from the pack beneath the sink and turn on the tap. Mum pricks the duck skin with a skewer. It looks like she's trying to kill it all over again.

She says, 'I know this is really strange, Spey, so thank you for being here.'

I scrub the carrot so hard, dots of sponge bristle are left on the skin. I turn the tap on full and rinse them down.

'Here he is,' Mum says brightly.

Yes, here he is, coming through the back gate into the garden. He's wheeling a bike, a rundown thing that looks ready to collapse. I suppose that's how he got here in the first place. A blue plastic bag's swinging from the handlebars. I want to stop looking at him, but it's hard. Technically, he's half of me, that part of me that's missing, but, man, we're so different. I can't see him in my face or my body shape or anywhere in my damn history. Mum's had to do everything. But, hey! He's bringing onions, so everything's all right!

Maybe it could never be balanced. He's got too much catching up to do. Mum's family have always been part of my life – Mum, my cousins, my small, loud grandma. (She says she has to be loud in case people trip over her. She wears bright orange trainers and her hair matches, so that's never going to happen.) Mum inherited Grandma's chin – it's made its way down to me – but her dad's height genes. I saw a picture of her in the Year Ten netball team in one of Grandma's albums. Mum's taller than all the others. I can see now that she's taller than Benni. I wonder if it bothers him?

I think it's going to bother Mum if I get much taller. She keeps reading about Black boys getting killed because of mistaken identity or just because. She doesn't want me to stand out and reckons that if I was tall, idiots would pick on me to prove themselves. I don't want to break it to her that short kids get crap too.

God! Maybe that's why Benni's really here – to help her with The Talks.

Mum has a whole long list of things to talk to me about. In Year Eight, I came home from school and she was waiting for me in the kitchen, right where she's standing now. I reckon she was there for ages, thinking it all over.

'I know things are hard for you,' she'd said.

Were they?

'Way harder than they were for me, Spey.'

Right. That's when I got it. Julius, from volleyball, he's got a white mum too. He'd warned me that it was due.

'I know that you probably won't tell me everything that's happening in your life,' Mum had said. 'Nor should you.'

Yes, definitely The Talk. Julius had told me it was just best to nod when she paused. *It's like she's telling you stuff you already know. She just wants you to know that she knows too.* So I'd nodded even when she told me why she'd fought to get me into a 'good' school which was mostly full of white kids. When I saw Julius at volleyball next time, I'd told him that Mum had been on the case.

'Best not tell her about light-skin privilege,' he'd said.

37

I had to look that one up. And, nope, I sure as hell wasn't going to go into that with Mum. I was never going to try and pass for white. Only North Korean, as long as I didn't have to talk to other North Koreans.

'Prove the racists wrong!' Mum had said. 'Get the best grades in your year. You know you can.'

And I had. But now I'm staring at the man she's trying to stop me becoming.

Benni leans the bike against our wheelbarrow and smiles through the window at us. He's heading into the kitchen. It's a small space. We're going to be so close. Right then, my stomach growls.

'Oh, no!' Mum says. 'We haven't had our Christmas breakfast yet.'

I'm happy for the diversion. 'What have we got?'

'I found the last ripe mangoes in London. There's posh yoghurt in the fridge and those croissants to heat up. It's enough for three of us.'

Three of us.

He comes into the kitchen and he is close, too close. I flatten myself against the cupboard as he passes. He slides past me and Mum easily. Maybe it's a prison habit. I suppose you don't want to step on the wrong person's toes. He leaves the bag by the sink.

'I'll give you the money,' Mum says.

'No!' He looks genuinely shocked. 'You've already helped out. And you're doing all the cooking. The least I can do is bring the onions.'

He turns to me and sort of looks me up and down. I want to meet his eyes, but I end up looking over his shoulder.

'Sorry, Spey,' he says. 'I honestly don't want to ruin your Christmas.'

'Did you think coming here would make it better?'

'Spey!' Mum's holding up the peeler like she's going to take my skin off with it.

'It's okay,' Benni says. 'I hate to think what I'd do if my father showed up unannounced.'

He and Mum swap looks. I just want to go upstairs again, but I reach round him to the fridge and take out the yoghurt.

Benni

Dear Spey,

Man, I'm gonna tell you now, I would rather stand in a dock knowing the sweatbox was waiting outside to carry me to pad-share with the most paranoid, stinking goon from the Aryan Brotherhood than put myself through that again. I knew it wasn't gonna be easy, and damn! You've really inherited your mother's hard-ass side-eye with extra-heavy attitude.

I'm glad you liked the trainers, though. It's good to know that Jordans are still a thing. They were top style when I was your age. Those old-school ones cost an arm and a leg, and, yeah, I know I owe you and your mum fifteen years of child support, but I don't think I could have hid how hurt I was if you'd just thrown them aside. Seeing you rush to try them on then catching yourself doing it, slowing yourself down and pretending it didn't matter . . . You looked like a proper kid. My kid.

But, Spey, what the hell have we got in common? Your mum was telling me about your grades and your ambitions, and I feel so proud and so helpless because there's nothing I can do for you. Of course, Gilda tries to make me feel good. She says I can show you what it's like to be 'resilient' and 'self-aware' and 'reflective', like she isn't all those things too. As well as more forgiving and kind than I should ever expect.

Anyway, I suppose I should tell you a bit more about me in case you ever want to know. Your mum knows some of it, but I told her not to tell you. I don't want her to sound like she's making excuses for me.

You probably know that I grew up in care but not how I got there. I suppose I wish now that I didn't know. My parents were married but they couldn't cope with me. They really loved me, though. I was told those two things, over and over again. They were both massive in my head, slugging it out like Godzilla versus King Kong.

Hey, Benni! Your parents really love you.

Hey, Benni! Your parents can't cope with you.

I was a baby when they gave me up. How bad could I have been for their love not to be enough?

When I was a kid, I used to watch families in supermarkets and parks to see what would happen when the kids played up. I'd see full-on tantrums, the ones where the kids threw themselves down in the middle of the aisle and just screamed. I saw one little monster shout the c-word at his granny in Sainsbury's but she still took him home. She didn't take him to her doctor's surgery and leave him and his carrycot on a pile of *Marie Claire*s like my mother did.

Man, I was only three months old. I could barely lift

my head, let alone start kicking out because I wanted more Wotsits.

Now the Better Dads guy is in my head saying, *Careful, Benni. This is for your boy, not you.* And that's the problem, Spey. I want to paint a glittering picture of your biological grandparents, but it's hard. I want to give you a gift that's even better than the Jordans. I want you to know where you come from. I want you to have an anchor, Spey, like I never did.

I thought about having one of those DNA tests so I could get more ethnic background. It's supposed to tell you where you come from, where you really belong.

I think it's too late for me, Spey. I don't belong nowhere.

Dee

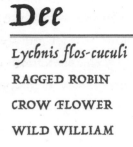

Lychnis flos-cuculi
RAGGED ROBIN
CROW FLOWER
WILD WILLIAM

There's music coming from the flat above. They're having a party. It started in the afternoon and it's been going all night. There's thumping on the ceiling and I think they're dancing. I don't dance. When I was in playgroup, they wanted you to do dances to some of the songs. We were all meant to do the same thing at the same time. I never moved the same arm or leg or hand as the other kids. Maybe I could have if I wanted to, but I didn't want to. Once, I thumped a girl on the side of her head. It wasn't deliberate, but she started screaming, so I thumped her again. That was deliberate. She was crying anyway so I didn't think it mattered. She said she didn't want to be my friend no more. I didn't care. I had Spey.

I don't like dancing because I don't like music. I kept getting glue ear when I was a kid and Nan said I was deaf for a bit, so maybe that's why. Music goes into my ears, but not together. It's bits of sound and voices. It's like when Nan broke up a jigsaw and shook it in the box so we could fit it together again. I can't put the bits of music together. I don't understand how everybody else hears something else.

Chez's older brother and his mates used to hang out in front of the dry cleaner's in the evenings. They'd play music really loud and swear at people who told them to turn it down. Nan was always out there having a go at them. Nan was pretty good at swearing too.

I want to think about Nan all the time, but it still hurts too much.

Nan showed me a ragged robin once. It was mixed in with some other flowers in a wild garden in London Fields. She said she liked ragged robin because it didn't try to pretty up. If it was a real person, no one was gonna tell it to tuck itself in. It was pink but not a soppy princess. I tiptoed past the other flowers, careful so I didn't crush nothing. I crouched down and tried to blow the leaves like it was a dandelion clock. The petals look like they're gonna float away, but they don't. Nan said they have to stay strong for the bees.

Spey

I don't want to get up. Fair enough, I never want to get up, no matter what day it is. This duvet's moulded to my shape like an alien presence. Seriously, if creatures from another planet want to conquer Earth, all they've got to do is disguise themselves as a cushy bed. Us humans would happily sink into them and stay there.

But, yeah, it's not just the sweetness of my duvet that's keeping me horizontal. It's the thought of facing him and her. I know I saw him go off on his bicycle yesterday evening, but he could have waited round the corner until it was safe to come back. He could be here.

I want to know and I don't want to know. Mum said she and him weren't planning to get back together, but what if the Christmas magic got to them?

Oh, god. What if he starts calling me 'son'? I can tell you something, Grandma's dancing back-up for Beyoncé before I call him 'Dad'.

Mum hammers on my door. It's so hard she must be using a real hammer.

'Thirty-second countdown,' she yells from outside.

She never walks right in. She says it's to preserve my privacy. I would have been happy for her to leave it there, but she didn't. After The Black Boy in a White Society Talk, I got The Porn Talk. I'd wished Julius had warned me about that one too, but apparently not everyone's mum sits them down for that discussion. Mum said she wanted me to be responsible with my privacy and it was important I knew that 'porn's not real and exploits vulnerable women'. With my shade of very light brown, it's hard to hide your blushing. I'm pretty sure she was lining up an I Don't Mind If You're Gay session as well. She kept leaving her laptop open in the kitchen with tabs open – UK Black Pride, UK Blackout, Stonewall and a couple of American ones I checked out afterwards, just because I was curious. The Sexuality Talk never did happen. Knowing Mum, she's still building up her browser bookmarks just in case. And she still does make a point of announcing when she's watching *Brooklyn Nine-Nine*.

'Time's up, Spey!' She eases open my door and peers around it. 'We need to get ready for Grandma's.'

Oh. Right.

She's wearing that bright red lipstick and I try to see behind her in case Benni's lurking in the background. Then I remember about Mum's lipstick. She says it's her warpaint to help her fight back against the snarky siblings' comments. I wonder who she was fighting against yesterday – me or Benni?

She says, 'You promised me Boxing Day pancakes, remember?'

No, I don't remember, but I need to keep her sweet.

'Mum?'

'Spey?'

'Is Benni . . . ?'

She raises an eyebrow.

'Nothing.'

She goes back downstairs and I head towards the bathroom. I check myself in the bathroom mirror. My non-afro is still non. Though not non-enough to lie flat. I'm heading towards Seth Rogen in *Superbad*. Mum reckons I should get cane row, but I really don't want the white-boy-appropriation comments by those who don't know me. Maybe I should get a DNA test and carry the results round with me to save the arguments. I did try and sneak a look at Benni's hair yesterday. There wasn't any to sneak a look at.

The kitchen looks like Santa's elves got bored of delivering presents and decided to carry out some heavy cleaning. The sink's completely empty; there's not even any food bits stuck to the drain strainer. I open the bin cupboard. The bin's empty. Yesterday, there was definitely a duck wing sticking out of a piece of foil. The dishwasher's full, though it's mostly pots. And it's definitely Mum's special stacking method, with everything falling into each other. I peer out the back door. The recycling bag's jammed – two wine bottles on top of the Advocaat bottle, a folded panettone box and loads of wrapping paper.

I take what I need out of the fridge. It's good that I don't have to reach round *him* this time. I whisk up the flour, milk and eggs and even melt a dribble of butter to add too. Just a pinch of salt, measured into my palm rather than shaken straight in. You don't want pancakes that make your mother heave. I can tell you that from experience. I heat up the frying pan and add a spoonful of oil. I wait for it to smoke before adding a ladle of batter for the test pancake. It turns from a splat to pancake-shape straight away. Two little bubbles erupt in the middle.

Mum comes into the kitchen. 'You're a proper expert, Spey.'

I flip it over and give it another minute before sliding it on to a piece of kitchen towel. Mum wraps the towel around it and takes a bite. She fans her mouth. I look down at the smoking frying pan then at the pancake and raise my eyebrows.

'Yes,' she says. 'But I'm hungry.'

I measure more batter into the frying pan. If you plan it properly, you can fit three in at once. I dig for the spatula in the mad drawer under the sink. Though finding anything in the mad drawer is an achievement.

Mum gives me a little smile. 'Benni put it there.'

She's pointing at a red pot with 'Utensils' painted on it in silver.

'It's from the work Secret Santa,' Mum says. 'I think it popped up last year too. Definitely the year before. I don't mind it. It's better than getting landed with the oven gloves that look like chicken heads.'

She hands me the spatula and I separate the pancakes and flip them over. Mum reaches past me to the sauce-and-spread cupboard. She takes out jars, one by one. Marmalade, lemon curd, chocolate spread and the posh honey. (Mum says you pay more if it's local bees. How come, when they don't have to fly so far?) She lines them up on the kitchen surface like she's hoping to shoot them down and win a prize.

'We need to fill up,' she says. 'Before we go out.'

And that's where our conversation starts to go wrong.

It seems that the price for staying home on Christmas Day is that you have to visit relatives the day after. Grandma always goes on about not getting any younger and how happy it makes her to see her family gathered round the table on Christmas Day. We only got a reprieve this year because my uncle had to pick up one of his kids from the airport yesterday. So Grandma's moved the celebration to today.

'We'll leave around eleven,' Mum says. 'Hopefully it'll be a clear run to Luton.'

And when we're there, we'll cram ourselves into the sitting room and I'll have to smile politely while the adults play kid Top Trumps. Mum always says she doesn't want to be drawn into it. Mum *always* gets drawn into it. Every. Single. Time. Mum looks dead proud when she reels off my grades and a whole list of ambitions that I've never even thought of. I carry on smiling so hard, my mouth nearly gets stuck. I must look like Barney the Dinosaur.

I think about January on Komodo Island. Okay, she's gone all the way to Indonesia to make absolutely sure she doesn't have to be in Luton. But if she can avoid it, so can I.

Me: Um . . . I don't want to go.

Mum: You know it makes your grandmother happy when you're all there.

Me: What about January?

Mum: She's six years older than you, Spey. She's an adult.

Me: You're an adult too, Mum, and you could decide not to go.

Mum: Don't be ridiculous, Spey.

Me: I don't see the difference.

Mum: She's my mother. I can't hurt her feelings.

Me: You're my mother. If you make me go, you'll hurt mine.

We pause while I rescue the pancakes. I scrape the burned bits out of the bottom of the pan and add more oil, then batter.

Mum says, 'The fact that January's not coming makes it more important for you to be there. I don't want Grandma to think that you don't want to see her.'

I bite down hard on a pancake. Luckily, it's one that's been cooling for a while.

'I will not argue about this, Spey. You will come with me as usual.'

More pancakes pile up. I just carry on cooking them. Mum takes crème fraîche and blueberries out of the fridge.

50

We stand there frowning at each other. I don't like what I'm going to say next. I know the real reason why Mum wants me there. It's because me and her are the real family. She's always done her own thing. Two kids. Two different dads. Both of them wastemen. And Mum's not in the least bit sorry, no matter how the rest of them try and make her feel. It doesn't mean they don't get to her – they do. I've seen her cry on the way home before. But, when she's there, she doesn't give them the satisfaction. Fi speaks Japanese and I'm mostly top grades. We're her armour. But now I'm going to send her to battle by herself, with nothing except lipstick to protect her.

Yeah, I feel properly crap about it. But after that stunt she pulled with Benni yesterday, surely she owes me.

I say, 'But things aren't *as usual*, Mum. Remember yesterday? How I came downstairs to find my long-lost father asleep on the sofa?'

Her eyes narrow. 'So?'

'I didn't give you a hard time about it.'

She opens her mouth to say something.

'Okay,' I get in quickly. 'I wasn't happy, but I did try. I wasn't rude to him, was I?'

'No, but—'

'It's not my fault if we didn't have anything to say to each other.'

'I don't understand what this has got to do with you coming to Luton with me today.'

'I'd just like a day to myself.' And then I have another thought. 'And what if Grandma asks about yesterday? I don't want to lie to her.'

I try and look like pure innocence. Mum presses her lips together. One day I'll tell her how much she looks like her own mum when she does that. I add another pancake to the stack. Mum takes it off and spoons over crème fraîche, blueberries and honey. Then adds another pancake on top. She presses it down. I turn away. I don't want to witness the carnage.

It takes her a long time to work her way through the mouthful. I realise she's done it deliberately so she doesn't have to talk. I've run out of batter so I turn off the cooker and help myself to another pancake. I opt for plain chocolate spread.

'Okay, Spey,' she says at last. 'I'll let you off this time. *Just* this time. But I'm going to tell you this for now – you're only ever allowed to play that card once.'

I nod. I try not to grin. We work our way through the pancakes. Mum's leaning against the sink and I'm on the corner unit by the cooker. Our words are stacking up like the pancakes but neither of us are saying them. Mum dots on the last blueberries and pours a honeyfall direct from the jar over her pile.

'Can you promise me something, Spey?'

Is this really a proper question? I can't help being suspicious. When Mum used to take me to primary school, she'd have a word of the day. She'd teach me it as we cut through the park. Now I realise it was to distract me from the shiny new play equipment that was shouting my name so loudly. I can't remember most of the words now. I didn't go to the kind of school where the other kids wanted to be your friend because you knew the meaning of 'meniscus'. But I do remember 'rhetorical'. Or, I remember Mrs Bodwin's face when she asked us if we *really* wanted to stay behind instead of going home. I'd asked *her* if that question was rhetorical. Her face wasn't a happy face. It reminds me of Mum's face now.

Mum's question is rhetorical. Saying, 'No, I can't promise you something, Mum,' isn't an option.

'What, Mum?'

'I want you to call your father.'

'My father?'

'Benni. If that's what you prefer to call him.'

'What's there to say?'

'I was there yesterday. If it's just the two of you, it could be different. A different dynamic.'

I don't want *any* dynamic.

'Well?' Mum says.

'I haven't got his number.'

'He's left it on a sheet of paper under the Christmas tree.'

'Like a present?'

She tears her pancake in two. She's planted those blueberries well. Not a single one falls off.

'It's sticking out from under the tree base thing,' she says. 'Don't be pedantic.'

Pedantic. Another word of the day. Luckily, I didn't try that one on Mrs Bodwin.

'You will call him, won't you?' (Also rhetorical.)

'We've got nothing to say to each other.'

'Start with "hello" and take it from there.'

'And what if it goes to nowhere?'

Mum's lips press down again. I take a bite from my pancake. It's at the cold clammy stage.

'If it goes nowhere,' she says, 'at least you both tried.'

I don't want to try. I tried pretty hard with her ex, Pete, and we didn't even have a DNA link. Then he turned out to be a dick.

'Well?' Mum says.

I swallow hard, trying to unclam pancake from the roof of my mouth.

'Because the other option is getting dressed right now and coming to Grandma's with me.'

'Okay,' I say. 'I'll phone him.'

'Good.'

Two pancakes are left. I offer Mum the plate. She shakes her head.

'I'm done.' She looks around the kitchen. The whisk is balanced against the measuring jug and batter trails across the counter to the cooker. My left sock is sprinkled with flour, along with the floor around it. When I move, there'll be a foot stencil.

'I appreciate the breakfast, Spey, but you better clear up before I go.'

Mum's hanging on as long as she can. Luton's calling her hard, but she's refusing to answer. Well, not until she's sure that the kitchen sink is food-bit free again. When I've cleared up to her satisfaction, I go upstairs and flick on my new Mac. Who cares if it's refurbished? It's still got excellent visuals and there's plenty of RAM.

Every time I look up from the screen, I see the trainer box. Jordans, though, and the right size. He must have checked with Mum. It's weird to think of them making plans together about me. It's weird to think about them being together at all. The Jordans are black and gold. They could have cost half as much as the Mac. He must have serious cash stashed away.

I pick up my phone. I have to make a call. I'm dreading it and kind of looking forward to it as well.

'What's up, Brutus?' Fi adjusts her camera so I'm not looking up her nose. 'Stabbed anyone in the back, recently?'

'Brutus didn't necessarily stab Caesar in the ba . . .'

Fi's grinning. She knows exactly how to push my buttons.

'And I didn't stab you in the back, Fi. What was I supposed to do?'

'Ah, Mr Big-Brain-Little-Brother,' she says. 'You are so easy to wind up. But knowing Mum, I'm surprised you didn't end up being called "Julius".' She grins. 'The downy-bearded one.

But, what's up? We've already done the Happy Christmases. We don't usually do a Boxing Day encore.'

She's in her apartment. It's tiny, but she says she doesn't need much.

'Are you by yourself?' I ask.

'Yeah. Not for long, though.'

We look at each other across the miles.

'We don't really do casual chats, little bruv. Talk.'

'What do you mean?'

'Come on, Spey! I've got to pay for my own internet and it's not unlimited.'

I take a deep breath and swallow down a big gloop of guilt. 'My father turned up yesterday.'

There's a pause. I'm not sure if it's an internet glitch or Fi's face having a shock-freeze.

'What?' she says at last. 'Like in real life?'

'Yeah.'

'And alive?'

'Yes!'

'And he's not Jesus?'

'What do you mean?'

'Making his big appearance on Christmas morning.'

'Yeah, Fi. Hilarious.'

'And you had no idea?'

'No.'

She laughs. Fi *never* laughed like that when she was in England. Not that I can remember. She might have with her friends, but she was always pretty angry at home.

'Oh,' she says. 'I don't need any other Christmas present after this.'

'You're welcome.'

She starts laughing again and I want to feel annoyed but it's a good sound, even if her mouth keeps the laughing shape for a few seconds after the sound stops.

'So you've come to me for advice?'

I shrug. And then just in case it doesn't come across clear for her, say, 'I don't know.'

'You want me to gloat?'

'You're going to anyway.'

'Yeah, bruv! Of course!'

'And it seems fair to tell you.'

'Indeed. I thought he was in prison or something.'

'He was on our sofa yesterday morning.'

Fi's hand claps to her mouth. 'He . . . he'd stayed over?'

'I don't know I . . . I don't think so.' This is not what I want to think about.

Fi shakes her head. 'Still, way to go, Mum.'

Is this finally going to be the thing that her and Mum bond over?

I say, 'I just don't know how I'm supposed to feel about it. You . . . you were really happy when your dad turned up.'

Her face goes serious. 'Why d'you say that?'

'Because . . . well, you always looked happy.'

'And your face always matches your mood, right, Spey?'

'No.' *But it was every Wednesday*, I want to shout. *You looked happy every Wednesday!* That's a lot of pretending.

'I suppose I was happy,' she says. 'In a way. I mean, I had a dad, like everyone else and he really cared about me. And then . . . well . . . as you know, Spey, I didn't have one any more. Thanks to you, Mum sent him packing.'

The guilt gloop is thicker and clammier than that last pancake. I line up an apology but I don't have a chance to drop one.

'Though I did,' she says.

'Did what?'

'I still saw my dad afterwards. I just didn't involve you.'

My apology sinks into the guilt gloop. It's all a confused mess.

'What's your problem, Spey?' Her big-sis radar can obviously see straight into my head. 'You made it clear that you weren't happy with the father situation.'

My face screws up at the memory of it. Mum striding across the grass then stopping dead when she sees Fi's dad.

'Having a flashback?' Tokyo-Fi asks.

Okay, maybe it wasn't a good idea to call her. But what did I expect?

There's a buzzing sound. Fi looks behind her. 'He's early, just for a change!'

'I'm sorry,' I say. 'For what I did to you.'

She smiles. 'It's all water under the bridge now. You were little and I shouldn't have made you keep a secret like that from Mum. The thing is, if I'd told her, she probably wouldn't have minded.'

The buzzer goes again.

'Look, Spey, I have to go, but all I can say is you just have to do what's right for you. Don't think about him or even Mum. You weren't born out of nowhere. They decided to have you, so you make your own decision. If you want to mug him off, do it. Turning up on Christmas Day – that's one helluva Messiah complex. But if you want to get to know him, be selfish, have your own reasons. And prepare for it to fail.' Another much longer buzz. 'Seriously got to go, but' – she winks at me – 'let me know how you get on. The curiosity is almost enough to make me fly home. Happy Christmas, little bruv!'

Just as Fi disappears, there's a knock on my bedroom door. If Mum and Fi got on better, they could have planned it.

'Thirty seconds countdown!'

'Come in!'

Mum's wearing her coat and she's added another layer of lipstick. A blue IKEA bag is slung over her shoulder. It's bursting with presents.

'You are going to call . . .'

'Yes, Mum.'

'I'll check.'

'I know.'

She stands there. 'Um . . .' she says.

I wait. What follows Mum's 'umm's is always unpredictable.

'By the way,' she says, 'this is for you.'

She holds out a brown envelope. It's A3 size and bulgy. I don't take it.

'Is it from him?'

'From who?' Mum looks genuinely confused. 'You mean your fa— Benni? No! Why the hell would he give me an envelope for you if he only saw you yesterday?'

'I don't know. None of it's normal.'

'Be sensible, Spey. Here.' She flicks it through the air. It spins twice and lands on the bed next to the Mac. Mum used to play a lot of frisbee when she was young. Her aim is good.

I pick it up. 'It went to our old address.'

'Yes. Luckily it wouldn't fit through the letterbox so they left it with Heather next door. She called me a while back but I only just got round to picking it up last week. Sorry, Spey. It's been a mad month, what with all the winter flu jabs and staff leave and everything.'

'Who's it from?' I ask.

'No idea.' She reaches out her hand. 'Pass it back and I can open it for you, if you like.'

I get up and go and kiss her on the cheek. 'Say hi to Grandma for me.'

'You're still welcome to tell her in person.'

'I'm phoning Benni. We have a deal, remember?'

'As long as *you* remember, Spey.'

I close the door after her, go back to my bed and pick up the envelope. It's pretty bulky and it looks like it came unstuck and was Sellotaped back at the sorting office. My name's spelled right – though it's only my first name. It's strange seeing my old block name and number. It's written in big black upper case letters. I sniff it. I don't know what the hell for. If it was full of anthrax, I'd be dead. Then so would Mrs Sutherland, my old neighbour. I bet she gave it a good squeeze before she handed it over to Mum. Or maybe she did open it and made the sticky-tape repair.

I tear it apart. The envelope's so knackered, there's no point being polite. As I rip it down the side, it sort of explodes. Not letter-bomb-and-anthrax explodes. Just loads of paper bursting out.

This is a joke, right? Though I've got no idea who's making jokes like this. *Do you know what's hilarious? Collect a bag of paper spam and send it to Spey's old ends.* I mean, seriously. Who would do this? I pick up a shred of envelope. The postmark's smeared, but it looks like it was sent in November. Mum really did take her time going round to collect it. I drop the envelope and prod the pile of rubbish. I've entered a Christmas multiverse. Somewhere in an alternative world, another Spey is chilled out in his room, setting up his Mac and yamming chocolate. But here I am with an envelope full of torn-up paper and a promise to call a dad I don't want.

I flatten out a piece of paper. It's a cut-out flower, maybe from a gardening brochure. There's a drawer in our kitchen full of garden centre leaflets. I try and unfold another scrap, but it's stuck to a longer piece of paper.

Oh.

It's a collage. I don't even have to unfold it to know that. It's stuck-on flowers and kids' drawings. Mostly dandelions and roses. And half of those drawings are by me.

I close my eyes for a second. God, I really am getting like Mum. She reckons it makes her thoughts clearer. This time, it works. I slide on to the floor and open one of the drawers beneath the bed. It's wide and deep and a bit cheap so the bottom's coming away from the sides, though that could be because of all the stuff I've shoved in it over the years. I take out the school books. There's a whole heap of them, mostly from Year Six, for some reason. And here's my old football boots, the ones with the removable studs. The studs *were* removed and mostly never seen again. And a neon orange bib. That must have fitted me when I was six. Oh! My SpongeBob ukulele! I loved that thing! Though Mum seriously regretted buying it.

I dig beneath that. Oh, god. It's the cardigan Grandma bought for my ninth birthday. I hated it on sight. It's dark blue with big buttons, like she'd wanted me to be Paddington Bear. Mum made me wear it for the Christmas Day family meet-up that year and after that, it went straight in the drawer. I'd even given it to Mum for the Oxfam bag, but she made me take it out. Somehow, she'd thought that Grandma would know. Actually, I wouldn't put it past my grandmother to have spies in every charity shop in east London. Just in case.

And here's what I'm looking for. I grab an edge, ease it out and lay it on the floor. It's been folded in half and it's not in the best condition – not surprising from all the crap that's piled on top of it. I open it up and stare at it.

Me and Dee made this.

Dee

Convolvulaceae

MORNING GLORY

BINDWEED

GRANNY-POP-OUT-OF-BED

All my thoughts are Nan, now. I want her in my head, but I know she's gonna leave and I'll feel sad again. Nan would never live in a dump like this, but if she was here, she'd go upstairs and knock on the door and tell them to turn down their party. She'd say, 'What sort of stupid-arse dancing makes you thump on the ceiling and disturb my granddaughter like that?'

Our neighbours used to say that Nan didn't care what anyone thought. They're wrong. She cared what I thought. She told me that there were bad things in the world. It was sad that I knew this already even though I was so young. She wanted me to believe that there were also many good things. They can be so tiny that you can't see them. It's like when you climb over a log in the park and your finger hurts and you have to look close to see what's wrong. But this time, it's a tiny splinter of good, buried in deep. Nan said you mustn't pull out the splinters of good. Let them bury

64

deeper and grow. It doesn't matter if you forget about them because they'll be there when you need them.

When we went to nursery, we'd walk through the car park behind the paint shop. There was a wire fence at the end and a long strip of grass where lots of stupid people chucked their rubbish. Nan showed me buttercups still growing there, and daisies and dandelions.

One day, Nan showed me a white flower. She said it's called bindweed because it clings on and won't let go. She showed me its tiny green arms grabbing the metal fence. It held on so tight, it strangled other plants. She said it's also called morning glory because the petals are like trumpets calling out to the sun.

The best name is granny-pop-out-of-bed. When you squeeze the green bit at the bottom, the flower pops out. It made Nan laugh because if she popped out of bed too quickly, she'd get dizzy and have to lie down again. When I heard her alarm every morning, I'd make her a cup of tea and turn the washing machine on while the electricity was cheap. Then I'd make sure she took her pills and help her choose her clothes. If her feet were cold, I would help her put on her socks. I liked helping her.

I never popped out too many flowers as I didn't want them to die, even though Nan said I shouldn't worry because it's a weed. That's a good thing. Weeds are tough and no matter how many times you cut them down, they keep coming back. One day, we walked past and we saw that the granny-pop-out-of-bed was gone and the grass strip dug over. The council had planted different flowers. They were all neat and in rows like school assembly, except for one that was squashed under a Supermalt bottle. I started crying but Nan said it was all right. Granny-pop-out-of-bed's got roots under the ground. It would have a little sleep then come back.

I feel like there's bindweed inside me. When I was at Chalkleighs, I tried to explain how I felt to my counsellor, Samira. I couldn't find the right words so I drew her a picture of the bindweed, climbing and grabbing at me.

Spey

That film *Tangled*'s stuck in my head. I seriously wish it wasn't. Mum made me watch them with her – *Tangled*, *Shrek*, *Frozen*, *Lilo & Stitch*. She said it was so I could see women were heroes of their own stories. I never asked, but I always wondered if Mum watched them for herself. Most of the princesses still end up with a prince, even if he's green and farts mud.

Tangled is about Rapunzel. Sort of. When I first met Dee, she had really long hair like Rapunzel. It was usually in plaits with pink bands at the end. I think her nan used to grease down the front but by snack time it was puffed up like a sneeze. Once, Dee was bending over her painting and a kid called Chez painted a white stripe up one of her plaits. I was sitting opposite her when it happened. I hadn't spoken to her before, because she used to scream if she was asked to share anything. She even had to have her own book at story time instead of looking at the one the teacher was holding. I shouted, 'He's behind you,' and she spun round and saw him.

Man, that was a mistake for both of them. Dee screamed because he was still holding her plait and it must have hurt when she moved so quickly. Chez let go of her hair but he

67

was still holding the paintbrush with white paint dripping over the floor. Dee picked up her beaker of paint water and chucked it over him. The boy got a faceful. Dee turned to me and grinned. I don't know why I remember this, but both her front teeth were missing and I could see right through to the back of her mouth.

There was a nursery worker called Laura. She took Dee outside to calm down, though she seemed pretty calm to me. It was Chez who was screaming, like she'd chucked fire ants at him, not water. I must have gone out to find Dee because I can remember seeing her next to Laura on a bench under a tree. Dee jumped down when she saw me. Paint was smeared across the front of her hair and her palms, like she'd tried to rub it off but it went in the wrong direction. She'd grabbed my sleeve and painted me too. Luckily Mum was never strict about that stuff. Now I reckon Chez's folks were less chilled about the mess, which is why he freaked out.

Dee had nosedived into the grass and I'd followed her.

'Look, Spey!' It was a dandelion clock.

I bent down to blow it but she slapped my cheeks so the air popped out too quickly.

'Don't blow away its hair.'

She just lay there staring at it and I lay there next to her. Then she asked me to tell her a story. I think I made up something about a tiny giraffe that ate nothing but clock fluff. I'm pretty sure I had to tell her different versions of that story for ages afterwards. After that, I was Dee's chosen friend. I didn't mind. I always wanted a proper sister. Fi was too old and treated me like a nuisance. Dee was easy if you let her have what she wanted, and that didn't bother me. Once, Laura had to call me in from outside because Mum was there. Dee wouldn't let me go and I started crying because I thought I was going to be in the middle of a tug of war. Dee's nan arrived and lured Dee away with a Calippo.

It was the only time I remember me and Mum walking home in silence. Usually, she made me stop and look at things – a fat caterpillar on the pavement or a weird potato sculpture on top of the bus shelter. By the time we reached our block, I had a big knot in my stomach thinking that I'd done something really bad. Mum passed me the usual mini yoghurt and sat down opposite me at the table.

She asked me if Dee was my friend. I'd tried to read Mum's face. I didn't know what answer she wanted, so I'd just told her the truth.

'She's my best friend.'

'Good.'

She'd kissed me on the forehead and I had no idea why. I still don't. Maybe she thought I was being kind. I wasn't. I think I just wanted to be like Dee.

Spey

My phone rings. It's Mum. I can't hear any noise in the background and then a car passes by. She must be standing on the street corner, close to Grandma's but just out of sight of the rest of them.

'How's it going?' I ask.

'As expected. Though it's fun trying to work out who knows January has a girlfriend and who doesn't.'

'She posts pictures on Instagram. She's not exactly hiding it.'

'Your Aunty Jacklyn isn't on Instagram, Spey. Though she's *most* vocal about you not being here today.'

There's a gap. I think I'm expected to say sorry I've abandoned her to deal with them all by herself. I can't. It's Mum's fault. She taught me from a very early age that it's wrong to lie.

She breaks the silence first. 'Have you phoned Benni yet? Because we had a deal, Spey. Only when your end is fulfilled shall I grant forgiveness.'

I really do think about lying now, but only for a microsecond. Mum's probably already checked.

'It's next on my list,' I say.

'A list of what, Spey? What on earth have you got to do?'

Pause. 'Oh, god. I thought our discussion about porn had done some good. Look, Spey . . .'

'Mum! No! I was talking to Fi!'

'Oh. Right. Comparing fathers, I suppose.'

The p-word had summoned a blush. The f-word's forcing that blush through harder. I'm going to come off the phone and see my burning skin attached to the screen. I almost ask her if she has a phone tap going.

Instead, I say, 'I still don't understand why you want me to call him.'

'To lose one child's father may be regarded as a misfortune. To lose both looks like you've got a deranged mother.'

'What?'

'It doesn't matter. Please, Spey. Just for me.'

'I'll do it after I've finished sorting out the laptop.'

'Spey, the mother giveth and the mother can taketh away.'

Being with her family really makes Mum go a bit strange.

'Phone him now, Spey!'

'Okay!'

'So then you can tick it off your list, right? I'll be back by eleven, latest.'

I'm tempted to say, 'Enjoy,' but Mum doesn't deal well with sarcasm at the best of times.

'By the way,' she says, 'Who was that letter thing from?'

I look at the bent and torn flowers spread across my floor. Two halves of one birthday collage.

'I haven't opened it yet. The Mac needs—'

'God, Mum's looking out the window. I'd better go back in.'

She hangs up.

I go downstairs and into the sitting room. There is indeed a piece of paper sticking out from under the Christmas tree. Benni's number is written large, under his name. I reclaim my space on the sofa, spreading across the whole seat. It makes me feel better. He may have had it for Christmas. I can have it for life.

I tap the number into my phone, take a deep breath and make the call. How long am I going to give him to answer? Two rings? Three, max. He answers in one and a half.

'Spey!'

'How do you know it's me?'

'Gilda gave me your number, just in case. Your name popped up.'

The same woman who gave me the lecture about privacy settings? I say, 'Oh.'

'I know it was a bit of a surprise,' he says. 'Me just turning up on Christmas Day and everything.'

A bit of a surprise?

'I thought you got here on Christmas Eve,' I say. He'd already looked well settled on the – my – sofa.

He laughs. 'No, definitely Christmas Day. I got to yours pretty early, though – around half-six. They were laying on Christmas at the place where I'm staying, but then your mum asked me around to yours. And I wanted to see you.'

'Why?'

'Because I've let you down. I've not been there for you. I want to . . . I want to make amends.'

'Why now?' I take a couple of quick breaths. 'Do you know what? It doesn't matter why you're doing it now. You've never been here for me before. I don't need you.'

'Spey, I've thought about you all every day I was locked up.'

'Us all?'

'Yeah. All of you. How I need to know you all so much better.'

'So how come you ended up here when there was us all to choose from?'

He doesn't say anything. Part of me wants to shut up. The other part carries on talking.

'Did all the others say "no"?'

'I didn't ask anyone else, Spey.'

'Right, Mum's the easy touch, then.'

I should hang up. I don't. If he does it first, I'll know I'm right.

'I want to make things good, Spey. Please give me a chance.'

'I'm fifteen now. You're too late.'

'I don't think it's ever too late.'

'What do you want from me, Benni?'

'I don't want nothing from you!' His voice rises, like I've finally got to him. 'It's what you can get from me! Boys need their fathers.'

'I've got Mum.'

'Yeah, and thanks to her you're an excellent young man. A real role model. But sometimes there's things you won't want to tell your mum.'

'And I should tell a complete stranger instead?'

I hear him take a deep breath, but he doesn't say anything.

'Me and Mum, we're good.'

'Fair enough, Spey. You know where I am if you need me.'

I won't.

We hang up at the same time.

Dee

Primula veris

COWSLIP

FAIRY CUPS

ST PETER'S WORT

I told Samira at Chalkleighs about the time Chez made his brother's dog do a shit on our vegetable bed. Samira laughed then she said, 'Sorry.' She said it was the shock that made her laugh. After that I didn't say nothing else. I wanted to tell her that I felt sorry for the dog, that it didn't mean no harm. It didn't even need to go to the toilet, but Chez stood there tugging on the lead and shouting at it.

I wanted to rescue the dog. It was called Jim Kelly. I knew because I'd hear Chez calling him all the time. Chez wanted him to be a fighter dog and made him hang from branches by his teeth. Sometimes Chez and Jim Kelly would follow me to the shops.

Chez told me that Jim Kelly would only eat raw meat and then lick the blood out the bowl.

Chez told me that Jim Kelly bit a road sweeper. The road sweeper had to go to hospital but didn't report it to the police because he was too scared of Chez.

Chez told my nan that he was coming for me and that she wasn't going to stand in his way. Nan laughed and told him that he was only twelve and he needed to behave himself.

The vegetable bed didn't have no vegetables left in it, not ones we planted, anyway. Someone smashed the courgettes and broke the tomato plants in half. There was a small bay bush. Nan didn't put it there. She thinks a pigeon dropped a seed and it grew. She tried putting a bay leaf in her porridge and she said it tasted nasty. She didn't mind other people taking them. She wouldn't want Jim Kelly dirtying them, though.

And once we found a cowslip. Nan found out that you can use it to make a face wash that stops wrinkles. We only had one so we decided to let it grow. And Nan said her wrinkles had made themselves at home. They weren't going nowhere.

There were other things in the vegetable beds. Once Nan found a knife. There's dog rose in there too. It kept trying to grow up the bean poles and Nan would cut it down and make me cry. Now I know that it's stronger than beans. It's got thorns like sharks' teeth.

I was worried when Chez put Jim Kelly in the vegetable bed. I thought he'd hurt his paw on the thorns. I was going out to help him but Nan was standing by the front door. It was closed but she'd pulled the curtain aside so she could see through the glass panel.

She told me to stay put. We'd clean up afterwards. It was

too late to worry about Jim Kelly because that bastard boy had already hurt the dog. It wasn't a dog, Nan said, it was a demon, because its owner was the devil.

Chez lifted Jim Kelly out of the vegetable bed and walked towards our door. Nan's breathing was louder than usual, even louder than when she walked upstairs.

She yelled at me to go to my room.

I didn't. I didn't want to leave Nan. It was me Chez wanted.

'Please, Dee,' she'd said. 'It's not safe.'

He came right up to our front door and stood there. His nose almost touched the glass panel.

Nan had shouted at him. 'You won't scare me, you little thug!'

He'd grinned, then hit the door hard. Nan jumped back into me. I'd touched her back. Her T-shirt was cold and sweaty. She took her phone out her pocket and said she was gonna call the police. The phone was shaking in her hand and she dropped it. Chez laughed, then him and Jim Kelly walked away. Nan let go of the curtain.

Nan said she wished I'd do what I was told. All she wanted was to keep me safe. As long as there was breath in her body, she was gonna make sure that happened.

Spey

Mum keeps saying that she wants a quiet life, just me and her going about our business, both of us working hard until I go off to uni. She wants me to study outside of London so I can see a different world. If 'different world' means Oxford or Cambridge, half my school want to go there, so I don't know how different it would really be for me. She's already ordered a pile of other university prospectuses to look through, even though I haven't even done my GCSEs yet. Bristol, Lancaster, Manchester, Edinburgh. Good universities to go with my good school. Good grades to give me good options.

'And do a course where you go away for a year,' Mum says. 'Taiwan, maybe. Or Berlin. If they still let British people in.'

I'd asked her if she's trying to get rid of me.

'Yes.' She wasn't even smiling. 'There's another world out there for you.'

'And what about you, Mum?'

Then she smiled. 'I'm just going to relax and enjoy my newfound peace and freedom.'

I wonder if Dee's nan ever imagined Dee leaving her and having a different life. Maybe she'd already imagined things the other way, with her dying and leaving Dee, but just not so soon. It's weird to think of her nan just . . . not being there. She took up space. Not because she was big. She was little, like my grandma. But, man, her voice was loud! Now I think about it, both me and Dee had grandmas that were always turned up full volume. After Dee's nan died, the local newspaper did a tribute. Mum showed me. Neighbours said she was like Big Mo in *EastEnders*, fair but tough, and if you needed anything, she was the one to ask. They had to fundraise for her funeral but they got double the amount of money they asked for. I don't suppose they gave the extra to Dee, or her mum.

Dee went to live with her Aunty Janet. I only know because it was on the same estate where me and Mum used to live. I'd already gone, but Moby stayed a bit longer. Me and Moby had started in reception together and we'd always been in and out of each others' flats until I moved away. He left the block a couple of years later, but we still stay in touch.

I message him.

U remember Dee?

Who?

The girl who moved in with her aunty

U mean the weird girl?

I start to correct him, but I don't want to dive into a long conversation right now. I delete what I was saying and start again.

What happened to her?

79

Don't kno. Think she was still there when I left, but u kno what my mum's like. She didn't want me mixing local.

Yeah, mine too. At one point, she threatened to move us to a place called Ditchling in Sussex if there was ever a sniff of gang near me. I'd looked up Ditchling. It's very old, has a cafe called The Green Welly and I would definitely have to learn to cut my own hair, because it doesn't look like there's a Black man's barber for fifty miles around.

I go back downstairs into the kitchen. The recycling bags are leaning against the back door and it already looks like a pigeon or something had a go at one of them. I can see the wrapping paper Mum used, tissue paper from the art shop with stars drawn on it and biodegradable string. I open the fridge. There are loads of leftovers from yesterday, posh not-so-freshly squeezed juice and Greek yoghurt and mince pies, salami and Italian ham from a deli and sourdough in the bread bin.

I wonder if Dee had presents. I wonder what she's eating. She didn't like to try new things.

I wonder if she's all right.

Man, why am I trying to trick myself? Dee isn't all right. I know that. Last time . . . I saw what happened to her. Yeah, just stood there watching like there was going to be credits coming up afterwards.

I close the fridge. I don't feel hungry any more. Dee's stuck in my head, though I don't suppose she left after that last time. She even blipped through my thoughts in English last month when we were doing *Romeo and Juliet*. Lionel was reading Juliet because Ms Ribon had decided to mix things up and reverse the genders. I'd already run through the passage at home and my brain had cut out until the rose bit – 'A rose by any other name would smell as sweet'. Lionel shouted the words so hard I'm surprised his spit didn't go right through the wall and coat Mr Gelicco in front of his whiteboard next door.

As Lionel was going full Juliet, I was back at Dee's sixth birthday party, me and her and those gardening catalogues in the sitting room. Mum and her nan stayed in touch for a while, even though we went to different primary schools. I was the only birthday guest; I was the only one Dee had wanted. I think her nan was pretty happy with that. She took us to the park and we went mad on the roundabouts and chased each other through those little fountains that spurt out the ground. We didn't even have swimming stuff because it was more fun running through them with your clothes on.

Dee's nan invited Mum round for tea afterwards. They sat on fold-up chairs on the edge of the communal garden in the middle of the estate. There were tubs of bright flowers in the garden and some high wooden vegetable beds. Dee showed me hers. She'd wanted it to be full of dandelions but they weren't allowed. Instead, her nan had planted a small rose bush and some raspberries. There was a *Bug's Life* windmill stuck right next to a wooden bug-hotel.

Mum was holding a small china cup. Dee's nan poured the tea from a teapot that was white with pink roses on it. The milk jug and sugar bowl were stripy blue and white. It made me think of *Alice in Wonderland*. There were even gold spoons like my mother was a visiting queen. I'd always thought that Dee's nan really was *the* Queen. Her face was wise, like a queen's should be. She made the rules and knew how to sort out arguments.

Dee and I were in the sitting room with a big plate of biscuits – chocolate Clubs and mini-Twixes and special Jammie Dodgers – for us. There was chocolate caterpillar cake waiting in the kitchen. I was glad Mum couldn't see how much sugary stuff I was scoffing down. The windows were open and we could hear Mum and Dee's nan talking and laughing outside. Dee and I pushed the rugs aside and spread a roll of paper across the floor. Dee emptied out a bucket of pencils and crayons, scissors and glue sticks.

'Help me,' she'd said.

We sorted the pencils and crayons into different colours – reds, oranges, pinks, greens, blues. She showed me a dark orange crayon with paper wrapped round the middle like a waistcoat.

'Lady Marmalade.'

I'd nodded. She laid it next to a pencil that was paler, like cartoon flesh colour. I started to organise the colours from dark to light but Dee nudged my hand away. She disappeared and came back with a pile of glossy brochures. She plonked them down and opened a page and pointed to the roses. They were orangey coloured too. They're still there, stuck to the collage up in my room.

'Nan says that's called Abigail.' Dee had jabbed another picture. 'That's Amanda.'

I must have nodded again like I usually did when I couldn't quite get what Dee meant.

She'd sprawled flat on the floor with me next to her. She copied the Amanda rose on to the paper with a yellow pencil, one petal at a time. Then she took a black pencil and drew a face, hands, trousers. She passed me the scissors.

'You do the cutting up.'

We started to fill the paper, cutting and gluing and not saying much to each other. Mum and Dee's nan were still laughing outside. I was sure I could hear their teaspoons clinking and dogs barking on the canal towpath that ran behind the estate.

Suddenly, Dee dropped her pencil and looked up. 'She's here.'

I strained. Nothing. Then I heard the voice.

'Dee-Dee! Dee-Dee!'

Dee's name had been changed into a song. I'd liked it. Dee held up a dark blue pencil.

'Roses can't be blue,' she'd said. 'Not proper blue. They won't let it.'

'Who won't?'

'Roses won't. Nan says they can be any colour, but they

can't be blue or proper black. But you can draw it.'

She thrust the pencil at me. I took it and started with a circle.

'Dee-Dee! Dee-Dee! Where are you?'

'Draw it!' Dee shouted.

'I am!' But I drew faster.

'Dee-Dee, didn't you hear me?'

The woman was younger than Mum. She looked like Princess Fiona with dark red hair and a green top, but there was a bruise across her eye and when she grinned one of her front teeth was missing. I think that confused me. Only kids like us or old people or pirates didn't have all their teeth.

But it was the smell. It made me want to cry. I knew it was Dee's mum and I didn't want her to smell like that.

'Gloria?' Dee's nan was in the doorway. I knew Mum wouldn't be far behind.

'I want to see my girl,' Gloria said.

'I know you do, but you can't just turn up, love.'

Dee's nan's voice was soft. The only other person she used that voice with was Dee.

'She's my girl,' Gloria said.

Dee snatched the pencil from me and started scribbling, dark blue, so fast and hard it was tearing the paper.

Dee's nan had put her arm around Gloria's shoulders. 'Of course you want to see her, love. But remember what the social workers said?'

'I gave birth to her! I have rights!'

Scribble, scribble, scribble. Dark blue streaking across the yellow and orange.

Dee's nan glanced behind her. Mum *was* there. I'd wanted Mum to make things right. We'd take Dee and the birthday cake from the kitchen and more biscuits and go to the park by the canal and play some more. Then when we took Dee home, her mum would have had a bath and she'd be in the garden drinking tea with Dee's nan. It would be all right.

Scribble. Dark blue across the floor beneath the torn paper.

'It's my girl's birthday,' Gloria said. 'And I remembered.'

Same way I'll always remember Lionel's Juliet. Ayesha was Romeo and really wasn't living the moment. I had to go over all her bits afterwards. There was one quote she didn't murder, about fate. Some stuff's just inevitable and there's nothing you can do to stop it. Maybe Dee's life was always heading a certain way. I couldn't have changed anything. Even if I'd tried

I go back upstairs and stare at the collage. Someone tried to fix Dee's rips with Sellotape, but the scribbles are so hard, they're shiny.

I don't remember leaving, but Mum must have ushered us out quickly. We might have got cake to take away with us. I don't remember. We didn't have Dee. And I don't think we sang 'Happy Birthday'. But something else happened before we went. Gloria bent down to have a look at our collage.

'That's beautiful,' she'd said.

Dee had snatched up the collage and shoved it at me. I think it was so big it kind of exploded out of her arms. Like it's just done over my bedroom.

'Take it, Spey!'

God, what had Mum thought then? Our flat was tiny and it was already pretty cluttered. I think she'd tried a polite 'no', but Dee had dropped it at my feet and crossed her arms.

'It's yours!'

I'd stared down at the paper spill. It was Dee's birthday. We were supposed to be nice to her and do what she wanted. I bent down to pick it up but Mum gently tugged my arm to straighten me. Dee's nan had looked from me to Dee.

'I think it belongs to both of you,' she'd said. 'Why don't you keep half each?'

Mum had agreed that it was a good idea. Gloria hadn't said anything. I think maybe she'd wandered off. I'd offered Dee the scissors to cut it. Nan had stroked her hair.

'Go on, sweetheart! Remember *Annie*? It's like the locket that got cut in half, so Annie would know her true parents again.'

We'd waited, then Dee had hacked the collage in two. When she handed me my piece, her nan had clapped. When Mum and I were on the bus home, I'd asked her if there was a different *Annie*. In the one I knew, Annie's parents had died but no one told her. When the locket got joined together again, it was all a lie.

Dee

Solanaceae

DEADLY NIGHTSHADE
DEVIL'S CHERRIES
BEAUTIFUL DEATH
BELLADONNA
BITTERSWEET

Deadly nightshade is in the same family as potatoes and tomatoes, but it's not food. It's a deadly poison and it's used as medicine. Nan said I should see the good in everyone, even nasty people, because people aren't always one thing. Then she said that people like Chez had no good in them at all. She said they were eaten up with their own poison.

Deadly nightshade has purple petals and it looks like a sad bell. It isn't the only nightshade. There's bittersweet too. That has a yellow anther and the flower looks like it's sticking out its tongue. Bittersweet berries are red, not black like deadly nightshade, but they're both poisonous.

Nan said that drugs are poison. My mum was infected with poison that made her ill and made her forget us. Now I'm selling drugs-poison for Chez. It's another reason why I don't want to think about Nan. If she knew I was doing this, she wouldn't stop crying. I make Nan leave my head when I count the wraps, carefully, like Chez showed me.

Then I go upstairs and over to the alleyway to deliver them. Chez says I must always take the money first because you can't trust junkies. He says I should know that already because of my mum.

Chez's like my dad. My dad's the one who gave Mum the poison and kept giving it to her. My dad's not her dealer no more. No one knows where he is. All the people Mum knows move around a lot, like she does. Like I do now.

Sometimes Mum went into rehab. When I was small, Nan called it 'Mummy's Get-Better Place'. She'd come and see me when she was better, then she'd go somewhere. She's somewhere now. She's been somewhere for a long time. Aunty Janet said it was best that she stayed there. Though she may be looking for me because it's Christmas. I look out of the window in case I see her walk by.

Once me and Nan were waiting for a bus and Mum passed us so quickly I didn't notice at first. Nan held my hand too tightly and I turned to see where she was looking. Mum was way down the street. Her head was down and she was wearing a little pink rucksack with a unicorn horn sticking out. I knew it was her because the bag used to be mine.

There's another nightshade called stinking nightshade. It's also called henbane. Henbane is good for magic potions because it makes you see pretend things and it makes you think you can fly. I want to see Nan and I want to fly, but for real.

Spey

The birthday collage. A heap of cut-out flowers and crayon from nine years ago. Why the hell have I been sent this? It's not like there's a note or anything to give me a clue. And it went to our old address, so whoever sent it didn't even know we'd moved. It's not like Dee's nan's just died and they're finally clearing out the flat. She passed away over a year ago.

I haven't got enough head room to think about this, not with so much Benni in there. It's not only my sofa he took over. He's bending up my thoughts. But Dee got in there first. I'd just stopped myself thinking about her. I suppose she chose me, that day at playgroup. I was the one she trusted enough to be her friend. I owe her.

That's my justification for where I am now, standing outside my old block. It's strange. It's in all my early memories, but I don't pass this way at all these days. I'm not avoiding it, but since Moby went, I haven't got any reason to come here.

It looks really tired. Maybe it was always like that, but I didn't realise when I was a kid. A good few flats are boarded up now. Mum says the council plan to demolish it and sell the land, but it could be years before everyone's gone.

I see the shop on the ground floor has got a new storefront

and a new name. It's now called Charlie's. When the door opens, it still looks like the same owner. He always wore his thick red jumper, no matter how hot it was. Mum used to call him Sam. I hope she wasn't getting it wrong all this time and his real name was Charlie. I go up the concrete ramp to the security door and tap the old code into the keypad. It works.

The foyer's clean. No lurking drug dealers. I used to wonder if Mum made up the stories about our neighbourhood crack houses, just to make me feel better about leaving here. When I'd Googled our old street it said they used to do a load of filming on our estate, when they wanted a certain kind of menacing urban. Moby was even an extra once.

I walk up the three flights of stairs. I can almost see me and Moby racing each other back down on the way to the park, with Moby's mum yelling from the top of the stairs. It's just as well neither of us fell over. We would have left half our faces on the concrete. Moby's mum was so strict she would have made us pick our bits of face off the ground while still giving us a full-volume bawl-out.

Loads of flats have made a real effort with Christmas decorations, even though I reckon half the families here are Muslim. The kids at our primary did assemblies for both Eids, Christmas and Guru Nanak's birthday.

The flat next to Mrs Sutherland's is boarded up too, good and proper, with a metal grille across the window and door. That flat used to be ours. I imagine jemmying off the grille and peering through the window into our old kitchen – the walls that Mum painted dark blue, the giant sunshine-yellow fridge-freezer cheap from Hoxton Street and the tiny bench table where we'd eat together. It was a while back and there'd been other tenants since then. No one had graffitied the grille yet, so the latest lot must have moved out pretty recently.

I knock on Mrs Sutherland's door. A woman sticks her head out. Her eyes widen.

'My god! Is that you, Spey?'

I nod and smile. She steps out of her flat. She's wearing thick green socks and slippers the same colour, like a grinch. It's mad, but Mrs Sutherland looks exactly the same as I remember. Perhaps I thought she was really old when I was little and she's grown into herself.

'You've got so big!' she says.

I suppose I've grown into myself too.

'I didn't think I'd ever see you round here again,' she says. 'No one ever comes back. Well, apart from your mum.' Her smile sticks. 'When she has reason to.'

Me too, Mrs Sutherland. I widen my smile. I realise I'm in Barney the Dinosaur territory again and narrow it.

'I'm really sorry to disturb you on Boxing Day, but I just wanted to ask about that parcel you took in for me.'

Mrs Sutherland's door opens wider and I hear music. When I say music, I mean the *Chitty Chitty Bang Bang* theme tune. My smile turns real. Dee's nan once bought us toot sweets and we got told off by the old bloke who lived above them. He'd said they made his dog scared. Then, of course, Dee insisted on seeing the scared dog. It was a really old thing lying on a blanket on the sofa. Its head rested on its paws and its face looked like it had seen the end of the world. Dee had plucked the toot sweet out of my hand and thrown them both in the bin.

A child joins Mrs Sutherland on the balcony. She's about four and dressed like Moana, with a broom for a paddle. She wraps her arms round Mrs Sutherland's legs. Mrs Sutherland strokes the child's head.

'Go back inside, Billie, it's cold out here. We're not really in New Zealand. You don't even have your shoes on.'

She picks up the child. Billie's bare feet wriggle like they're still trying to walk.

'Mummy's making milkshake. It should be ready by now.'

She sets the child down and they run off. Mrs Sutherland turns her attention back to me.

'There's not much I can say, Spey. It was early last month. They' – she nods towards our old flat – 'were still there. They were always out, mind. The postman was always asking me to take things in for them. I was happy to at first, but they never called for them. I always had to knock on their door. I almost said no again until I saw it was for you. I called your mum straight away. She took her time getting here.'

'I'm sorry about that.'

'It's not your fault, is it? I hope it wasn't anything

important.' A blender whirs in the kitchen behind her. Mrs Sutherland glances back then at me again. 'Is there anything else, Spey? I don't get to spend much time with Billie, you know.'

'Yes. Sorry. It's just that I think the package came from Dee. I wondered if you knew where she was.'

'Dee?'

'Her Aunty Janet lives round here. Dee moved in with her after her grandma died.'

'Oh. That Dee.' Mrs Sutherland folds her arms. 'Poor Janet. She really didn't deserve what that girl put her through. Why do you want to know?'

'Dee was my friend.'

Was.

'Why would a boy like you get tangled up with a girl like Dee?' She gives me a long look. 'Isn't that why your mum took you away from here? So you wouldn't get tangled up in trouble?'

I keep my face blank. 'Is Dee still round here? Or her aunty?'

Mrs Sutherland shakes her head. 'That girl never listened to a word Janet said. She was still hanging around with those little thugs from St Mabel's, wouldn't come home at night, wouldn't tell anyone where she was. Social workers had to move her right away in the end, and from what I heard, that didn't help much, neither.'

'What do you mean?' I'm trying so hard to keep my

face friendly, it's actually hurting.

She leans towards me. I don't think she realises she's licking her lips. 'Druggie. The apple doesn't fall far from—'

'Is her Aunty Janet still round here?'

'No. After the girl moved out, she sold her place back to the council and moved.'

'Thank you.' I turn away, letting my friendly face drop.

'One minute, Spey!'

Friendliness back on.

'I do have Janet's address, if you want it.'

'Yes, please.'

Mrs Sutherland disappears into the hallway behind the front door. She reappears holding an address book and her glasses. As she slaps on her glasses, I realise that one of her eyelids is smeared in sparkly green eyeshadow. She notices me staring and laughs.

'Billie turned me into a princess too.' She waves the book. 'Me and Janet still send each other Christmas cards.' She flicks through the pages. 'Janet really tried her best to help the girl.'

I didn't. I could have, but I didn't.

'She even followed the girl all the way down to the seaside. That's what social workers thought would sort the girl out, a nice little holiday by the sea.' Mrs Sutherland stops on a page and stares at me over her glasses. 'But Janet said it's just as bad there as it here. And I read about it too. All these kids brought down from London to sell drugs.. I suppose it's easy money. No one wants to have a proper job these days.'

'Um . . .' Ums are good for holding back words that might kill your conversation. Mum taught me that. She said I might need to use it on a teacher or two. 'Do you have the address?'

'Yes. Just let me jot it down for you, Spey.'

Mrs Sutherland leaves me standing there again. Moby lived on the other side of the block, up on the sixth floor. He reckons that his old flat's boarded up too. His mum told us she saw the Gherkin being built. And how one Christmas they lit it up so it looked like there were baubles hanging from it. Now you can't even see the Gherkin because of all the new towers.

'Here you go.' Mrs Sutherland hands me a whole sheet of A4 with an address written on it in pink felt tip. I don't tell her that I could have just taken a photo of her address book on my phone.

I glance at it. 'Hastings?'

She nods. 'I'm going to take Billie down when it gets warmer.'

I tuck the paper into my coat pocket. 'Thank you, Mrs Sutherland.'

'It was lovely to see you, Spey.' She closes the door.

Dee

clematis vitalba

WILD CLEMATIS

TRAVELLER'S JOY

OLD MAN'S BEARD

It's not Christmas no more, even though the party upstairs is still going. It's Boxing Day. Nan said it's called Boxing Day because kids stop playing with their new toys and muck about with the boxes instead. I used to like Christmas with Nan. We'd put up our tree and decorations on the first of December and I'd have an advent calendar with chocolate behind each window. On Christmas Eve, we'd go for pie and mash in Hoxton Street then catch a bus into central to see the lights.

When I was at Chalkleighs, Samira asked me to tell her about my happy memories. I could have told her about Christmas, but I told her about my flower book instead. Nan gave it to me. It was for my birthday. Spey was there but Mum came round. I told Samira that I didn't want to see Mum so that's not my happy memory. Mum wanted to kiss and cuddle me, but Nan wanted her to have a bath first. They ended up shouting at each other and the man upstairs called the police.

After Mum went, Nan and I finished the birthday food and she gave me my flower book. She said it was from her and Mum. There was even writing inside the cover.

Happy birthday, Dee-Dee. We'll love you for ever. Nanny and Mummy xxx

Nan said there were thousands of stories about flowers and we could find them together. We started with old man's beard because I liked the name. It can make more than 100,000 seeds. I asked Nan how much 100,000 was, so she took me to the Arsenal stadium and told me to count the seats. It was too hard. I kept forgetting where I was. The guide told us there was room for 60,000 people. Nan said I had to imagine that there was half as many seats again. The guide also told us how they took care of the grass on the pitch. They had to make sure it was perfect for the players with no weeds. Old man's beard is a weed. It couldn't be perfect with no weeds.

I told Samira that I like old man's beard because it's very good at getting planted. I saw old man's beard in the woods near Chalkleighs. Maybe a pigeon dropped a seed or a squirrel brought it on her fur. The seeds are tough. They don't care where they go as long as they find a place to grow. Samira asked me if I thought I was like that. No, I'm not. I didn't go to Chalkleighs by accident.

They took me to Chalkleighs after what happened in the shopping centre, though they were planning it before. Chalkleighs was near the seaside and it had a garden. There were sunflowers and an apple tree and a red rose bush climbed up the back wall. Samira said the rose had been blooming there for nearly twenty years because there was a sunny aspect. She found out the name of the rose for me. It's called Danse de Feu. It means fire dance.

There were supposed to be three girls staying at Chalkleighs, but one of the rooms was empty. The girl it belonged to was called Jasmine. She was in hospital and they weren't sure if she was coming back. The other girl was called Spencer. She'd been there for two months and told me she'd had enough. She kept running away. Once, the police found her in London. Another time she was gone for two nights and came back by herself. After that, she said she didn't want to run away again. She wanted to be my friend.

I didn't want to be Spencer's friend. She shouted at everyone. When they brought her back from London, she locked herself in her room and wouldn't come out. I put in my earbuds and turned up my music but I could still feel her kicking the wall. It made me shiver.

My social worker said there weren't any suitable school places for me yet. I didn't mind. I don't like school. I found a path at the back of the police station that took me into the woods. I had to bend my head so I didn't get scratched by the blackberry bushes. It was too early to eat the berries. They were just red and green bubbles. I came off the path and walked until I couldn't see any buildings. Then I sat down on an old tree trunk.

When Nan was upset, she said that life was like a deep hole and you threw your happiness in it and it disappeared. She said the hole gave you back your happiness. If you filled it full of love, all the happy things would float to the top and you could fish them out and enjoy them again.

Spey

Dee's moved out of London and she's near her aunty. She's not alone. I don't need to know anything else. It's not like I can add to her life. And, no, I'm not ignoring the bit about drugs. Mrs Sutherland could be making it up. *Apple doesn't fall far from the tree*. Right. It was easy for her to make Dee part of county lines. It's been all over the news in the last few months. I didn't even know what it really was until a year ago or so. The first time I heard someone say 'county lines' I thought it was an American thing, kind of sheriffs in old police cars chasing criminals to the borders of the next state. I haven't even told Michael that.

But, be truthful, Spey. Forget Mrs Sutherland. Did you ever think Dee might get caught up in crap like that?

Yeah. I did.

On the bus home, I go through my contacts to see if there's anyone else who'd know Dee too. There's a girl called Ashleigh who's got a bit of a following for her hair stuff. She went to our playgroup. We were never really friends, but she messaged me last year about a gig her sister was playing. I DM her.

> Remember that girl, Dee, from nursery?
> Any idea what happened to her?

Though I'm the one who probably saw Dee the most recent. Then there was the time about six months before that. It must have been before her nan died. I was cycling down the canal path towards the Olympic Park. I was supposed to be playing in a volleyball tournament in the Copper Box and was already running late.

I was bombing along, way faster than I should have been. I kind of swerved through a tunnel and almost bumped a girl into the water. She hadn't flattened herself against the wall like some of the other pedestrians, or marched purposefully towards me, staring me in the eye like she was daring me to even try squeezing past. She was crouched on a strip of grass on the edge of the towpath. I knew it was her before I realised it. I think it was because she was so busy doing what she was doing that she didn't notice me, even when I slammed on the brakes and stopped with my front wheel almost touching her knee.

'Dee?'

She looked up and grinned. 'Hello, Spey.' She pointed to some yellow flowers. 'Primroses.'

I propped my bike against a lamp post. She straightened up and came over to me. She was carrying a courier bag over her shoulder. She opened it and took out a book. It was thick, with a hardback cover.

'It's about wildflowers,' she said.

'Not into roses any more?'

She'd handed it to me. 'Wildflowers are stronger. Especially the ones like dandelions and daisies that no one wants. Nan says that the only difference between a flower and a weed is judgement.'

I could really imagine her nan saying something like that. No! I'd actually heard her nan say something like that. I flicked through the book and the names came back to me.

ALEXANDERS

CLEAVERS

MONKHOOD

RAGGED ROBIN

SHEPHERD'S PURSE

SILVERWEED

YARROW

'I remember this book,' I'd said. I knew there'd be a chocolatey fingerprint by '**SCARLET PIMPERNEL**'. I'd put it there the first time Dee let me look through it. Dee had freaked and Mum had to come and take me home. I don't think I went back to Dee's many times after that. I also knew that there was an inscription in the front cover. The book was a birthday present from Dee's nan and mum.

I'd handed it back to her. Dee didn't seem to mind that we hadn't seen each other for ages. I'd felt weird, like I could have tried harder. I was asking her all this stuff about which school she was at and if she still saw anyone we both knew. She didn't really say much. I suppose I don't blame her. If I'd cared, I'd already have known. I would have had her number and messaged her to meet up like I did with my other friends. It was like we were standing on different sides of the canal, heading in opposite directions.

There was something about the way she'd looked too. She'd always been quite little, but Year Eight is when it all starts changing, for different kids at different times. If you'd made us all line up against a wall, we'd look like a wonky heartbeat. I'd had what Mum called a growth spurt. I was one of the taller kids, though it turned out that I'd peaked too early. My voice was still trying to sort itself out. I could have done both 'Bohemian Rhapsody' *mamma mias*, though not at the right time.

Dee looked like a Year Five, still little and still with long hair, though not in plaits. It was loose and clumped a bit at the back, like she hadn't managed to get a comb there. She was wearing a light blue tracksuit but the knees were stained from where she'd been kneeling.

I'd said, 'Are there just primroses round here? Have you found anything else?'

I think she'd said something about a cowslip in her vegetable bed and opened the book to show me what it looked like. Then cow parsley and hogweed and scarlet pimpernel. Scarlet pimpernel! I'd almost laughed. We'd made up a story about scarlet pimpernels, but I hadn't wanted to tell Mum because I thought 'pimpernel' was a rude word. A dog barked and Dee had looked away.

103

'That's Jim Kelly.'

'Who?'

A boy was walking towards us. He had some sort of staffie straining at its leash. It was wearing a harness so it didn't choke, but the boy still kept his arm by his side like he enjoyed seeing the dog pull hard. As he came closer, I saw he was a few years older than us.

I'd asked her if he was Jim Kelly. She'd laughed and said that was the dog. I recognised the boy. He was Chez's older brother. He used to come with Chez's mum to pick up Chez from nursery. He didn't look much different – just taller and angrier. He stopped right in front of us. Dee reached out her hand to the dog. I almost grabbed her wrist to stop her, but the dog just licked her fingers. The boy pulled the dog back. It gave a little whine. Dee asked him to leave the dog alone, but he ignored her. He was too busy eyeing my bike. Mum had bought it for my eleventh birthday. It had been too big then, but now the saddle was raised to the highest it could go and my knees hit the handlebars.

'A piece of shit,' the boy said.

I didn't bother replying. I could see how he was playing it, just waiting for any crap reason to show how tough he was. I wasn't going to risk getting a knife waved at me because I was upset that he didn't rate my bike. I thought he'd carry on walking but he grabbed Dee's arm so quickly that she dropped her book. His grip was tight; I could see her skin bulging through her sleeve. I felt my own fingers tense, even though I had no idea what I was supposed to do.

'Chez's looking for you,' he'd said.

I'd forced out a smile. 'Mum would love to see you, Dee. It's been ages. You can come back home with me, if you like.'

Dee had looked confused. 'Why does your mum want to see me?'

'Yes,' the boy asked quietly. 'Why *does* your mum want to see this?' He'd waved Dee's arm. I'd swallowed back my anger and told him that me and Dee had known each other from way back. I'd picked up Dee's flower book and offered it to her.

'Come on!'

The boy had yanked Dee towards him. He'd given me this smug smile, like I was supposed to be impressed that he was holding the dog with one hand and Dee with the other. As if either of them could have fought him back. Bastard. Dee had taken her book and he'd let go of her. I'd tried to make eye contact, but she'd slid the book into her bag and looked up at him. Then she'd walked away with him.

I'd stayed there for a bit, even messaging Julius to say I was too late for volleyball, but the squad was one short and they needed me. I had to go. Now. So I'd got back on my (apparently shit) bike and carried on my way, along the towpath until I could turn off. Then raced through the marshes, off the path, on the grass and grit, faster and faster until my legs hurt and my brain didn't want to explode any more.

Dee

Anthriscus sylvestris

COW PARSLEY

QUEEN ANNE'S LACE

MOTHER-DIE

It's morning, but it's still dark. I tried to turn the light on, but there's no electricity. I've still got candles from last time. Later, I'm gonna check Ingram's room for matches, or a lighter and some food. I'm hungry, but I won't die because I'm hungry.

I almost died because I was too small. Nan has pictures of me when I was a baby. I was born too soon and she said I could have fitted inside a shoe. I was in hospital for a month after I was born. That's how long Nan was in hospital before she died. A month. They didn't think I'd be able to breathe by myself. I can. Though sometimes I sound like a monster. That's what my mum says. Nan said I should ignore her, but I don't mind. When I hear my breathing it's like my heart is beating; I know it works. Until it stops like Nan's did and then I'll be dead.

Samira asked me if I thought about death a lot. I didn't before Nan passed, but then I went to see Nan just after it happened. I wasn't scared, just sad, even though she'd been asleep for nearly a week and even Aunty Janet said she wouldn't wake up again.

I've forgotten to charge the phone. I only have a tiny bit of battery left. I have to message Chez. I have to tell him that Ingram's gone and he's locked me in the flat. Chez will be angry with me, even though it's not my fault.

I'll wait. Maybe Ingram will come back.

Spey

I go home and get my Mac to do everything I need it to and then I just sit there. I've piled everything back into my drawer apart from the birthday collage. I've also worked out the one thing that was bothering me. How did whoever sent it know *where* to send it? I remember Mum saying we had to leave but Dee's nan taking back my half and writing her address on the back of it. She'd asked Mum for our address – our old address – to write on Dee's. It's still there. I wonder if Mum knew even then that she planned to move us away as soon as she could.

My phone buzzes. I'm ready for Mum to check up on me again but it's Michael. He's heading out to the skate park later to check out Phoebe's new board. I message back and tell him it's going to be full of screaming kids.

> **Nah, Spey. Good reason why we're waiting for sundown**

I think I was meant to bounce back a vampire joke. I don't feel like being funny. He messages again.

> **U with granny?**

No

> **If u don't wanna come, just say, man**

I call him. He picks up straight away.

'Something going on, Spey?'

'I just . . . Look, can I ask you about something?'

He laughs. 'Something or someone?'

'Someone, but . . .'

'That Danaii girl. She back on the scene?'

'No. I used to know a girl called Dee and . . .'

And it all spills out. Well, not all of it. I don't mention what happened when I was at the market with Danaii, but I tell him about Dee's mum and her nan and how I was her only friend. Then I tell him about the collage and how I think Dee's maybe caught up in county lines stuff on the coast. There's a pause, then Michael whistles.

'That's a lot of information, Spey.'

'Yeah.'

'A girl you haven't seen for years has sent you a cursed collage.'

'Come on, man.'

'What do you expect me to say?'

I seem to be having a lot of conversations today that aren't going the way I want. 'I don't know. I just don't know what to do.'

'Yes, you do. Leave well alone. You don't owe her anything.' I can almost hear him thinking. 'Or do you?'

I say nothing.

'Silence means secret baby, right?'

I don't mean to laugh. 'No, man, it's serious. I saw her by the canal a couple of years ago. She was with one of the boys from her old estate. I'm pretty sure she was in trouble, but I didn't do anything.'

'Was he bashing her?'

'No! He was just . . . It didn't look good. I tried to get her to come with me, but she didn't.'

'So you did do something. What else were you supposed to do, bruv? Get shanked for her? That's police business or social services or stuff.'

I heard a bell ring.

I say, 'You on the bus?'

'Yeah, heading out to Phoebe's a bit early.'

'Oh.'

I hear the bus door open.

'I get you want to help her,' he says. 'But you don't even know if she wants your help. You don't know where she is and you sure as hell don't know who she's mixed up with. Unless you've got some badass brutha on your side, don't do it.' He's sounding a bit breathless. He must be in a hurry to get to Phoebe. 'Look, I reach. You coming down later?'

'Um . . . Maybe.'

'I take it that means no, Spey.'

'It's just . . .'

'You called for my advice, bruv. Just say no. Your conscience may be hurting you now, but your chest's gonna hurt even more when it's got a knife sticking out of it.'

Michael hangs up and I lay back on my bed. My hand dangles over the side and sweeps along the collages. Michael's right. I should just shove them both in the drawer with the stud-free football boots and forget about them. Even better,

110

I can dump them in the recycling with the bottles and penguin wrapping paper.

I open my eyes and look across my room. If Air Jordans could stare, they'd be screw-facing me right back. One of the tongues is poking out from between the laces like it's harbouring an opinion. *Boy, don't even think of putting your foot in me until you stop being so stupid.* I want to yell back that I'm not being stupid. But I don't, because yelling at trainers *is* stupid. I am thinking, though, that sometimes things hook themselves into your head until you sort them out. That's what's happened with all my Dee thoughts. Even if I chuck away the collages, it's not going to get rid of . . . Man, it's not going to get rid of the truth. I could have helped Dee twice and I didn't.

But what the hell am I supposed to do? Challenge some hard-ass drug lord to a battle? I could barely look Chez's brother in the eye, or Chez. I don't know anything about this stuff. Mum's done too good a job with me. I don't think I even know anyone who's been arrested.

I sit up, so quickly my eyes blur. *I don't know anyone who's been arrested?* Seriously? 'Professional criminal' is half my damn DNA. He may not be a badass brutha, but then, I don't know, do I? Maybe Mum made him tone himself down to meet me. It doesn't matter. I'm not going to call him. I've done it once. I've said what I had to say. I'm not going anywhere. I'm going to stay here, explore the leftovers and catch up on some *Tower of God*. I glance over at the Jordans again.

Boy, you really gonna tuck into posh ham and Italian Christmas cake while your friend's in trouble?

Yes! I am! I go downstairs, pull off a chunk of panettone and chew. The cake's soft, but it doesn't want to go down. It's like there are so many Dee thoughts they can't stay in my head and are spilling out into the rest of me. I go and sit beneath the Christmas tree. I chew and I chew and I chew. Then I do it. I call him. He sounds really happy to hear from me. I can hear a bird singing and dogs barking in the background.

'I'm chilling in the park,' he says. 'Some of the lads overdid the Christmas spirit last night and their headaches are making them grumpy. It's only a matter of time before something kicks off.'

Funny, this is the first time I notice why Mum makes him sound like Hagrid. It's nothing you'd notice without listening hard.

I say, 'About earlier . . .'

'It's okay, Spey. Like I said, it's up to me to make amends. It shouldn't be easy. Do you . . . do you want to meet up?'

'No. Well, yes. It's just . . . a friend's in trouble. Or I think she is.'

And the story comes out again. Well, nearly all the story. I don't mention the market. It still sounds downright stupid, though. Two bits of paper got reunited and I think a girl's being owned by a drugs cartel.

I wait for him to laugh, but he says, 'So you want to go and find her, then?'

Yes! No! I just wanted to tell you because . . . Because I wanted him to talk me out of it too.

'You think she's caught up in county lines?'

'Maybe.'

'Look, I've got a friend. Sol's made it his business to find out about these operations and try and close them down. His niece got caught up with it when she was younger. I'll call you back, Spey.'

He rings off. I lie down on the carpet next to the tree. When I look up I can see Jiji staring back at me. I don't know what sort of luck I want him to bring.

Benni phones back half an hour later. I'm still lying under the tree. He says that Sol's up for it. He's already trying to find out who's running some of the operations on the south coast.

Already? Benni really did mean we'd try and find her? I sit up slowly. Pine needles are stuck to my hands.

'You got the aunty's address?' Benni asks. 'She's in Hastings, right?'

'Yes.'

'We'll head there first, then.'

'Now?'

'Sol's got the car, so we have to work to his schedule if we want his help.'

'Right. I . . .'

It's all running away from me.

He says, 'Have you told your mum about this?'

'Not exactly.'

There's a pause and I take the chance to slip in something about it being a good idea to head down to Hastings, but not on Boxing Day. Wouldn't it be rude to suddenly burst in on someone else's Christmas?

'Okay, Spey,' Benni says quietly. 'I get it. I'm sorry. I've jumped in and set things in motion when I should have just kept my mouth closed and listened.'

'No, it's just . . .' It's just what? I keep going over the times I've let her down. Now I'm persuading myself to do it again when maybe I've got a real chance of setting things right. Because it's not only Benni who's making amends, is it? 'I'm just worried,' I say.

'Of course,' Benni says. 'I'm not surprised. We're in expert hands with Sol. That's why I called him. But I understand if you don't want to go. Have a think about it and—'

'No,' I say. 'I want to do it.'

'Okay. But I'm not taking you anywhere without your mother knowing. Call her now and I'll text you where to meet us.'

I put the phone down on the rug next to me. I rub my stomach. It feels like that panettone's turned itself back solid again.

Dee

Arum maculatum

CUCKOO PINT

LORDS-AND-LADIES

PARSON IN THE PULPIT

When I lived in London, I could see the canal through the gates at the back of the estate. When I lived in Chalkeighs, I could see the sea from the path at the top of the woods. Now I'm here, I never see the sea at all. Chez says I'm only allowed out to sell the drugs. Ingram has the money to buy the food and electricity and gas because it's his flat. Sometimes I went to the shops to help him and I would see the sea. I had to turn my back on it when we walked home.

I was supposed to like the seaside. That's what everyone said before I moved to Chalkleighs. Even Aunty Janet said it. *You're lucky because you'll be near the sea. I might even join you.* I don't know if I like the seaside, but I do like the sea. Before I moved to Chalkleighs, I thought the sea was blue. Sometimes it is blue, but sometimes it's silver or white or all those colours at the same time. When there's a sea mist, the boats are ghosts.

Samira said that you could download an app if you

wanted more information about the boats. I think she forgot that I wasn't allowed to have my phone as it would stop me being safe. I didn't mind. I didn't want more information about the boats. I just liked to watch them pass by.

Samira found me a book about plants in the sea, things like seaweed, algae and plankton. I read the page about coral. It looks like a plant but it's really tiny animals. It's lying. It's just pretending to be a plant. I didn't want to read it no more so I left the sea-plant book on the table. I went to my room, took my flower book out the special drawer and went for a walk in the woods. I followed the path to the top of the hill, just before the woods end. I could hear the hum from the pylon and the electricity station. I was turning round to look at the sea when a boy yelled from behind me. He was riding a bicycle, free-wheeling down the hill and I only just had time to jump out of the way. I saw his face for a moment. It was full of smiles. I wanted to be as happy as him.

I stayed off the path and pushed my way through the brambles. I sat down on an old log and looked around. There were loads of brambles, but I could see ground-ivy and dried-up bluebells and ferns. I took my flower book out to check the ferns. There are many different sorts but people think they're all the same. There was a lady fern and male fern. The book says that male fern is the strongest.

'You are so hard to follow!'

I looked up even though I knew the voice. I'd heard it

shouting. Spencer was pushing through the brambles.

'You're always alone! I thought I'd keep you company.'

She swore when a bramble pinged back and scratched her. I told her that she didn't have to push so hard.

'Well, don't just sit there, help me!'

I didn't want to. I wanted her to go away. She swore again. I thought it was at me, but she was trying to wipe away the blood on her arm. When she stood there in the bushes, it looked like she was wearing a green skirt. Her hair was bright pink. It made me think she was like a giant flower pushing herself out of the ground. Sometimes bramble flowers are pink. Nan and I used to see them when we were walking along the canal. Sometimes cow parsley turns pink too. It can be called nosebleed.

Spencer said, 'Sorry, Dee. I didn't mean to shout at you. I've got a big mouth. Sometimes I can't help it.'

Spencer smiled at me. I didn't smile back.

'Come on, Dee! These bushes are scratching me up bad. I'm not gonna have any skin left. Please give me a hand. I won't bother you, I promise.'

I thought about her kicking her bedroom wall so hard I could feel it.

'Please, Dee?'

That was a whisper. She touched her arm and smeared the blood. I left my flower book on the log and went over to help her. I told her to try and go backwards a little bit, then held the bushes apart. She was wearing little denim shorts and her legs were scratched too. She looked down at them then at me.

'This is your fault.'

I said it wasn't. I hadn't asked her to come.

'I went through all this so we could be friends. What's wrong with you?'

I told her I didn't want no friends. They usually want something.

I went and sat down again. She came and sat next to me. 'Yeah, Dee. Truth. Don't trust no one.'

I wanted to read my flower book, but I couldn't with her watching me. I was going to put it in my bag but she snatched it out my hand. She was so quick, my fingers went snap in the air.

'I always wondered where you went when you disappeared. I thought you were with some boy or something, but you're here.'

I wanted my book back. She turned a page over too hard. I heard the sound of paper tearing in my head. My buttercups and harebells and knapweed, torn right through.

I said, 'Give it to me.'

She flipped back to the cover. She looked at me, then down at the writing.

'Awww,' she said. 'That's sweet. It's from your mum and your grandma.'

I nodded.

'Maybe I should call you Dee-Dee now.'

I didn't say anything. I just wanted my book.

'Are they into this flower stuff?'

I nodded again. Only Nan was, but I didn't want Spencer to know anything else about me.

Spencer told me that when she was a kid, she used to pick the petals off her aunty's flowers. They'd been in big pots on her aunty's balcony.

'Man, Dee, she loved those flowers. I'd take the petals and I'd mix them with flour and salt and stuff and pretend it was food for my dolls. Then I'd forget about it and my aunty would find it all mash up and stinking at the bottom of my cousin's wardrobe. I don't know why I always left it there. Maybe I just liked making her mad. And, man, she was already mad as hell because I'd left her flowers all naked.'

An ant walked across Spencer's leg. She flicked it off. I thought its feet would be sticky because of her blood.

'What's that?' She pointed to a flower hiding by a bramble bush. 'It looks like it's got a hood on.'

I went and kneeled down next to it. I couldn't help it, but I smiled up at her. I'd never seen one in real life before.

I said, 'It's got loads of names. Like cheese-and-toast and devils-and-angels.'

'Cheese-and-toast? It looks damn poisonous.'

'It's cuckoo pint too.'

'Why?'

'I don't know.'

'A pint of what?' She took out her phone.

I said, 'Why didn't they take your phone away too?'

She laughed. 'They can only take the phone they know about.'

She came and crouched next to me. She'd left my book back on the log. It was open and face-down on the wood. If the log was damp, it would leave a stain.

Spencer laughed again. This time it was so loud it made me jump. A robin that had come to check us out flew away. She showed me her phone then read it out.

'"Pint" is a shortening of the word "pintle", which means "penis". It's supposed to look like a dick.' She squinted at it and giggled. 'A bird's dick.'

That made me laugh too.

Spencer said, 'So, Dee-Dee? Do you reckon we can be friends?'

Later I read more about cuckoo pint, in case I see it again. Its seeds get spread by a fly that lives in cow shit. The spiky bit inside the hood heats up and smells like that too, to make the fly come to it. After it's flowered, it gives you red berries and they're very poisonous.

Spey

Benni asked me to meet him in Shadwell, but it takes longer than I expected because engineering works means it's buses instead of trains. He told me to wait outside when I arrived, until him and Sol came out. Benni says that it's good that Sol has the car because there aren't any trains on Boxing Day. I never thought about that. I usually just get tubes and buses.

Before I left, I called Mum. I almost didn't do it, just because he told me to. Is this my life now? Playing parent ping-pong, with each of them telling me how to treat the other one? It's not like I'm even getting any credit for all the years I've been good. I am probably the least stressful teenager in east London.

My call went to messages. I called again. Messages. She couldn't be driving home yet. It was way too early. The only reason she'd leave too soon was if there'd been a big family pile-in – and she would definitely have messaged me earlier on if anything like that was going down. I called again. She picked up.

'Oh. Spey.'

'Mum? Is anything wrong?'

'Not exactly.'

I could hear music.

'Is that *Little Shop of Horrors*, Mum?'

'Well, we were playing charades and it came up and, you know, we suddenly all realised we haven't heard it for ages.'

And was that my grandmother in the background singing 'Suddenly, Seymour'?

'Look, I was going to call you,' Mum said.

'It's okay. I did it.' Twice.

'You did what?'

'Called Benni.'

'Oh, yes. That's good.'

Grandma was seriously giving it some. If Seymour was actually standing beside her right then his eardrums would have suddenly combusted.

'Your Aunty Miranda brought out the Advocaat,' Mum said, 'and we made snowballs. And, well, I'm really not driving anywhere tonight. I'll be back first thing in the morning. Sorry, Spey. Will you be okay?'

For a second, I forgot to answer. Mum was having fun with her family?

'Spey?' She was just a bit too loud. 'Are you there?'

'Yeah, sorry. I'm fine. I actually phoned to tell you I'd be meeting up with Benni.'

'Oh! Wow! That's fantastic. Seriously, Spey, it's what I hoped for. I don't think . . .'

Grandma must have been right next to Mum. It sounded like she was offering both of us sweet understanding. Mum carried on talking.

'. . . what we needed. No grouchy teenagers cramping our style.'

'So does that mean I don't have to come next year?'

'Don't push your luck, sweetheart.'

Luck's been pushed now, Mum. I'm sitting on a bench literally freezing my arse off waiting for Benni and his vigilante mate. The street lights flick on, but it's not properly dark, so they're just smearing the rain. I stand up and sit down again. Even in those few seconds, it feels like Frozone brushed his hand across the bench. I see a kid watching me from a balcony on a block opposite. There's a Christmas tree next to them, its lights blinking on and off. They don't look away when I stare back. God, I'm in a staring match with an eight-year-old. Who am I?

I take out my phone to see what everyone's up to. Luckily, Mum's not on Instagram, because god knows what her feed would look like. Shauna's posted a picture. She's cuddling her baby sister on her lap and reading her *Clive is a Librarian*. I send her a thumbs up. Meanwhile, my own thumbs are being chewed away by the cold.

'It's all sorted.'

I look up. Benni's with another guy, who nods at me without smiling. He's already big, but zipped up in his jacket, he's almost cuboid. He's got half an eyebrow missing. I don't know if his barber slipped or he got scarred. This man doesn't look like he'd tolerate a barber with wobbly hands. He's had an ear stretcher through his left lobe. I didn't know people did that any more. I can see right through the hole to the fence behind him.

'This is Sol,' Benni says.

I know. The bus journey gave me plenty of time to check him out. He popped up on a a website about inspirational black men. Mum's always sending me links to sites like this as she obviously knew that my own father would not live up to the ideal. Nor would Sol. He's not featured as one of the inspirational ones. The main post's about a bloke called Gary Westsett who joined a gang in Wolverhampton when he was thirteen. His stressed-out mum went in hard and sent him to live with his granny in Jamaica, but he just got in with the badmen there. He was in prison here and in Jamaica, then after he'd had a couple of kids he decided enough was enough. He started up an anti-gang organisation and now gets pulled in to advise politicians. There's a picture of him between two white blokes in suits holding one of those giant cheques.

Sol was in the comments. He didn't even use an avatar. Real name, real unsmiling face. He's going on about selling out and rewarding the criminals and ignoring the victims. He says that county lines needs direct action. *You can't trust the police nor the politicians nor the teachers nor the social workers. All of them are in it for the money and an easy life. If you want to wipe out those lowlifes poisoning our children and prostituting our girls, we need to be vigilant. We need to be ruthless. We need to take the fight to them.*

So it seems like we're taking the fight to Hastings.

At the end of Sol's comments, he says: *Every young woman is a queen, even if they haven't had a chance to shine yet.*

Dee, a queen? In a different world, maybe, she'd be a flower queen, standing in a field of ox-eye daisies and poppies with a crown of dandelions on her head. Man, if it wasn't for Dee, I wouldn't know what an ox-eye daisy was.

I stand up but don't know what to do with myself because Sol doesn't offer his hand or even really look at me. He walks off up the street.

I say, 'He's not very friendly.'

'He knows he's got a job to do.'

'Right.'

If Benni knew me, he would have understood that 'right' straight off. It meant 'this bloke's seriously terrifying and I don't want to get in a car with him'.

I say, 'How do you know him?'

I'm whispering, even though Sol is way ahead and can't hear me.

'I knew his brother first.'

'Is he a gangbuster too?'

'Nah,' Benni says. 'Richie's pretty much the opposite. But we've got to get a move on. We need to pick up Sol's niece from her mum's.'

He leaves me and hurries after Sol.

*

125

I don't know how I managed to fall asleep. It's not like the car's super-deluxe or anything, though I don't know what I *was* expecting. It's probably best not to take the fight to drug dealers in a BMW X7. We don't want to stand out.

Back in Shadwell, I'd slid in behind Benni and shut the car door softly. Sol looks like he'd appreciate a door slam as much as he'd appreciate a loose-fingered barber. There's a kid's seat right in the middle at the back with a blanket crumpled across it. It was so cold when we got in the car, I wanted to take the blanket and cover myself. I didn't think Sol was going to like that, neither. The engine started and hot air blew round us as we pulled out into the street. I closed my eyes, then opened them quick. Sol likes his music loud. East London trickled past, a mash-up of buses and cars and roadworks. Sol and Benni were talking but the back speakers were drowning them out. I seriously wanted to know what they were saying.

And that must have been it. Even with bass so strong it was making my skin shake, I fell asleep. It's probably from living in London. Our old estate was never quiet. And Sizzla's way better than a kid screaming because his dad touched his marble run. The only problem is that I dribble when I sleep. I know because there's brown marks all over my pillows. I mean – not just the pillowcases, but right deep down into the pillows themselves. It really pisses Mum off because you can't wash pillows in the washing machine. They turn into weird lumps that you can't fix. We tried. So she adds a pillowcase and then another one until the seams are stretching like Wolverine's vest.

I realise I've been dribbling in Sol's car, but I haven't got a pillow to dribble over, so the spit's stuck to my cheek and slimed across my sleeve. Luckily there's no stains across his upholstery or I'd just get out and walk home now. My thigh's hurting from where the child seat's been digging in. The car's stopped moving. Someone bangs on the window. They do it again. That must have been what woke me up. I try and straighten myself, a reverse slide up. Then I see it's police. Sol and Benni have disappeared. It's just me in the car and a cop on the outside.

I sit up even straighter. The engine's off so I can't open the window. I open the door and almost fall out of the car. Dead leg, man! It's just as well I forgot to undo the strap. My legs are cramped and my neck feels knotted like a balloon. I unclip the seat belt but stay there. If I try and stand up, they're going to think I'm on drugs. That's if they don't think that already.

There's two cops, one woman, one bloke. The woman bends down to get a good view into the back. The man stays upright, like he's going to play leapfrog over her.

She says, 'I'm PC Holding. We saw you in the back there and wanted to check if you're all right. What's your name?'

My tongue moves inside my mouth. Speaking needs four things. First, air, working its way up my lungs. Second, vocal cords (they seriously don't look like guitar strings – man, I was so upset when I found out). Third, my tongue, mouth and lips have to get synchronised. And last of all, I need my brain, the supreme overlord of everything. I think my overlord went on holiday when I was sleeping.

I try to nod, even though that technically isn't the answer to her question. Gravity takes my head down but it sort of jams there. Then I worry that it's going to spring up like a jack-in-the-box and bash PC Holding's nose bridge. I rest my chin in my palm and persuade it up. Really carefully.

PC Holding asks again. 'So, what is your name?'

She says it a little bit slower and a little bit louder while touching her name badge.

My tongue slaps a few syllables around my mouth and a name falls out. I think it's mine. The cop behind her writes it down in a notepad. Great. Official police interest. That's going to please Benni. I don't think Sol's going to be brimming with Christmas joy if he sees them taking notes about his car, neither. But, seriously? Where the hell are Benni and Sol, anyway? Have they dumped the car and me with it? Am I some sort of decoy? I jerk upright and PC Holding jumps back. I think she lands on the guy's toe because he flinches.

'Easy,' he says. I don't know if he means me or her. In those American crime shows, you're supposed to keep your hands in sight to show you're not carrying a gun. Though in The Talk, Mum did point out that black and brown kids get shot dead by the police in England too. That haunted my dreams for a while afterwards. I flex my fingers and lay them flat on my knees.

'Sorry,' I say. 'I was asleep.'

'Are you unwell?'

'No.' The supreme brain overlord is finally in the Uber home back to me. That's five decent words I've managed and four of them were in the same sentence.

It's the guy's turn. 'Who's driving the car?'

'Benni's friend.'

'Who's Benni?'

'My . . . um . . . father.'

The cops swap a look. Yeah, I wish I was lying too.

'And who is Benni's friend?'

He's the man who says, *You can't trust the police nor the politicians . . . All of them are in it for the money and an easy life.*

'Um . . . I don't really know him. We've only just met.'

They swap another look. Do they honestly think I can't see them?

'How old are you?' PC Holding asks.

'Fifteen.'

'And where's Benni now?'

I look around but try not to be obvious, in case she really thinks I have been abandoned. Or taking the piss. He obviously isn't in here.

'I think he must be with his friend.'

'The one you don't know because you've only just met?'

'Yes.'

Then there they are, walking out of the building behind the

129

policeman's shoulder. There's a tall, cross-looking girl with them.

'He's there,' I say.

PC Holding spins round like a siren's gone off. Benni and Sol walk towards us. Their faces are blank. The girl looks like she's breathing in drain stink. Benni's eyes flick to me then away again, like he's sending me a secret message on a light ray and I'm expected to catch it and read it as it passes. Someone needs to tell him that it takes a good long while before you can read each other like that. None of them acknowledge the police. Sol goes straight to the driver's side and opens the door. PC Holding straightens up. For some reason, I say, 'Thank you,' to her. She nods to me and steps back. Her partner's scribbling in his notebook, glancing at me like he's trying to draw my portrait. Benni belts up. The girl slides in on the other side of the car seat. Sol starts the engine and we pull away. I want to look back but I'm sure PC Holding and partner are still watching us and they might think my backwards glance is a call for help.

I lean forward and rest my arms on the back of Benni's seat. Benni breathes in like he's going to say something, but Sol gets there first.

'What did they want?'

'They were worried about me.'

'Dream on, boy. They were nosing.' I catch his eye in the mirror. 'What did you say?'

'I was asleep. They woke me up.'

'And?'

'What's he gonna say?' Benni asks.

'I'm asking the boy, not you. Well? Spey?' The way he spits out my name it's obvious he's not keen on my mum's choice, neither.

'I didn't say anything. I told them I was all right.' And my name. I think.

'That it?' Sol says.

'Yeah.' Though, god, I seriously wish I'd given them Sol's name now.

We turn the corner on to a one-way road. Sol takes his time steering between the cars parked-up on both sides. I grab glances at the girl. This must be Sol's niece, the one who was rescued from county lines. She's black – well, more black than me and Benni, and her hair's twisted into bantu knots. Every single hair is under control. The ear I can see is full of studs and loops and there's a small tattoo just behind it. Her hair's styled tight so it stretches the ink. I don't know what it's supposed to be. I can't imagine a conversation where I'd ever dare ask her.

Benni throws a quick glance back at me.

'This is Astrid,' he says. 'Sol's niece.' Yeah, Benni. I kind of guessed that already.

Spey

We've hit gridlock on the motorway. Everyone must be escaping their families. Well, everyone apart from Mum, who seems to be having a great time with hers. I suddenly want to message her, but what am I going to say? *Hey, Mum, I'm stuck in a car with Benni's mad gang-busting mate whose got a niece who must have hated me before she ever met me.*

Oh, and I'm hungry. So hungry.

Benni's nodding his head. His lips are moving too, but I can swear his words don't match J Hus's. I don't even know how I know this tune. Mum banned J Hus as soon as he hit jail for being a potential bad influence on me and I was never into him enough to sneak a listen on my headphones.

Astrid is slumped towards her window, still doing an excellent job of not knowing I exist.

Benni turns round. 'You know this track?'

The car moves half a wheel forward and stops sharp. I sway forward and stay there. My mouth is close to Benni's shoulder. It opens and starts talking. My mouth, not Benni's shoulder. Though this whole situation is so weird, a talking shoulder wouldn't be out of place.

I say, 'Mum hates this stuff.'

'Yeah. I know. She thinks rap's all about money and

sex— um . . . sexist. But sometimes you have to listen to what people need to say.'

'You think I should go against her?'

Benni shakes his head hard. 'I didn't say that!'

Astrid snorts. 'J Hus is an idiot. I don't know why y'all arguing over him. Thinks he's a big man 'cause he carries a knife in a shopping mall. I mean, Westfield, man! What was he gonna do? Cut up the leggings in Primark?'

Sol changes the music. That should be it, but it's like something's burning in me. It's like Benni can get Mum to serve him up Christmas lunch one day then brush her away the next, just because he's sitting next to some tough gangsta-fighter.

'I wrote a song for Mum once,' I say.

Astrid glances over at me, eyebrows raised.

Benni twists right round. His jacket slides across the seat. 'Did you?'

'Yeah. For Father's Day.' I pause. He doesn't react. 'When I was eight.'

He still doesn't say anything. I reckon there's a whole thread of bouncebacks running through his mind. And when he's chosen the right words, he'll still have to find the right tone.

'What was it about?' he says at last. Tame and safe.

'Mum. Because she had to be my dad too.'

Sol turns up the music and Benni sits straight again.

Astrid twitches her neck the minimum amount she needs

133

to show that I am now officially seen by her. She's even smiling. Sort of.

'How did the song go?' she asks.

I try and read her face, but since I've only seen half of it for the last hour I've got no idea what she's thinking. And it's not like I'll be killing our conversation. She isn't exactly . . . verbose. (Another one of Mum's avoid-the-shiny-new-slide words.)

'I want to write a poem about my ma, who's gotta be the things that both parents are, I'm gonna make her cake and cups of tea, cause of all the things she does for me.'

Astrid raises her eyebrows. '*Fresh Prince* beats, right?'

'Inspired by.'

She laughs. 'I did the same thing for my mum.'

'From *Fresh Prince*?'

'Yeah. For her birthday. So this is a story about my mum, she's got lovely hair and a perfect bum.'

I breathe in her laughing air and it starts to work on me. Something pops out that sounds like a giggle.

'Why do you think it's funny?' she asks.

I'm imagining my mum's face if I ever voiced an opinion on her bum. Once she got over the shock, that would be one massive Objectification Of Women Talk. And probably Porn Talk Part Two. Astrid goes back to looking out the window and the laughing gas evaporates.

'It's brutal,' she says.

'My lyrics?'

She flips up the tight seat belt so she can turn right round to face me properly. She does it with her little finger and it bends back so much I think it's going to snap. When she's comfortable, she lets the belt fall back in place.

'Going country. Not just for you, but your family and anyone that really cares about you. Though you don't care at first. It's all eating out and new phones and jokes. You get the best attention, especially if you're a girl.'

I think of Dee and my stomach bumps. 'What do you mean?'

'Don't play stupid. You and your mates ever chirps up a girl? It's like that. More boys, less girls, big time chirpsing.' She tips her head sideways. 'Yeah, you know what I mean.'

Technically, I don't chirps. My mother might hunt me down and kill me. I have, however, been in the presence of mates who do.

'What's your friend?' Astrid asks. 'White? Black? Turkish?'

'Dee? She's white.'

Astrid shrugs. 'She's gonna be valuable. No one searches little white girls going about their business. She got parents looking for her?'

'Her mum's around sometimes. But . . .'

'Drugs?'

I nod. 'I think her aunty tried to help.'

'The problem is you don't always know you want to be helped.'

'I suppose so.'

'But she's luckier than some. She's got you.'

The music shifts. It's a Christmas track. Sol turns it down. I wonder who the hell put together his playlist. *If you like J Hus, try Wham!.* Benni peers through the gap between the seats. I think he's going to say something else about my Father's Day poem. He's had long enough to work it out.

Instead he says, 'I tried to write poetry in prison.'

'Like Oscar Wilde?' It pops out my mouth before I can do anything.

I tap my lips like I'm trying to nudge the words back in and snap them shut. After a couple of years watching *University Challenge* with Mum, I know stuff, stuff that lurks in secret corners of my head then jumps out when I'm not looking. It's the stuff that can make you look like a show-off or get you a beating in certain schools. Though not in my current one. Michael's mentored a Year Seven who's read Kafka in the original German, without being German.

'Yeah,' Benni says. 'Like Oscar Wilde. Though I never got to see Reading jail from the inside. They closed the place down a few years ago.'

There's a little pause. Should we be bonding over the fact that we both know that Oscar Wilde wrote *The Ballad of Reading Gaol*? And that neither of us expected the other one to know it? (Okay, *I* didn't expect *him* to.)

'What happened to your poems?' I ask.

'I've still got them in a notebook somewhere. We had a writing group. I can't remember which prison.'

Because you've been in so many.

'The tutor was a guy called Manji. He gave us all a notebook of our own. Half the lads couldn't read or write, but that didn't matter. Either the tutor or one of us did the writing for them. He used to read to us – love poems, war poems, sonnets, limericks, all sorts of stuff. He said he wanted to expand our minds beyond the prison walls. We lost guys along the way, of course. They were shipped out or just couldn't be arsed and their notebooks ended up as roach material. And sometimes there weren't enough screws to take you down to the library, even if you were virtually begging to go. I always went if I could. It was better than sitting on my jack for twenty-three hours a day.'

Benni turns back and looks at the road ahead. We're stuck behind a tanker but it seems clearer after that.

We stop at a service station. Sol doesn't ask us. He just stops, but no one complains. I suppose it's for petrol, but he parks nearer to the shops. There's a Starbucks, a chemist and a SPAR, all with fairy lights in their windows, though the chemist is closed. Benni and Sol get out and follow the signs to the toilet. I don't really need to pee, but I need to pee even less now they're both heading that way. I still haven't worked out if I want to know Benni any better, so we're nowhere near the stage where we can have a casual side-by-side piss with Sol as our screwface wingman.

Astrid unclips her seat belt and opens the car door. She

strides towards the smokers' shelter and smokes. Proper cigarettes. I'm shocked and I don't understand why. I've seen people jacking up harder stuff than tobacco when I've been heading through the park to school. Mum said there was a dealer on our block when I was little. He'd almost be handing packages to his customers over my head as she wheeled my buggy through the foyer on the way to the childminder. But no one smokes any more. Not cigarettes. Astrid does, though. And she doesn't make a performance of it, like some of the posh kids when they're rolling up a spliff at parties. She does it like she's swiping a password or brushing her teeth, automatic. Pack out of bag. Cigarette out of pack and in mouth. Pack back in bag. Lighter out of pocket. Cigarette lit – and breathe. She glances over at me and sees me watching. She doesn't look away. I do.

When I look back again, she's on the phone.

I wonder if that's what Dee's like now, hugging a wall, in a cloud of smoke. I can't imagine it. Dee smoking – nah. She just didn't do the things that other people did. That's what confused everyone. She didn't follow the patterns. She made her own. Sometimes I thought there were two Dees, the human-size one and then a tiny one inside her head surrounded with levers and dials. (Yeah, like the Arquillian jeweller in *Men In Black*.) The outside Dee looked like any other girl, but the Arquillian-jeweller Dee saw a different universe.

Benni and Sol are coming back, both at the same time,

like they really did synchronise in there. Sol's rubbing cream into his hands. Benni's shaking his like he passed the only towel to Sol.

'I'm going to get some snacks,' Benni says.

Good. I should go and help him with his selection, but that feels too father-son normal. Sol comes back to the car. He ignores me and calls over to Astrid.

'You coming?'

She's on her phone too, having a conversation that isn't making her happy. She kills the call.

'Is there a problem?' Sol says.

His phone buzzes. He takes it out his pocket and checks it. 'Shit.' He turns back to Astrid. 'You message your mother?'

'What d'you mean?' Her arm drops and she balances the cigarette in her fingers, away from her body like she's scared of catching fire.

'How does she know who we're travelling with?'

'Because he was standing right next to you in her sitting room.'

'You know what I mean?'

'Sorry, Uncle Sol. I don't.'

'He didn't have a badge with his name on it. I don't remember saying "Benni" at all at your mother's. For good reason.'

'And she noticed.' Astrid takes a puff but turns her face away when she exhales. 'She got worried and asked me.'

'And you told her?'

'Of course I told her! When y'all ask me questions, I tell truth. Wasn't that what we agreed? Or am I the only one keeping that part of the deal? Am I supposed to tell the truth all the time, except for when I lie for you?'

Sol looks over at the SPAR. Benni's on his way out with his snack-loaded bags. 'She told your dad. I just got a message. He's on his way.'

'What?'

'He wants to meet up with his old friend.'

Astrid kills her cigarette – murder with extra violence. 'It's not my fault.'

'No.' Sol nods towards Benni. 'It's his.'

Sol heads back to the car and we follow. He gets into the driver's seat, belts up and starts the engine. We all take the same places we had before. I thought Sol would tell Benni about Astrid's dad, but he just jacks the music up again. I want to get my hands on that snack bag, but now definitely doesn't seem like the time to ask. I should have brought the rest of the panettone and the ham.

Twenty minutes later, Sol turns on to a slip road. Benni looks over at Sol, but Sol just carries on driving.

'Isn't the motorway quicker?' Benni asks.

I check Astrid but she's back on the 'ignore Spey' vibe.

'Sol, man!' Benni says.

I thought I understood the balance here. Sol brought the car and the expertise. Benni brought the mission and the snacks. But Sol's shifting along the seesaw to show how he's got the power, and Benni's small and light. I want to whisper in Benni's ear, tell him that Astrid's dad's on his way to us and no one seems happy about it. I don't, because I'm on that seesaw next to Benni, my legs dangling in the air until Sol lets us down. I watch the lights streak past the window. Random houses, headlights on the parallel country road, then bright spots of red cats' eyes between the road and hard shoulder.

'Sol! What's happening?' Benni's shouting.

Sol just carries on driving like he's got a Benni-filter turned up full.

'Are we turning back?'

We take an overpass, shoot round a roundabout then it's another slip road. A sign flashes by. Thirty-three miles to London.

Benni sees it too. 'If the plan's changed,' he says quietly, 'drop me and my boy off at the nearest station.'

I am not your boy! Oh, and there are no trains. That's why we're in the bloody car!

'Sol!'

'You bother me again, Ben, and you're gonna leave this car without me opening the door first.'

'Uncle,' Astrid says. 'Don't.'

I don't want to be in this car any more.

Benni sits back in the chair so hard I'm surprised I don't see his spine poking through the upholstery. Sol whacks the

141

music up so hard he must be revving the engine on beats. I lean towards Astrid.

'Who's your dad?' I ask her.

'The man who brings trouble.'

'Like mine.'

'No, Spey. Nothing like yours. Yours is sat in front taking bad-mouth from my uncle because he wants to help you. Mine . . . nah! Never gonna care about no one except his sweet self.'

I want to open the window. Just a millimetre for a nanosecond to cool my hot red face. Astrid doesn't seem bothered that she's made me blush. Or she doesn't care.

'It's up to your dad to tell you his business.'

He's not my dad! I swallow it back. I don't want to hear any more about what she's got to say about that. It doesn't make things all right just because hers is even crappier than mine.

'We're here for Dee,' she says. 'Let's talk about her.'

I nod.

'What's your plan when you find her? Those boys aren't gonna let her go easy. She's an asset.'

'An asset?' I shake my head. 'Like Bourne.'

I meant to say this in my head, but my mouth opened and spilled it out. Luckily, a man shouting 'jungle' on Sol's mixtape covered up my idiot words. But god, I wish Dee was a trained assassin like Bourne. She'd have easily taken out Chez and those bastard gangboys that prowled her old estate, strangled them with her bare hands, or shoot them with a long range rifle in Waterloo station.

Astrid's still talking. '. . . property. She belongs to them. You want to take away their goods.'

'Dee isn't goods.' Though it seems like she was always being passed around like a package with the wrong address.

'Of course I know that,' Astrid says. 'But you need to understand how they think.'

And suddenly, I want to know – what's the worst that could happen to her? Who will she be when I find her?

'What was it like when you . . .' When she what? Went country? It made it sound like a hotel in Cornwall. But what else can I say? When you dealt drugs? Sold crack? '. . . when you were part of a gang?'

She laughs, a quick snort like she's holding back most of it. 'You studying to be a lawyer, Spey?'

'What do you mean?'

'The way you're checking your words. *Part of a gang*? Like being part of a samba crew or trampolining club?'

'No. I didn't mean . . .'

She turns back towards the window.

Five minutes later, we're off the motorway and heading into a town. I don't catch its name. I check my phone but the battery's run out. I must have turned the torch on by accident again. And running all those Christmas vids earlier probably didn't help. We turn into a Quik Inn car park. Sol turns off the engine and gets out. He strides across the car park to the reception.

Benni looks round at me. 'I'll sort this out.'

I don't say anything. I don't even want to meet his eyes. Sol being such a dick to him is a secret we can keep separately. He stabs the seat belt release button and shrugs himself free. The seat belt whirs back into place, the metal clasp clanging against the inside of the car. He gets out and follows Sol's trail. Astrid gets out too, but she goes and sits on the low wall between the car park and the street. She hoists her bag on to her lap and starts rummaging until she finds her cigarettes. I wish I could just vault into the driver's seat and go on my way. Instead, I let myself out and join Astrid on the wall. I keep a good distance between us, though.

'What's happening here?' I ask.

'How do I know? It's not like Uncle's telling me nothing, is it?'

'Is your dad here?'

'Nah.'

'So why have we stopped?

She holds her fingers to her temples. I'm surprised the cigarette doesn't singe her hair. I've heard that some edge control gel is pretty flammable.

'Okay, Spey! I'm psychic! I'm tuning into Uncle Sol's thought waves and he tells me . . .' She drops her fingers and looks at me. 'Part of a gang.' She laughs.

'What?' I sound like a cross six-year-old.

'You think Dee's *part of a gang*?'

'No, not really . . .'

'But I was?'

'No, I didn't mean . . .'

'Like I sent the top man in the Fallgate Boys an application form offering up my services? Then I took an exam to see if I was qualified. I'm lucky I passed, right? Or I wouldn't have been part of it.'

I stand up and roll my shoulders. I don't need her stress. It's not like I invited her to come with us. All she's brought is attitude and now, it seems, trouble. I'm going to plug my charger into a socket in the reception and once I've worked out where I am, try and get away from here, with Benni or without him.

We hear men shouting. Me and Astrid look towards the Quik Inn door at the same time. I think half the town must be looking towards that door because that's one mad ball of noise rolling towards us. Then it bursts out on to the steps, two grown men yelling at each other. Two grown *Black* men yelling at each other like they want to summon the police helicopter from Hackney right now. They stop at the top of the steps, both of them fists clenched.

'No, man!' Benni shouts. 'You know I can't deal with that right now!'

'You lied to me!'

'What did you expect?'

'I expected you to be truthful! You said you and Richie had come to an arrangement. I know my brother. I know how you can't trust the man. But I trusted you, Benni! You see the position you put me in?'

'What was I supposed to do?'

'Tell the damn truth! That's what.'

'You don't understand.'

Sol glances over at me. 'Yeah. I do. But what do I do now? Hide you in my pocket?'

Benni lets his hands relax. His arms flop by his side. 'We could just carry on driving.'

'With my brother's daughter in the car?'

'You didn't have to bring her, Sol.' I see Benni tense up again. 'Or was it deliberate? You know Richie wants to find me, so you brought Astrid as an excuse—'

Sol grabs Benni by the shoulders and pushes him against the wall. I should do something. I should dive in between them. I should call Sol off. *Call Sol off?* I can't even find enough voice to cough right now.

Astrid runs over to Sol's car and opens the driver door. She bangs it shut hard. Sol lets go of Benni and looks around. I was right. The man doesn't like hearing his car slammed about. Astrid's eyes are wide and she's breathing so hard she doesn't need cigarettes to make the air smoke. Sol lets go of Benni and Benni wipes his jacket collar like he's cleaning off Sol's handprints.

'When's he gonna be here?' Astrid asks.

'He can't get wheels 'til morning.'

'So we're staying here?'

'Yeah.' Sol glances at Benni. 'Or head back to London.

Anyhow, it's too late to pitch up at some poor woman's house in Hastings. She wouldn't open her door to us lot.'

I could have told him that Dee's Aunty Janet had a sister on crack and – well – Dee. She must have been used to all sorts of people knocking her door at every hour. I don't, though. I watch Astrid head to reception, followed by Sol.

Benni's still arranging his clothes. I look away and keep looking away even when I hear his footsteps coming towards me. His slightly beaten-up shoes stop near my flash new Jordans.

'Sorry,' he says.

'I could have been in Hastings already.'

'No, you couldn't,' he says. 'That's why you asked me.'

'I wish I hadn't.'

'Fair enough.' He walks past me towards the stairs.

Dee

chenopodium album

ᏘAT HEN

LAMBS QUARTERS

WHITE GOOSEFOOT

I've got ten per cent battery left on my phone. I can't charge it because of the electricity. I've got messages too, but I can't deliver nothing because I can't get out the front door.

I should phone Chez.

They're gonna phone Chez.

I'm supposed to deliver up to Kemp Town. If I don't, someone else is gonna take over. Chez said I better not let that happen.

Samira at Chalkleighs made me make a list of the things I thought I could control and the things I thought I couldn't control. I couldn't control who came to Chalkleighs. I couldn't control Spencer and Anissa. But she said maybe I could work on how I control the way I deal with certain situations.

Anissa moved in because Jasmine went somewhere else after she left hospital. There was another girl after Jasmine, but she only stayed two days because she was an asylum seeker and had to go somewhere else too.

I thought Anissa and Spencer would be friends, but Anissa didn't want to be friends with no one. The second morning she was there, she came downstairs and started shouting at me and Spencer when we were having breakfast. She said she was sure that someone had been in her room when she was having a shower. If she ever found who it was, she was gonna break their fingers.

Then Spencer got cross and threatened to break Anissa's stupid face.

Then Anissa said that she knew proper gangstas that could shoot Spencer through her skanky heart and never get caught.

Then Spencer said— Man, I didn't care what Spencer said. I didn't even care that she batted the cornflakes and orange juice off the table and specks of it dripped over my jeans. I left them all yelling – Spencer and Anissa, then Milly and Abi from Chalkleighs, who were trying to calm everything down but were shouting too.

I went to the woods. I walked to the top of the hill, even though all the shouting had made me feel tired. I found my usual place and sat down on the old tree trunk. I couldn't see any flowers this time, only leaves. A kid had dumped a fairy house in the place where the cuckoo pint was. Someone should have told that kid that fairies don't live in cardboard boxes. Why would they when they could live in a real tree? The kid had made a proper effort, though. They'd cut out real windows and stuck on curtains made out of pink material. The front door was painted bright red. It was shiny too, like they'd used nail polish.

I used to paint Nan's toes because it made her feel dizzy when she tried to bend down and do it herself. She liked silver and gold. She said colours like blue and purple and red made it look like an elephant had stepped on her foot. I think that's because I wasn't very good at nail polishing and loads of it would end up on her skin. She didn't mind. She said anything made her ugly feet look better. The nurses asked me if I wanted to paint Nan's nails the night before she died, but I said no. Nan was sleeping. She wouldn't have been able to choose the colour. Samira had asked me if I feel guilty about that. Of course I don't. I didn't know Nan was going to die. And if I had known, I'd have been trying to change everything so she didn't die, not spending time trying to paint her nails.

I sat there on the log in the woods and closed my eyes. When I close my eyes, it's like my ears open wider. I could still hear the buses going down towards the sea and the pylon in the electricity station humming on my skin. It must have been play time for the primary school on the other side of the woods. I wondered how many of them kids were screaming because they were happy and how many just wanted to get the bad stuff out. I suppose that's what Anissa and Spencer were doing this morning, shouting to get the bad stuff out. But I've got enough bad stuff of my own. I didn't want to catch their stuff too.

I heard a swear word and opened my eyes. Spencer was coming towards me. She stood there for a moment, wearing her bramble skirt. She rubbed her bare arm and scrunched up her face.

'Man, this is when I need a can of petrol, Dee. Splash it all over, get out my lighter and *whoosh!*' She waved her other arm in the air. 'All of this thorny crap would be gone.'

I didn't say nothing. She made a face at me and started pushing her way towards me again.

'I was just joking, Dee-Dee.'

I wanted to close my eyes again but I knew that you don't close your eyes when girls like Spencer are around.

She said, 'I love nature, I really do. And if I *did* have petrol and a lighter, I'd go into that stupid bitch Anissa's room, and set fire to that. If I was lucky, she'd still be inside.'

She sat next to me. I stood up.

'Don't go! I've only just got here.'

She grabbed my hand and tried to pull me down again. I stayed standing.

'You swapping friends, then, Dee? You're gonna be hanging off Anissa's tail now?'

She stood up again. I stepped backwards and felt something squish. My heel had kicked the fairy house into the tree.

'Awww,' Spencer said. 'Look what you've done. Them poor kids!' Then she gave me a smile. It wasn't her big angry

151

smile. It was like one she'd kept as a secret. 'I know you didn't mean to do that. You're like me. You know what it's like to have someone mash up your stuff. My older brother was a maniac when Mum wouldn't give him money. He used to kick in our doors and jump on my toys. All kind of mad-boy shit. Once him and Mum were fighting about the microwave. I mean, proper fighting. Ross held one side, and Mum held the other side and they were pulling it like it was a cracker. Then Ross let go and it dropped on Mum's foot. They had to take her to hospital because she broke some bones and I went to stay with my aunty.'

She took another step. I reached behind and touched the tree bark. I dug my fingernails right in until I could feel splinters. Spencer stopped in front of me and put her hand on my arm.

'We all go through shit, don't we?' She shrugged. 'That's how we end up in places like Chalkleighs. And that's why girls like you and me deserve fun.'

I knew she wanted me to nod, so I did. I thought maybe she'd go away then.

'Do you think about the bad stuff, Dee?'

I shook my head. I tried not to. Samira had said that my bad memories were part of me. She couldn't take them away, but she could help me put them in different rooms in my head. I only had to visit them when I wanted to.

Spencer put her arm round my shoulders and pulled me away.

152

'Hey! You haven't got your book today!'

'It's in my room.'

'You have to be careful, Dee-Dee. I reckon Anissa won't think nothing of having a snoop round your room.'

I was careful. The drawer was locked.

I didn't mind leaving the wood. I didn't want Spencer filling the space there. Even though she was smiling, I could feel her angriness. It was like the hum from the pylon. We cut through the back of the leisure centre to the main road and walked downhill towards the sea. I was supposed to see Samira at eleven-thirty but I didn't know what time it was because my phone was still locked in the office.

I asked Spencer where we were going.

'To the pier! For fun!' Spencer looked up at the sky. 'It feels like I've just broken out of prison. No Abi breathing down our back telling us to tidy up or do our homework. No Samira trying to get us to stress out about things that happened ages ago and don't matter no more, anyway.'

I thought about Samira sitting in the office right now, waiting for me. I'd promised her I'd let her know if I couldn't make it. I pulled my arm away from Spencer's.

'What?'

'I'm supposed to tell Samira if I can't see her.'

'Well, phone her, then!'

'They took my phone.'

Spencer gave me another big smile. 'Well, there you go. It's not your fault.'

She took my arm again and pulled me on.

I didn't like the pier. It was too loud. It was like the stones and the sea and the gulls were shouting at everyone. We walked past the kids' rides and places selling coffee and a closed-down restaurant, right to the end. I couldn't see the big boats on the horizon, because there was a mist. It looked like the sky was melting into the sea. We had to stop walking or we would have fallen off the edge.

There were seats at the end of the pier. I could see the backs of people's heads. A bald man. A woman in a blue headscarf. A baseball cap over a hoodie. Spencer held my arm tighter. She was holding me so close her elbow dug in my side.

'Look who I brought!' she said.

'Good one, Spence.'

The person wearing the baseball cap turned round. I didn't need to see his face. I knew that voice.

'Hello, gorgeous.' Chez came towards me. He ran his finger from my hair down to my chin like he was looking for a scar, or trying to make one.

Dee

Sonchus asper

PRICKLY SOWTHISTLE

SPINY-LEAVED SOWTHISTLE

HARE'S LETTUCE

I couldn't move. Samira told me before it was normal to feel like that. She'd said it's our brains telling us to run away or stay and fight. I couldn't fight. I always lose. Then my brain switched. It shouted, 'Run.' I kept my head down so I could see my feet, and make sure they were really running. The sea and the stones and the gulls were still shouting but my feet were thumping too. They sounded like the angry man who lived next door to me and Nan. He used to bang on the wall when our TV was on.

I thought Chez was gonna follow me, but when I stopped and looked back, all I saw was other people looking at me. I walked back up the hill to Chalkleighs and went straight to my room. Samira had pushed a note under my door. She was going to be at Chalkleighs until one o'clock if I needed her. After that, I could use the phone in the main office if I needed to call her later in the afternoon.

I didn't need Samira. I needed Chez to go away.

But he'd been looking for me. He'd just found me. He wouldn't go away.

I unlocked the drawer in my desk and took out my flower book. I closed my eyes and opened it. Prickly sowthistle. It looks like baby dandelions and no one notices them. They're everywhere, like in the cracks in the pavement and in the gardens that no one wants. The seeds spread in the air and they've even been found on the under-bit of planes. Birds eat them and poo them out. So do cows and earthworms.

I thought about what Spencer said. We'd all been through shit. That's why we were at Chalkleighs. But shit can take you to places where you can grow.

Chez knew I was there. He'd found me. He thought I'd be too scared to tell anyone. And I was, but . . .

I had grown.

I could tell Samira. She said everything was confidential unless I was in real danger. Then she'd have to tell someone, to make sure I was safe. I didn't know if I was in real danger.

I put my book back into the drawer. And then the fire alarm went off.

I went on to the landing. I couldn't see no flames or smell no smoke, but Abi came and took me downstairs and into the car park. I thought maybe Spencer had done what she said she was going to do and set fire to Anissa's room. Like I said, you should always keep your eyes open when

156

girls like Spencer are around because they always have *their* eyes on you.

I heard the sirens getting closer and a fire engine pulled into the car park. The firefighters ran out and ran into the building, though I still couldn't see no smoke. Someone poked my back. It was Spencer.

'You ran off, Dee. I thought we were gonna have some fun.'

I said that I didn't want to have fun with Chez.

'But he wants to have fun with you.'

We watched Abi do the head count. Then Spencer'd smiled that angry smile. 'Man, Anissa's gonna hate this. Strangers stamping through her stuff, looking for fire.'

I asked Spencer if she'd started the fire.

'How could I? I was with you, getting ready to have some fun!' She stayed behind me, whispering straight into my ears. 'But what if it isn't in Anissa's room? What if the fire's burning in your room right now, Dee? Can you save your little flower book?'

Prickly sowthistle grows everywhere. So does bindweed, creeping up and grabbing. It was pulling at my insides, like flames. The pages would be burning, smoke filling my drawer until my flowers would be ash. I tried to run towards the building but Spencer pulled me back.

'You're not allowed to go in, Dee. It could be dangerous. But you don't have to.' She let go of me with one hand and dug into the pocket of her playsuit. 'I'm your friend,

157

remember? I've got your back.'

She held up my flower book. I tried to grab it but she moved it away.

'Friends. I've got your back and you've got mine.'

She was not my friend, but I nodded.

'Yeah, best friends for ever, Dee.' She pushed the book into my hand. 'But take care of your stuff. You never know who's gonna cause you trouble.'

Spey

I haven't stayed in a hotel in England before. I've stayed in loads of overseas ones and Mum even took me to Edinburgh to the festival when I was in Year Six. One of her friends was in a play there, but we had to leave it early because of the swearing.

I'm not sure if this is even a hotel. In the adverts, Quik Inn go on about being different from other hotels. It's on the laminated welcome sheet pinned next to the sink too. *Quik Inn. Comfortable and affordable, for travellers who know the value of money.* The room is tiny. You can step out of bed and into the shower. I mean it. One step. As long as you don't knock yourself unconscious tripping over the toilet first.

The sink is outside the bathroom and there are two plastic cups wrapped in more plastic balanced upside down on the tap. I'm not sure where you're supposed to put them when you unwrap them. Maybe on the toilet seat. There's a flat screen TV on the wall above a kid-size desk. If I take a step back – a small one, because I don't want to crack my spine on the sink – and hold up my phone, it covers the whole screen. So, yeah, I might just as well watch a film on my phone – but I can't because there's only thirty minutes' free Wi-Fi.

The remote control's on the desk and I click the TV on.

The visuals are sharp but the sound is shot. I scroll through the menu. There's nothing I want to watch, anyway.

My phone buzzes.

> **Hi. It's Astrid. Want to go for a walk?**

Anything's better than being stuck here. Even hanging out with a girl who seems to hate me. Though since she must have asked Sol to ask Benni for my number, she couldn't hate me that much. That takes effort.

> **Ok**

> **Watch out, tho. Last time I saw Uncle Sol he was in the foyer with ur dad**

My dad. She's not going to give up on that, is she?

The way they were earlier, I'm surprised I can't hear police sirens. I open the room door a crack and stick my head out into the corridor. Nope, no shouting. They might have taken their fight outside or be having a quick rest before starting on each other again. I go back into the room and close the door. I head over to the window, unlock it and pull it up. The view outside is car park, but not the same one we parked in. It must wrap around the building. That's a lot of cars. There must be a whole load of travellers who believe those adverts about knowing the value of money. I grab my room swipecard, the light clicks off and I clamber out. I land on a grass verge. Well, to be accurate, on the rubbish on the grass verge. I pull the window down, but leave a tiny space in case I need to hoist it up and get back in.

I follow the car park round to the front. Astrid's waiting by

Sol's car. For a second, I think she's going to hot-wire the engine and drive us off, but she nods at me and walks away.

'Where to?' I ask.

'I think I know this place.'

'Right.'

She doesn't say anything else and I don't ask, even though I'm dying to know.

I say, 'The room's a bit basic.'

She looks at me and raises her eyebrows. I'm beginning to wonder why she ever bothers lowering them when she talks to me. 'I've seen worse.'

Right, she did say 'walk' not 'talk', but this is way too awkward.

'I was worried about bumping into your uncle so I climbed out the window.'

She glances at me, then laughs. 'Serious?'

'What about you?' I ask her.

'I went through the front door! Your dad stormed off to his room and Uncle Sol disappeared.'

We're out of the car park and on to a main road. It's dark for a main road, even though there's loads of cars. The street lights don't feel bright enough and it's colder than London. I wish I'd brought my gloves.

'Is it a secret where we're going?'

She laughs. I'm glad. It stops me feeling so stressed around her.

'Not really. We're going to the station.'

'Seriously?'

'Yeah.'

'There aren't any trains.'

'I know.'

We cross over the road and climb up some steps to a footbridge over a railway track. Our footsteps clank like stormtroopers. Astrid is just ahead of me. I catch up with her.

'Why the station?'

'I want to remember something.'

We clank down the other side of the bridge and head through a parade of shops and restaurants. Some are closed for Christmas, but a tapas place is open. It looks like there's more staff than eaters in there. The KFC's got people, though. It makes me smile. I think about Fi and her Tokyo Christmas. Mum hates chicken shops, so every time I go in one, it's like I have to dodge past an invisible Mum stretching out her arms to bar me. According to Aunty Jacklyn, they're nothing but gang hideouts and you can tell by the menu whose territory you're in. It depends on whether the laminate's gloss or matte. Give Mum her due, even she rolled her eyes at that one. This KFC must be neutral territory because the menu's on a board over the counter.

The shopping parade's pretty busy. Astrid weaves round everyone like she's got a built-in anti-crash device. We come out on to a wide pedestrian street. It's even busier here, probably because it's where all the pubs are. The lamp posts are wound with Christmas lights that join overhead into bell shapes. The lights flash on and off to make it look like they're ringing.

'It's just up there,' Astrid says.

Yeah, I can see the station at the top of the hill. A few taxis still wait in the rank. I suppose it's so people know where to get one. Maybe Uber hasn't made it to these parts yet. The station's closed, but there's a small wall outside. Astrid sits down. So do I. Again. It's as cold as the bench in Shadwell.

She says, 'All the stations start to look the same after a while. It doesn't matter if they're big or small. There's gonna be a WHSmith, a coffee place, a pasty shop, and if you're really lucky, a Krispy Kreme stall.'

'Did you go to a lot of places?' I listen to my words as they come out, hoping that there's nothing to stress her out again.

'Yeah,' she says. 'Loads of places. And the thing is, it's not like they dragged me screaming to do it.' She looks at me. 'I wanted to. Or I thought I wanted to.'

She slides her bag down her shoulder so she can find her cigarettes. I wait for her to go through her routine and take in a lungful of smoke. When I got the Drugs Talk, Mum said that the hardcore anti-smoking adverts around when she was a teenager really worked for her. That, plus working in a doctors' surgery. If she saw me sitting so close to Astrid, she'd report the girl for attempted murder.

'I hated school,' Astrid says. 'I think our year group was the one that made at least ten teachers change their careers.

I could swear that my old chemistry teacher works for Deliveroo now.'

'Did you get any GCSEs?'

Shit! I seriously just asked that? Am I really turning into Mum?

'Nah.' She shakes her head, making a wobbly line of smoke. 'I could have if I'd got my head down, but . . . what was the point?' She waves her non-smoking hand towards the station. 'All this seemed more exciting.'

'Krispy Kreme doughnuts?'

There's a pause. A long one.

'In every flavour possible, Spey.'

There's a laugh in her voice and I breathe out. It's like her cigarette smoke is drawing out all my hidden stupid. A car pulls into the slip road next to the station. It's a police car. I see the cops' faces as they slowly drive towards us. I grip the wall. I can't help it, because my first thought is that they're looking for me. That one in London was taking a pad-full of notes. Just as my mouth opens to let out some more stupid, Astrid's spare hand covers mine, tangling our fingers together. My voice cuts out and it's just as well the wall is low, I would have hurt myself badly from falling off in shock.

Astrid leans towards me, whispering in my ear. 'There's nothing wrong with us chilling here. Having a bit of privacy. Getting away from our folks.'

My voice hasn't reconnected yet.

The cop car passes by. Astrid straightens up and releases my hand. My brain sweats confusion.

'There's a whole load of stuff goes on in places like this,' she says. 'Folks like to pretend that it only happens in London or Manchester. Look a bit harder and you'll see it all around these little towns too. But you have to play the game, never look suspicious, especially if you've got anything on you. It's gonna be easier for Dee. A white girl's gonna fit right into those seaside towns.'

Dee fit in? Astrid's never met her. And I *was* being stupid about the police. They couldn't find the guy who broke into Shauna's dad's garage even though the security camera caught him full in the face.

I say, 'You reckon there's really stuff going on in places like this?'

She laughs. 'I know it does. This was the first place they brought me. You know that Spanish food place we passed? That's where we went.'

I nearly ask, 'Who's "we"?' But for once, my brain jumps in on time.

'I thought we were heading for the KFC. Man, I already had my foot through the door checking the best deal on wings. They had to come and pull me out. "Nah," they said. "We're gonna celebrate."'

I wait for her to carry on. I want to hear but I don't. I know it's not going to end well, but . . . Well . . . Astrid is here. People come through this crap and out the other side.

So I do say it. 'What happened next?'

'The Spanish place was closing up,' Astrid says. 'I don't think they'd been that busy. It was November and cold and dark. No real Christmas vibes yet. Suddenly, all us lot pitch up. Enough of us are white not to worry them too much and they let us in. The boys go mad ordering everything off the menu and the waiter gets this look on his face. He says he wants the money in advance.'

My stomach pulls, like Mum's in there twisting my gut herself. *They're going to look at you differently, Spey. You have to behave.* And me never reminding her that it depends if they notice my Black side.

'Then?' I say.

'Nothing at first. Then Foster says, "You better get the manager." Foster's the boy who's leading business down these ends.'

'Does the manager come?'

'Yeah. We all go silent and I realise how much noise we must've been making. The manager comes and he's an older bloke, maybe same age as my granddad. About sixty or something. He's wearing a waistcoat and a suit like a proper mafia don. Foster gets off his stool and he walks towards the manager. Then him and the manager hug.'

I'm picturing it. But the scene's not taking place here. It's in the Bronx.

'So you got all the food?' I say.

'And beer and wine. I don't usually drink alcohol, but I got a cocktail because it was a tenner and they were paying. I didn't even like the Spanish stuff that much. I just wanted one big plate of food, not all these little things you had to share, your rice and potatoes and meat all separate. My friend, Liz, though, she loved it. They paid with a big wad of notes, but I don't think that waiter got no tip. I walked past that place a few times afterwards. I even just looked in now. I never saw that waiter in there again.'

'You reckon Foster was a regular?'

'Yeah. And a big spender too. No one was asking our age when we were getting drinks poured for us.'

'You stayed down here?'

'Yeah, no Quik Inn for us. We got put up in a rental place, with a fridge full of food, flat screen, everything. I thought one of the boys was planning to stay over, but . . . nah. Nothing.'

One of the boys planning to stay.

'No. Roman stayed.' Astrid laughs. 'He was Liz's boyfriend. It was his idea that I came down here with her. Lucky we had our own rooms, but I had to turn my music up really loud.' She sighs. 'Then the next day we started selling.'

She said it like it was flogging plastic trash in pound shops on *The Apprentice*.

'The stash was kept in Liz's room. She had one of them old-school DJ record boxes, a silver one with a key. They trusted her to do the weighing and packaging and stuff. I just delivered it. I made two hundred quid for a couple of days' work. Of course I was gonna go back.'

I can't work out if my next question is one of the stupid ones or not. I ask it anyway.

'Is it all about money?'

She kills her cigarette. This one gets more mercy than the other ones.

I say, 'Because I don't think Dee really cares about money.'

Astrid stands up and stretches. 'To be honest, I don't know if I really did, neither. It wasn't like I was spending it on nothing much. Though it was good to know it was there. It was just . . . I don't know . . . so damn exciting doing something that was so . . .' She laughs. 'So bad.'

That's not Dee, neither. She never really cared about good nor bad.

I say, 'In the car, you said it was really brutal for your family. What happened when you went home?'

She perches on the wall again. She reaches for her bag but doesn't open it.

'Mum was furious. She'd called the police and everything. She said that if I ever pulled a stunt like that again, she was gonna throw me out.'

'But you did.'

'Yeah, but it was never like the first time. When I came back, there wasn't no cocktail or potato omelette. Foster gave me the leaflet for McDonald's delivery and said I had to use my own money if I wanted food. They were pretty damn clear about what would happen if a penny of their money went missing.'

'Did Liz come back with you?'

'No. We kinda stopped being friends. I mean proper friends, like we'd been before. I don't know if she felt guilty about what she'd got me into or was just jealous. Jealous of what? I don't know. I was stuck in some cruddy flat near an industrial estate. The guy who lived there was on a three stretch so Foster and his mates were paying the rent for him. They didn't pay no electricity nor gas, though. It was on a key and no one was gonna buy more than they needed so it ran out on my first night. Total darkness. One of Foster's boys passed by with takeaway. He said he'd put some power on the key, but I had to pay him back.'

'Pay him back?'

She sighs and looks me full in the face. 'Yes, Spey. Pay him. It's funny, that's the bit that really stressed out Uncle Sol too.'

I feel myself blush.

'And that was the way it ran,' she says quietly. 'Different places, different flats, all of them manky. Different boys trying their nastiness.'

'And your mum?'

'She kept her word, which is more than I did. She gave me loads of chances but I kept pushing her, so in the end she had to follow through and told me to pack my bags. Man, I even saw it like it was a good thing, I was breaking free.

My sister, Andrea, she was going to uni, but she wasn't really free. She still needed Mum's money and her room back for holidays. Me, I wasn't gonna depend on no one.'

I risk a question. 'What about your dad?'

She laughs. 'My dad? Man's too busy running a line through prisons like they're tube stops.'

'The way everyone talks about him . . . I don't know, it sound like you should be untouchable.'

'Nah.'

I wait for her to say more, but she's fallen silent. I wonder if I'm going to be meeting her dad in person soon enough.

I say, 'What do you think they'll have been doing?'

'Selling. Delivering. Whatever they tell her to do.'

'Dee's never been good at doing what she's told.'

Astrid gives me a sideways look. 'This is really confusing me, Spey. The boys don't like a girl who isn't compliant. How did she end up in this thing? Was it a boyfriend?'

My stomach jolts like the Christmas leftovers want to see the station car park. 'I don't think so. She used to live with her nan and when her nan died, she ended up in care.'

'Did they carry her to one of those homes outside London?'

'Yes.'

Astrid sucks her teeth. 'Some of them places are like Argos for gangstas. You select your goods, you pick them up and you take them away.'

'I told you. Dee isn't goods.'

'And I told you, I know that.' Astrid stands up. 'Maybe she

170

doesn't. She might not think she's worth anything better. That's why I'm here. To make sure she does.'

Dee's nan would have fought wars for Dee. But when she died, who else could fight that hard?

'She's gonna be tough to find,' Astrid says. 'Sometimes the boys rent out Airbnbs. Other times it's a crap flat when a junky's in rehab, or still living there but don't care who's occupying their spare room as long as they're getting paid for it. One time they took over the place of some poor old guy with a lung disease. I was supposed to tell his neighbours I was his new carer.' She yawns. 'I suppose we better get back. We're gonna need all our energy for tomorrow when my dad lands.'

We walk back through the parade of shops. The tapas bar is still open and seems to have had a last-minute rush. I can hear the noise from outside. Astrid's looking at the KFC menu.

I say, 'But you got out of county lines, though.'

'Yeah, that's down to Uncle Sol. He made himself an expert on all the operations, all cross the country. He always managed to track me down. He kept turning up on my doorstep asking me to leave with him. After three years, I listened.' She sighs. 'Man, I'm hungry. You got any money?'

Benni

Dear Spey,

How are you doing? Are you feeling it?

Four walls.

A small bed.

A sink.

A small box of cornflakes for breakfast and a plastic tub of orange juice. Or a tub of plastic orange juice, because the tub and drink are gonna taste the same.

A door that locks you in, though this time you keep the key, if you can call this scrap of plastic a key. I've got too used to keys that go clang. Lots of them. All the damn time.

And the bathroom may be small, but at least it ain't communal and you can take a dump with a door to close. There's no padmate on the top bunk holding his nose.

I know you're still wondering why I turned up on your doorstep offering you a father you don't need or want. Okay, I know I'm making amends, not just to you, but to all of you, and I will too. I am going to make it up for not being around, for being so far from the role model you and your mum deserved. But I'm gonna admit it. I'm being selfish too. I want those secret moments, the ones I hear other men talking

172

about. Like seeing their kids' first steps, or rubbing their gums when the first teeth are coming through. Then this afternoon in the car, I caught sight of you in the mirror and I just wanted to crack up. You were all bent over, neck crook sideways, fast asleep. What are you gonna say if I tell you that you got that from me? One-man cell, two-man cell, landing full of hyped-up hard men banging up their pads, me – I learned to sleep through all of it. So, yeah, Spey, maybe that's what we've got in common. We can both sleep through an apocalypse.

And, man, when you finally opened up that box of Jordans. Looking at all those expressions sweep across your face. Surly – shock – joy – surly again when you see me watching you . . . it took me right back to when I was fifteen, before I set foot in one of Her Majesty's establishments. Not long before, though.

I was so pleased I could do something that would make you happy. I only wish I could tell you that you don't get nothing for nothing. No. That came out the wrong way. Not you. Me. *I* don't get nothing for nothing. You, Spey, don't owe me no debt for the trainers, but . . .

. . . and this is a bit I'm gonna edit out. But I need to say it out loud or else I'm not gonna let myself believe it. The trainers did cost me. More than they ever should. I fell right into the trap so damn easily. I thought I knew all the tricks. But I have to remind myself, I'm in the situation that I am because I let myself get taken for a fool.

I didn't have no money, Spey. You've probably heard how they push you out of prison with just £46 in your pocket. It's been the same amount since before you were born. But my problems started before that. The first time I hit that prison reception, man. They bring you straight from court and your head is ready to explode. You want to cry and punch the wall at the same time. You know everyone's eyeing you up, trying to work you out, the screws, the boys, everyone. I didn't have no one topping up my account so I've got to choose. Do I buy toothpaste or a little bar of chocolate to sweeten my day?

But prison is a hustle. There's always gonna be some baron offering to help you out then expecting you to pay him back double. And that first time, Spey, I was sinking. I took what was offered because I didn't think I'd survive.

And that's when Richie . . . Well, you don't need to know.

You asked me to help you, Spey. I'm gonna see that through. Then after that . . .

We'll see, won't we?

Spey

Okay, the Quik Inn bed is comfortable. I slept well, though Mum says I can sleep on the edge of a razor. I've just been woken up. My phone's vibrated so hard it made my pillows shake. Sometimes I wonder if my phone's really alien technology, where the out-of-planet supervillain wants to trigger earthquakes in London.

It's a message from Benni. He says we need to go.

I stare up at the ceiling. There's probably someone lying in a bed right above my head. And someone above that. What if the floor gives and the top one plummets through the floor on to the one below that, and then the next one and the next one? And here I am on the ground floor, lying here waiting for all the trouble to land on top of me.

My pillow shakes again. This time it's from Astrid.

> My dad's gonna be here by 8

Who is this man? Is he going to storm through Quik Inn brandishing nunchuks and a machete?

More vibrations. Benni's calling.

'Can you come up to my room, Spey?'

'Why?'

'We need to leave.'

'With Sol?'

175

'Please. Just come. First floor, 107, it's closer to the stairs than the lift.'

He ends the call. I'm supposed to obey without question, like he's got proper parents' authority over me. But I pull on yesterday's jeans and hoodie and, yeah, it's going to be the same pants and socks. I suppose I could have rinsed out the pants, but they were never going to dry on time. Sol would appreciate a wet-pants patch on his back seat as much as he would have appreciated my sleep dribble yesterday. I unplug my charger and tuck it into my rucksack. I wish I had a toothbrush. KFC gravy doesn't leave in a hurry.

I follow the sign to the stairs and head through fire doors into another hallway. I think I've found the service stairs, but I don't care. I go up them and out on to another landing. I'm by room 102. Further along, a door's open and Benni's waiting. He has his jacket on.

'Ready to go?'

'With Sol?' I ask again.

'I'll explain later.'

'No.' I go into his room. His bed's barely mussed, like he only slept on top of it. One of the plastic cups has been used. A tiny disposable toothbrush is lying next to it. He sees me looking at it and roots around in his jacket pocket. He pulls out a small plastic bag and hands it to me. It's another mini toothbrush with toothpaste.

'They sold them at reception,' he says.

I take it but I don't want to brush my teeth in front of him.

I don't know why. It always feels like a private thing.

He smiles as he turns his back. 'You'd never survive a double cell.'

'Just as well I never intend to be in one.'

'Good.'

I open the pack and empty the brush and tube on to my palm. They remind me of the toys you'd get in a nursery school. And suddenly, it pulls at me again. I'm coming over all shy about brushing my teeth in front of a witness when I should already be in Hastings looking for Dee. I go over to the sink and start on my teeth.

Benni's chatting away. 'I once had to share a cell with a Norwegian kid who'd been done for dealing ecstasy in a gay club. He seriously shouldn't have been inside and when I walked into that cell, the look on his face . . . I knew that every American prison film the boy ever watched was playing through his head.'

I scrub hard at a piece of chicken that must have married my back tooth. In the end, I yank it out with my fingers.

'In the three days we were stuck together,' Benni says, 'he never met my eyes, never used the toilet, never said a word except to God. I suppose I could have told him that I was as scared as he was, but one thing I knew for sure about prison was you don't tell anyone when you're scared.'

I finish brushing my teeth. I can't see a towel so I wipe my mouth on my sleeve. I go and sit down on the bed. I feel a bit bad for messing up its neatness.

'Tell me why we're sneaking out of here like something out of *Chicken Run*.'

'Out of what?'

'What's with you and Astrid's dad?'

'It doesn't matter. He's nothing to do with this. I knew Sol could help. *That's* what matters.'

'But it can't do, can it, if we're creeping out of here without Sol?'

'Sol needs to stay here and deal with Richie.'

'I'm not a kid! You don't have to hide stuff from me!' Even when I was a kid, I knew when adults were telling kid-lies – the stories they spun that left you with more questions.

'We were in the same foster home for a bit. Then we met up again in prison. He's helped me out now and again.'

'So why are you running away from him?'

'Because things can kick off when he's around. He's . . . unpredictable. You've seen how Sol can be. Richie's a hundred times worse. He'd just hold us up.'

Benni takes both our toothbrushes from the side of the sink and chucks them in the bin. 'We can get the train direct to Hastings. Do you want to find Dee or stay and meet Richie?'

We grab our things and head out the back exit. I'm not sure if guests are supposed to use it, but the door's wide open. The cleaner having a cigarette by the wheelie bin isn't too bothered by us, neither.

Benni stands looking up and down the road. It's starting

to rain. 'Any idea where the station is?'

'Yes. I do.' I have a thought. 'Don't you need to pay for our rooms?'

'It's on Sol's card. I'm gonna pay him back.'

'And Sol's all right with that?'

'Don't worry about that, Spey. I'll sort it out.'

Dee

Mercurialis perennis

DOG'S MERCURY

BOGGARD POSY

DOG'S COLE

When I was at my first primary school, my teacher used to tell me that I should take time out and think about my behaviour. I couldn't understand why. If I've already done the behaviour, why should I think about it?

Then Nan explained it to me. I need to think about how my behaviour affects other people. I told her that other people's behaviour affects me. When Lacie pulled my hair, I pulled hers back but I didn't lie about it like she did, so I always got told off. Matteo swore at me and I swore back, but I did it louder. So I was the only one that got told off for that too. Nan went to the school and had words with my teacher. I waited in the corridor outside the classroom. Then Nan took me home and I started another school the next week.

I'm thinking about my behaviour now. Chez said he didn't remember that I chucked water at him at playgroup. He even laughed loud when I told him, like I'd made it up.

But I hadn't. I don't think he forgot, neither. The water wet up his clothes and put poison about me in his head.

Some plants are poisonous all the way through. Every bit of them. They don't make medicine. They make you throw up, or turn yellow and even die. When they find a place they like, they bully out the other plants and take over. They don't even smell good, neither. They smell like they're rotten.

The firemen didn't find no fire in Chalkleighs. Abi, the manager, was angry as hell. She took us all into her office one by one to tell us it was wrong to waste the fire service's money and time. It was irresponsible. She sat far back in her chair like she thought I would spring at her. I told her it wasn't me who pushed the alarm and then let her carry on talking.

When I went back to my room, Spencer was waiting for me. My flower book was in my pocket so it didn't bother me too much. The room in Chalkleighs never felt like my proper room. I was just borrowing it until they decided I didn't need it no more and someone else could have it.

Spencer emptied her leather bag on my bed. It was phones and money. One of the phones was an iPhone, still in its box. The other one was old and scratched. The money was notes folded in half in small plastic bags. Spencer pointed at them like she thought I hadn't seen phones nor money before.

'Chez really wants you back, hun. You know our boy gets what he wants. Especially as you two've got previous.'

I'd put my hand in my pocket and held my book so tight some of the pages bent over. I imagined squashing it all between my fingers, petals and leaves and seeds and poison, then holding up my arm and seeing it run down my elbow and drip on to the floor. I let go, so my fingers were just resting on the cover.

I thought about all the flowers that no one notices. Like nightshade and sowthistle and cranesbill and dandelions. They grow in the places where no one can see them or sometimes people see them so much they stop seeing them. But they still grow and they grow tough.

I had grown. No one had seen it.

I didn't need Spencer emptying her bag on the bed and telling me what I should do. I didn't need Chez standing on the pier and yelling at us. I thought about how my behaviour affects other people and how Spencer and Chez's behaviour affects me. Nan said that she was proud of me for standing up to Lacie and Matteo. I should never let bullies get the better of me.

I walked out the room and down to Abi's office. She let me call Samira right away. I'd told her that I was in real danger. She'd said she had to report it. Later, when I went back to my room, I saw that Spencer had taken the phones and money away.

Spey

The station is open again, though the Krispy Kreme stall isn't. I don't know what we could have done if trains weren't running. Hitch-hike? Like me and Benni were going to pick up rides.

Benni stares at the ticket machine. 'Do you know how to use this thing?'

I look at the screen. In theory. 'Yeah.'

'Why've they got to make it so hard?'

I check the departures board. The Hastings train leaves in twelve minutes. Benni scratches his head like a cartoon character.

'You should just be able to buy a ticket,' he says. 'From a real person.'

'You can,' I say.

We both glance back at the ticket office. A queue snakes backwards and forwards, full of people with suitcases on wheels and supersize plastic bags with sales logos on them. If you straightened it out, it would stretch out of the foyer and across the street to the theatre opposite. I didn't notice it last night with Astrid. *Dick Whittington*'s playing. Me and Mum saw at least three Dicks in the Hackney Empire. And, yeah, she even giggled when we had to yell, 'Get up, Dick!' Benni's got no idea about all the stuff he's missed with us. Though it's hard to imagine having a parent sitting on either side of me instead of just one. I got used to sharing an armrest with a stranger. Even the one time Pete came with us, he sat on the other side of Mum and kept going on about how stupid it all was.

I slide in front of Benni and stare at the ticket screen. Man, there are so many types of tickets.

'Don't folks like to talk no more?' Benni asks.

I carry on staring at the screen. What do we need? A return, right? But not coming back here because we'll be returning to London. Or I will. Who knows where Benni will be heading. But won't we need an extra ticket to bring Dee back?

'They've got that woman's voice in buses,' Benni says. 'She tells you the stops so the driver doesn't have to say nothing to you and you don't have to say nothing to them. And no one asks for directions, even when they're proper lost. They just stand there in the middle of the road turning their phones upside down and round and round, almost getting dashed down by a lorry because they won't ask a breathing human the way.'

Yeah, Benni, I need a 'young people are crap' lecture right now, because that's really going to help me work out Off-Peak, Super Off-Peak or Anytime. I tap Anytime. And maybe we should just get singles and work out the rest when we get there.

'You weren't . . .' I lower my voice because there's a woman queuing up close behind us. 'You weren't away for that long.'

'Eight and a half years? Imagine yourself when you're twenty-three. How different's the world gonna be then? When I first got a phone, it was just calls and messages and . . .' He laughs. 'And Tetris. I always loved Tetris. It was one of the things I missed most while I was away.'

Not me nor Mum, then. Or even any of his other kids. Just dropping blocks. I carry on staring at the screen. Two singles to Hastings. How the hell do I do that?

Quantity. There it is. I increase the number of tickets to two. Do I get a discount? Am I a student or child? I'm not even going to bother asking if Benni has any discount cards. I push confirm and the price flashes up.

We both say, 'Shit,' at the same time and it feels . . . wrong. Maybe your first synchronised swear should be a moment you bond, but . . . no. I don't really swear in front of adults. I don't really swear much, full stop. Not since I told Mum to 'fuck off' when she made me wear socks I didn't like to nursery. I'd never told Mum it was Dee who taught me that, but I think she guessed. The look on her face and the really loud, 'What did you say?' must have shredded my blaspheme brain-cable, because swear words don't often make it through.

I realise me and Benni are both holding our hearts too. I let my hand drop.

Benni says, 'We get a carriage on our own for that much, right?'

185

The woman queuing behind us clears her throat.

'Um . . .' she says. 'I was wondering if you're nearly done. It's just that my train leaves in six minutes.'

I need to start all over again. I jab the button to reset.

'I just need to collect,' she says. 'I'll be quick.'

I step aside. 'Go ahead.'

She quickly moves in front and I slide back behind her.

'Our train goes in nine,' Benni mutters.

'When's the next one?'

He squints towards a departure board. 'Looks like an hour and a half. Reduced service.'

The woman taps away easily. Surely a ticket machine can't be *that* hard to work out. I take out my phone and tap in *What train tickets should I buy?* I see Benni's watching me. *No, I'm not using it for calling or messaging. Or even Tetris. Is that all right for you?* I scan the results. He is right, though. It would be simpler just to ask someone. But there's no one to ask. So Off-Peak means not rush hour. It pretty much looks like rush hour now, with everyone leaving their Christmases behind. I tap for more info, but the site says I should use their online planner or check with a member of staff. THERE IS NO MEMBER OF STAFF!

The woman in front takes her tickets and glances behind and smiles at me. 'Thank you.' She gives Benni a quick look, but her smile is gone.

There's more of a queue now. I'm not letting anyone else go ahead. I line up tickets. Two Off-Peak singles. I'm fifteen so

I still count as a child. Yeah, the child who's sorting all this out because the adult has no idea.

'You got enough money for the tickets?' Benni says.

'I bought the railway line. It seemed cheaper.' It comes out automatically. Mum and I used to fire film quotes at each other when I was little.

He gives me a sideways look. '*Inception*? The airline thing?'

'Yeah.' I wasn't expecting him to recognise a changed-up quote from a Christopher Nolan film.

He says, 'Tom Hardy was pretty popular inside. What with Bronson and Bane and The Krays. *Inception* didn't have quite as many fans. I liked it, though.'

Inception and Oscar Wilde. That's probably going to be as good as it gets for us.

I use my phone to pay. I hear Benni breathe out loudly but he doesn't say anything.

There's a whir and a patter as the tickets fall into the holder. One at a time. I reach in and grab them.

'Three minutes,' Benni says. 'And we better damn well get a seat for that price.'

A whistle blows on the platform and we run. A man's legging across the concourse to another platform, his trolley bumping behind him. He's yelling for the guard to hang on and she does. Seriously, she stops the train from pulling off long enough for the man to throw himself through the nearest door. She bangs it shut after him. I honestly didn't know that it was possible for a train to wait for a passenger. I thought trains were like buses and drew extra power from seeing people run to catch them. The faster you're running, the more juice for the engine. And it all gets forfeit if the person actually does catch it.

Our guard's one of the normal ones. His hand's in the air, his whistle's in his mouth and he's not making eye contact with anyone sprinting towards the open doors. Me and Benni run. It's a race. A race to catch the train. Just. The. Train. But as the guard blows his whistle and yells at us to stand clear, I dodge in front of Benni through the door. Benni leaps in behind me as the doors snap shut.

'That was close,' he says.

He's sweating.

'Yeah,' I say. *And I won*.

We puff our way through a couple of carriages. They're pretty full of people and luggage. We finally find two seats opposite each other. Benni nods hello to the girl he's plonking himself next to. She nods back and pushes her earbuds in tighter. The guy sitting opposite her lugs his bag off the free seat and balances it on his knees. He doesn't even look at me as I sit down. The train pulls out of the station and I sit back, making sure I don't knock shoulders with him. I close my eyes to shut out his jiggling bag. Benni's toes are jammed against mine under the table. Outside, the rain seems to be beating the same time as the train.

We stop. A slow creaky stop. I open my eyes. A train speeds towards us and the station. That's okay, then. We're held up on a red signal.

The other train disappears and we stayed stopped.

The boy next to me reaches for his phone on the table, but the girl next to Benni is quicker. Hers is already in her hand.

'There's been a landslide,' she says. 'Not on this line, but the diversions are causing delays.'

Benni opens his eyes. We're looking at each other. He shifts his legs so his knees bang mine. I look out the window. The rain was just starting when we left Quik Inn, but it's serious now.

I say, 'Did you miss it?'

He looks confused. 'What?'

'The rain. While you were in prison.'

The rucksack on the boy's lap gives a little jiggle even though we're not moving any more. I see him glance at Benni then down again.

Benni shrugs. 'That's a strange question.'

'Back in the hotel, you said I'd never survive a double cell.'

'Something you're never gonna find out.'

'Yeah, but . . .' How do I say it? I've never sat opposite my father before. Not even at Christmas dinner. Mum arranged it so he was at the end and me and her were opposite. Maybe he held me when I was a baby, high in the air, looking down at me. But now our knees are touching. We could be staring right into each other's faces but we don't know anything about what's in each other's heads. 'I just wondered what it's like, being stuck in a cell.'

'It's boring,' he says. 'That's the worst of it. I've been in some places where you're locked up all day, all night . . .' Now he's looking out the window. 'I missed the sunshine most. If you were lucky, you'd get outside for an hour or two and I liked that, just standing there with the sun on my face.'

I want to ask him if he ever wrote poetry about it, but I don't know how that'll sound. Well, I do. It'll sound like I'm taking the piss.

My jiggling neighbour manages to nudge me without touching me.

'Please,' he says.

He picks up his rucksack and I ease myself out from my seat and stand in the aisle while he slides past. I move into his seat and Benni shifts so he's next to me. Now I have to try not to knock knees with the earbuds girl. Rain hits the window, blurring the tracks that we're still not moving along. My father's even closer.

He says, 'Were you one of those little kids that loved jumping in puddles?'

'I suppose so.' Though don't all little kids?

It was Dee who really loved water, though. There was a wet-play area at our nursery. She refused to wear the little plastic apron thing and the staff gave up trying to battle her about it. Her nan usually brought spare clothes with her, just in case Dee was too damp to take home on the bus. Once, Dee stuck her face in the water tray, arms out behind her like a Naruto run, and didn't move. Laura shrieked so hard everyone stopped playing. She ran over to Dee and pulled her out.

Dee was grinning. 'My face was swimming!'

'Yes,' Laura had said. 'It was.' Laura definitely hadn't been grinning.

The train intercom pokes us with static. I can't quite catch the words. Benni's frowning and listening hard. When the crackle stops, he sighs.

The girl opposite me pops out her earbuds. 'What's happening?'

'They reckon we're stuck here for another twenty minutes,' Benni says. He pats my shoulder. 'I know it's a pain, Spey, but we're still on our way.'

Of course we are, if 'on our way' means stuck just outside a station. I wonder what Sol and Astrid are doing. Has Richie the Ninja arrived yet? Maybe they're all heading back to London. I fire a quick message to Astrid. I won't hold my breath for a reply.

Dee

Hydrocotyle ranunculoides
FLOATING PENNYWORT

Nan and I saw it when we were crossing the bridge over the canal to go to the Olympic Park. It was all across the top of the water. There was so much it looked like we could walk across it. Nan and I didn't know what it was at first. We tried to find it in my flower book when we got home, but it wasn't there. We found marsh pennywort, but not this. Nan had to go on the internet to find it. She found out that floating pennywort shouldn't have been in the canal. It was a nuisance. It had crept in and taken over.

Aunty Janet wanted to make everything all right after Nan died, but both of us were sad and both of us were angry. They'd crept in and taken over both of us. I couldn't stay inside her flat. I'd go back to my old estate. New people were living in me and Nan's old flat, a man with two little boys. When the curtains were drawn, I could see he'd painted our sitting room a different colour. That made me feel better. It was their place now. It didn't miss me.

The council had taken away our vegetable beds because they were being used as bins. One time, I saw Chez. He stopped to talk to me, but he didn't have his dog, Jim Kelly. He said that Jim Kelly had got knocked down by a car and died. He was surprised how sad that made him feel. It made me feel sad too.

Chez said he was sorry that Nan had died and that he really meant it. He'd been nasty to us because he was having a hard time at school and his mum had left with his little sister and his dad and older brother were angry with him all the time. He'd taken it all out on everyone. When Jim Kelly died, he grew up. The dog had made him a better person.

The next time I saw him, I went back to his flat and we played video games. I wasn't very good at them, but he showed me how to get better. I started going to Chez's instead of going to school. Sometimes his dad was there, but he didn't mind about me. Even though we were in Chez's bedroom, he didn't want sex. He said he had enough girls already. He just wanted me as his friend. That was more important to him.

One time we went to see a woman who lived on a boat on the canal in Islington. She had puppies for sale and Chez wanted one. She asked him some questions but because he didn't answer them in the way she wanted, she wouldn't sell him one. He threw his can of Coke at her window. Then he snatched mine out my hand and threw

193

that as well. He shouldn't have done that. The woman cared about her puppies. But Nan says – said – that I shouldn't always hold my anger all inside. It can cause damage. Chez's anger jumps out of him like it's too scared to stay inside. It causes damage too.

Sometimes Chez asked me to help him and his dad out, taking stuff to people. I'm not stupid. I knew what the stuff was. They said it was easier for me as no one was gonna suspect a girl like me. Chez's a bit Turkish and a bit Portuguese and a bit German, so I don't think no one would suspect him much if he didn't try and screwface them out all the time.

Another time, we were in Chez's room. He'd lit up a spliff and was trying to teach me how to smoke, but I didn't like it. It hurt my chest and made my mouth taste nasty. I didn't hear the front door open because Chez had music on. When it stopped I heard a voice I knew.

'That's my mum,' I said.

Chez sort of smiled but he didn't say nothing.

'Maybe she's looking for me,' I said.

He stroked my cheek. He'd never done that before and I didn't like it. 'She's looking for something, Dee, but it ain't you.'

I told him he didn't know for sure, but he said he did and his dad was taking care of it. I wanted to see her. It couldn't be an accident that she'd gone there when I was there too. Even if she didn't know it, something in her head told her I was close. I tried to get up but Chez pushed me back on to the floor. His hand thumped into my boob and it hurt. He was still holding the spliff and it almost burned my chin. He turned the music up again and sat there watching me.

'When's she ever come to your aunty's, Dee? I mean, man, that's her own sister. She knows where you live if she wants to see you. She didn't even come to her own mother's funeral, yeah? The grandma who cared for you since you were a baby. You told me that yourself. So why's she gonna come just for you?'

He'd just cotched out, smoking his spliff.

I told him Mum wasn't allowed to just turn up and see me. Aunty Janet didn't trust her in the flat in case she took something.

Chez said, 'I'm doing you a favour, then, Dee. She's gonna break the rules if she sees you. I'm stopping her, right?'

I didn't want no favours. I wanted to see my mum. The anger kept going round and round inside me, getting stronger and stronger, but there was nowhere for it to drain out.

I tried to leave the room but Chez grabbed me. I kicked him and he fell backwards. I ran out of his bedroom but I couldn't see my mum, so I ran out of the flat. Chez was yelling at me and calling me names. I didn't see her outside, so I kept running and running and running, until I'd run back to Aunty Janet's. She wanted to know why I was so upset, so I told her how I'd heard Mum's voice in Chez's flat.

Aunty Janet called the police. I wish I hadn't told her. The police went to Chez's flat and he started to hate me even more.

Spey

The train manager's just walked through the coach and said we'll be heading off in another five minutes. Benni settles back in his seat like he really believes it.

'So, how's it going at school?' he says.

This? Now?

Benni, you didn't make it to parents' evenings or secondary school open days or take me to the theatre or museums or galleries to top me up on all the things that Mum said school wasn't teaching me. If you had, you'd know – you'd know exactly how school was going.

'Fine,' I say.

'Your mum sent me some copies of your reports.'

I turn and look at him. Mum stayed very quiet about that. He nods.

'You're an amazing boy,' he says. 'And you've got a smart head on you. Top marks across the board. Full house.'

I almost expect him to ruffle my hair. He sighs and looks past me out the window. It's the same out there as it was twenty minutes ago. Rainy. What did he expect I'd be like, though? That I'd inherited a crim gene and that no matter what Mum did, my path was already set for youth offending?

'It couldn't have been easy,' he says.

'What couldn't?'

'School. Playing the game. Unless . . .' He gives a little shrug. 'Unless things have changed since I was a kid.'

I have no idea what to say. How do I know what it was like when he was a kid? I mean, I know the general stuff. No internet, CDs as high-tech, people smoking on buses and stuff, but him? I don't even know where he was living. Or who with.

'What game?' I ask.

'The game that stresses the hell out of teachers. I was that kid who asked loads of questions and got pissed off when they didn't get answered. Though saying that, it probably bothered me way more than the teachers. I was never at a school long enough for them to know my name.'

'How many schools did you go to?'

'I've got no idea. I moved around a lot.'

'Why?'

He fiddles with the strap on his bag. 'It's a long story. Maybe I'll tell you properly one day.'

'What about now?' I say. 'We're not going anywhere soon.'

'I suppose so.' He wraps the strap tight round his finger and lets it go. 'It's just . . . I do want to tell the story properly. There were these classes in prison about how to be a better dad. They suggested . . .' He stares down at the table.

'They suggested that you shouldn't tell me?'

He shakes his head. 'Not exactly. I want to find the right

words.' He takes a deep breath. 'I was just a baby when my parents put me in care.'

'Parents? Both of them?'

'Yes,' he says. 'They were married.'

'Married?'

He puffs out his cheeks. 'Everyone's surprised at that bit.'

'I just thought . . .'

'Desperate single mum, abandoned by the dad . . . yeah. It's the tale you hear the most. Not mine, though. It's usually easy to get babies adopted if the parents agree, but not so easy for the little brown kids. Social services were pretty strict about matching you up. I completely get that. They didn't want me to be the lonely little black boy in a family full of white people. There was a mixed-race couple in Bristol who were interested in me but the woman fell pregnant halfway through the assessment so they didn't need me any more. Of course, I didn't know that at the time. I was busy being a two-year-old.'

Benni as a two-year-old. I can't even imagine it. 'How did you find out?'

'I had a look in my social services files when I hit twenty. You think it'll give you the answers to everything, but it doesn't.'

Benni's bag strap has come loose in its buckle. He taps the metal prong against his thumb – not hard, but I can still see his skin bending in. How long do you have to do that before it makes a hole? He stops and tightens the strap again, then rests his hands on the table.

'When I was a kid, I believed the story.'

'What story?'

'*The* story. That a real family is a mummy and a daddy and you in the middle. That if you work hard at school you'll get a brilliant job. If you fail at any of it, it's your fault.'

'Which subjects did you do?'

He laughs. 'Can't remember. I don't think I turned up for any exams. But if there was a prize for winding up teachers, I would have aced it. School's just part of the system, spreading those false stories.'

'So you're saying I shouldn't bother?'

Benni's eyes widen. 'No, no, no, no, no! Jesus!' And for a second he looks like he's really seen Jesus strolling down the aisle towards him. 'Your mum would kill me if she thought I was putting that idea into your head. With her bare hands.'

'Mum says I'll always have to work harder than the white kids.'

I glance down at my own hands. The skin that melanin forgot.

Benni notices and laughs. 'Yeah, Spey, people are gonna make up their own minds about you. The way you speak, the way you cut your hair, the way you carry yourself . . . Well, unless you're gonna have "I'm A Black Man" tattooed across your forehead, then you know what they're gonna think. And don't have the tattoo, Spey, because then your mum will kill *you* with her bare hands.'

'And you think looking white makes things easier?'

I say it a little bit too loud. He's giving me a puzzled look and I want to tell him about how Mr Sanguon, the history teacher, got so fed up of my questions that he made me lead a discussion about The Alternative Winston Churchill and how he wasn't everyone's hero. The head of year is standing right next to him, looking on all proud, like Mr Sanguon hadn't been teaching that Winston was God before I started my questions. Then Vinnie coming up to me afterwards laughing his arse off telling me that I just got played. *Yeah, Benni, maybe I do know the game.*

I turn to him, making sure my voice isn't too loud this time. I don't need a whole load of strangers staring at us.

'Mum made me go to a supplementary school for a while,' I say. 'It was on Saturday mornings. I didn't know anyone at my secondary school because Mum and I had only just moved to the area. Everyone was meeting up at the weekends. They'd ask me along but I couldn't go and I didn't really want to tell them why.'

Benni nods. 'Sometimes our business is our own.'

'Mum said that she hadn't known anything about Black history, so she wanted to make sure I did. And maybe, yeah, it taught me to play the game.' Though I don't think Mum really knew that there was a game. 'The thing was, I was the palest kid in Saturday school. The first time I walked in . . .' Every single face had a 'why-the-hell-are-you-here?' look. Luckily, Mr Derek knew exactly why I was there and made me welcome in a way that none of the others could argue with. 'But sometimes it's like I'm expected to flash a screenshot of my DNA results just to prove who I am.'

Benni makes a laughing sound but his lips are pressed down tight.

I carry on. I realise that all of this is rolling out of me because I've never had a chance to say it before. 'Then we started hearing about all the bad things that white people have done to Black people. I know it's true . . .' I take a deep breath. 'But it made me feel weird about Mum. I know what happened in Africa and America and Trinidad and Jamaica was really bad, but Mum didn't do it. It's not her fault. And sometimes I think I'm expected to take sides.'

Benni starts fiddling with the strap again. 'Did you ever tell your mum how you felt?'

I shake my head. 'I kept trying to work my way up to it, but in the end I didn't have to. After a couple of months, she picked up some Saturday shifts at the surgery and I used to stay over at my aunty's from Friday night. She was over in Sydenham, too far away to take me.'

'I'm sorry,' he says. 'I know how crap it is when folks see you and have an instant opinion about you.'

I take a sneaky look at his profile. He's medium brown, not that tall, no piercings nor gold teeth. His hair is buzzcut low. I wonder what people see in him. The boy whose seat I took must have already been sifting through his judgments about us before I announced Benni's prison time. He made his exit pretty quick.

Suddenly, Benni turns and grins at me. 'You know I met your grandma once?'

I blink hard. 'What? On purpose?'

'Yep. I went round her house. And lived.'

Neither Mum nor Grandma have ever told me *this* story.

'It was before she moved out of London. Me and your mum had been shopping in the big Asda in Leyton Mills. Just as we were going through the tills, we spotted your grandma heading to the exit with a massive trolley full of stuff. I mean, seriously, we had no idea who she was planning to feed with that lot. And there was no way she could get it home on the bus.'

'She usually called a cab,' I say.

A different driver every time, because none of them drove safe enough for her.

'Yeah, that's what your mum said. But I'd borrowed a mate's car. How could I let her struggle? Though . . . I don't know. Maybe we should have left her to it. The devil looks after his own.'

There's a silence between us.

'Sorry,' he says. 'That's disrespectful about your grandmother.'

'Mum says worse,' I say.

'I know, but . . .'

I wait for him to say how family's family and you should defend them anyway. He doesn't.

'So we gave her a lift home,' he says. 'And we helped her unpack. Well, I did. Your mum had just found out she was pregnant and didn't want to tell no one yet. So when I'd finished carrying everything out – and, man, your grandmother's trolley was like one of them wells where you throw down the stone and wait for ever to hear it reach the bottom – deep, man! – then I get introduced.'

He's pushing the strap out the buckle of his bag. I look out the window. Blurry fields streak past. We must have got going again without me noticing. The girl opposite me has fallen asleep. One of her earbuds is dangling down by her cheek.

'Your mum introduced me to your grandma as her "friend". There was you, already starting to grow inside her and that's what she said. "Mum, I would like you to meet my friend, Benni." '

'What did you expect her to say?'

'I don't know. I didn't expect her to go into full gory detail, but "friend"?'

'But what, though?'

He doesn't say anything. 'I suppose you're right,' he says at last. ' "Meet the father of your new grandchild," was hardly gonna make her jump for joy, was it? Especially if she hadn't known I existed before I lifted her bags of baked beans out the boot.'

'Maybe Grandma would have started asking questions.' Grandma would definitely have asked questions. 'Maybe

204

Mum wanted to save you from that.'

'You've got a wise head on your young shoulders, Spey. It's hard to believe you're my son.' He grabs my arm so quickly his bag almost falls off his lap. 'I mean, it's not that I think that you're not my son . . .'

'I get it,' I say.

He lets my arm go. He's got a serious grip. My sweatshirt must now be part of my skin.

'I wish . . . I wish . . .' He's tapping the buckle prong again. This time it's his forefinger. 'I wish I could have been there for you before. I've wished it every damn day.' He stops tapping. 'Did you ever tell anyone about me? Where I was?'

'Yeah.'

He looks happy and confused at the same time.

'Really? You weren't ashamed of me?'

'I didn't know I was supposed to be. Every Black History Month in primary school, they'd wheel out Rosa Parks, Nelson Mandela and Martin Luther King, so I kind of thought that prison was a good thing. When I was in Year Two, we were doing our assembly and I was reading out the Nelson Mandela bit. I finished by announcing to the kids and teachers and parents that my dad was always in prison. The kids didn't care, but my teacher looked like she was going to throw up.'

'Shit.' I thought he'd laugh, but he looks embarrassed. 'Sorry.'

'For what?'

'Everything, I suppose.'

The only sound for a while is the train and some loudmouth on his phone halfway down the carriage.

I say, 'What is prison like?'

'I thought you made it clear that you weren't planning a stay.'

He gives me a little smile. I smile back.

'Because everything I know is from *Shawshank Redemption* and *The Blues Brothers*.'

I say it light, like it's a joke, but he looks at me like I'm serious.

'You really want to know? Well . . .' He's playing the buckle like a piano. 'When I was on remand I shared a pad with an old guy who called himself Mitchum. He was seriously into his African superheroes. You seen *Black Panther*?'

Once in the cinema with Mum, once with mates. Then a couple of more times on Amazon Prime. 'Yes,' I say.

'Mitchum had a poster of Killmonger on his wall. You remember when he's ready to fight T'Challa in that Golden Jaguar vibranium suit?'

'Yeah,' I say. *Benni knows it's Golden Jaguar? Do they even mention that in the film?* That's Oscar Wilde, *Inception* and *Panther*. Maybe three's a lucky number for us.

'This guy used to worship that picture,' Benni says. 'Like it was Jesus.'

'What? Say prayers to it?'

I'm kind of joking, but Benni says, 'Yes. Actual worship.

He'd ask Killmonger for strength, confess his sins to him, pray for him to look after his grandchildren, all that stuff. He treated Killmonger like the Messiah.'

I don't know if I'm allowed to laugh. Maybe the guy had a mental health problem and it was his way of staying calm.

'I got moved to a single cell, thank god,' Benni says. 'But my old bunk was taken over by a young guy who'd just converted to Islam. He really couldn't get his head round Mitchum praying to this poster. He thought it was deep, deep wrong.'

Now I seriously don't know what I'm supposed to feel about this story. I try and read Benni's face, but a small frown and a smaller smile and no blinking? I've got no idea what that means.

'What happened?' I ask.

'Prison's jam-full of locked-up angry guys,' he says. 'Mitchum and this boy, Cassius, tried to talk it through. It's not like you can get away from each other in that tight little space. You've got to hear each other breathe, snore, fart . . .' He kisses his teeth. 'I mean, I dreamed about giving Mitchum a slap, all the damn time. But I held it down. You can't afford to kick off when you're living nose to nose. Maybe if I was religious, I *would* have cracked after so many days seeing Mitchum praying to Killmonger. Cassius did. They ended up punching each other all the way to A&E. That's what prison's like. All the damn time. Everyone trying to hold it down until they can't no more.'

So why did you keep going back?

I think he sees the question on my face.

'Maybe I got so used to being Benedict Charles, prisoner number AX4261, I didn't think about it no more.'

Benedict? My father is called Benedict? That would fit right in at my school.

'I was a prison boy. That was me. Because what the hell else could I be?'

If we were in *EastEnders*, I'd put my hand on his shoulder and tell him that he was my dad, and that's all that mattered. I just sit there with my hands on my lap.

'I don't want to be that old man worshipping my Killmonger poster, picking fights because I ain't got nothing else. I need to change, Spey. I need to do better.'

He opens his bag properly. He rustles round inside, then takes out a couple of packets of crisps. He offers me one. They're crinkly and ready salted. I look at them.

'What?' he says. 'You don't like these ones?'

I thought I was the only person in the world who did like them.

'No,' I say. 'They're fine.'

We both open our crisps at the same time. They give a little gasp like they're surprised they're wanted by anyone.

Benni

Dear Spey,

I've got all these thoughts and I want to sneak into the loo to record them on my phone. But it's gonna be weird if I stay away so long, so I'm gonna keep them in my head for now and try and remember them for later.

I didn't mean to tell you so much about Mitchum and his Killmonger love. At least I didn't give you the full rundown about Cassius tearing down the poster and shanking Mitchum with the broken end of a toothbrush. You don't need to know that crap but it's like all these stories are pressed up inside me and they jump out before I know it. And I didn't run my mouth off about Black Mamba and all them other drugs, and how my mate, Afan, put his fist through his TV set when he was off his head or when a newbie on the induction wing had a seizure in the mess hall while some of the boys watched and cheered.

What *do* I want to tell you, Spey? Prison wears you out, man. All of it. The cells where you're either caged up on your Jack Jones or stuck with a padmate you don't know from Adam, sleeping so close you can almost touch each other's noses. You know there's no doors on the toilet,

209

right? You just hope your padmate keeps a good diet.

But you know what's worse? The biggest decision you're gonna make inside is whether you buy the decent soap or a packet of crisps from your meagre earnings. And even then, you've got to have enough earnings to let you make that decision. Some of the lads make a decision about either keeping their head down and getting on with their time or being the rebel and riding it out on basic. No TV. Minimum visits. Nothing to remind you you're human. That was me in the first few years. Who cares if they take away your visits when you ain't got no one to visit you in the first place?

That's all done now. I've made promises. I'm never going back.

And things aren't all bad. I could show you a picture of the hostel where I'm staying. It isn't as bad as these places go, and I've stayed in a few. The manager's Polish, so he organised a decent meal for Christmas Eve because he wanted to show us what he grew up with. There's a couple of Polish lads staying there and they really appreciated it. Then some of the other lads who've got family in different countries started talking about their old Christmases. Spey, man, I'm an expert in Christmas across the world now! Put me in that black chair on Mastermind and I'm gonna score top points!

I didn't say nothing, though. I know what Christmas should be and I've had some good ones. But I've never shared a turkey with someone who's not being paid to have me there. Not my foster carers, nor the children's home or the prison or the hostel. And I felt . . . I don't know. Time's running out. I came to your house so I could feel like I was part of a family. I'd already got your trainers. So I phoned your mum and, yeah, you said she's a soft touch. That's not a bad thing at all, Spey.

Earlier this year, I met your sister, Becks. I keep taking sneaky looks at you to see if you and her look alike. I can't see it yet. Maybe my genes will power up when you're a bit older. Becks, she's got a good head on her too. And a loud mouth. That's not a bad thing, neither. No one's gonna mess her about.

And you, Spey, I'm so proud of who you are and what you can do. You're gonna be this blazing star and my heart's gonna burst with happiness knowing your life can be so good. Did you know that your mum sent me a picture of you in your primary school Christmas play? It took a while to get to me because I'd moved prison. You'd probably started shaving by the time I opened that envelope. But I held that picture and stared at it and wondered how you and me could ever be related. I don't mean the way you look. Man, me of all people know the different ways that genes can go a bit mad. Your mum had sent a card too. She said you were chosen as the narrator because you were the best reader in the class. It's just you there, dressed like Charles Dickens with a top hat and a waistcoat and a book in your hand. And me, barely read two books in my life. I knew things had to change. It was you who made me go to those poetry lessons. I know about Oscar Wilde because of you.

I want to tell you all that, Spey. I will. When we're ready.

Spey

As we pull into Hastings, it feels like something's changed. It's stopped raining, so that's helped. But I mean with Benni. Of course, I don't feel like I've suddenly gained a father. But it's like when me and Mum were hanging up the baubles on Christmas Eve. The trees's just a plain fir, then we made it something else. It's like me and Benni have finally started something but we're not fully decorated yet.

The station barriers suck up our tickets and we head out. We stand by the bus stops outside the station and find the address that Mrs Sutherland gave me. Dee's Aunty Janet lives about twenty minutes' walk away.

'Hastings isn't a big place,' Benni says. 'Especially if you're used to London. But it's got a few hills.'

'Have you been here before?'

'Yeah. Thirty years or so ago. I reckon it's changed a bit, though.'

'Good or bad?'

A woman in a hijab races into the station. Benni smiles. 'For good.'

'We need to head this way,' I say. 'There should be a shopping centre near here.'

There is. With a queue outside for the Primark sale.

Benni says, 'Have you let your mum know where you are?'

Shit! Mum! The snowballs should have worked their way through her system by now. She'll be leaving for home.

'Unless you want me to tell her,' he says.

I look at the map. Eighteen minutes to our destination. All I've got to do is get to Dee's Aunty Janet. If I fall into an argument with Mum, it's going to take way longer than that.

'Yes, please,' I say.

'Just one minute.'

We tuck into the doorway of a closed-down dry cleaner. I reckon Benni's like Mum and can't message and move at the same time.

'I'm just gonna say that we're in Hastings looking for your friend Dee. I'll make sure she knows you're safe with me.'

Looking for my friend Dee? He's really telling her the whole truth? Mum's seriously going to have something to say about that. And that something is, 'Come home right now, Spey,' no matter how safe he tells her I am.

He taps out the message. Using just one finger. Pausing after every letter. There's time to tell him to stop. Or give her less detail. *Or lie?* Because even if he doesn't know what's going to happen next, I do. At last he presses 'send'.

He breathes out. 'Hopefully, she'll . . .'

My phone buzzes. It's a message from Mum. The first word is 'Spey'. If it starts with my name, it isn't good.

Benni's phone rings. He looks at it, then at me. He mouths, 'Your mum,' and answers.

'Hello, Gilda!'

I open Mum's message.

> **Spey, come home now. You cannot disturb this poor woman's Christmas looking for a girl you haven't seen for years.**

I start to type 'Dee's in trouble' then go back and delete it all. What's the point? Benni's already having the discussion and already losing it.

'Gilda . . . No . . . He's right next to me. I won't . . .'

Benni nods and opens his mouth but Mum's voice rules. I can actually hear her. I look down at the empty reply box on my phone. I could tell her the whole story, about why I need to go to Dee now, about the time I saw her by the canal, and then in the market . . .

Nothing I say will be enough for Mum.

'Okay, Gild! I'll tell him!'

Benni glances at me and shrugs.

I can smell hot dogs. I spot a mobile food truck outside a church and by the look of the pictures plastered across it, it's selling sausage sandwiches. The serving shutter's still down, but there's definitely frying happening behind there. My stomach rumbles. The plain crinkle cuts must be digested right down to atom level by now. I tap Benni's arm and point to the truck. He nods.

'Of course,' he says to Mum. 'I understand . . . all these years . . .'

I walk towards the truck. Someone's whistling along

215

to Mariah Carey behind the shutter. I glance back. Benni's turned towards the wall, his phone pressed to his ear. I walk past the truck and carry on walking. I turn the corner by a church and Benni is out of sight. I cross a main road. I can see the sea. I head towards it and walk down the steps to the pebbles.

The sea's churning beneath the pier struts like it's going to keep harassing them until the pier gives up and collapses. I film it for a few seconds then send it to Fi. She replies straight away with a picture of an ice-cream vending machine. I don't know when we stopped using words and went for pictures instead. Fi messages me again. This time she's holding her ice cream and about to take a bite. Her boyfriend must have taken it from that angle. I'm a crap brother. I'm jealous of her. I want to be thousands of miles away from Mum and Benni, just thinking about myself and ice cream.

Another message flashes up from her. This time it's actual words.

> So u and daddy are father-son bonding by the seaside, then?

How do u kno?

> Mum sent me a message. She must be mad. There's loads of typos

I'm looking for my friend Dee

> The crazy nursery girl. So I heard. Is she in the sea?

She wasn't crazy.

> **Sorry. I didn't mean that in a bad way.**
> **I remember Mum saying that she always**
> **did her own thing. That's good.**

I squint into the distance. I can just make out a massive boat on the horizon, maybe a cargo boat full of shipping containers. How deep is the sea out there to keep it all afloat?

> **You bottling out, Spey?**

Why do u say that?

> **Because ur sitting on the beach messaging**
> **me instead of looking for her**

Her aunty lives in Hastings

> **But ur sitting on the beach Instead**
> **of knocking on aunty's door**

Maybe Mum's right. I should leave
her alone. I didn't think it thru

> **Maybe. But can you find Dee without her?**
> **Good things can come from snap decisions**

Like staying in Japan and leaving your little brother to deal with the fallout? When I don't reply, I think she's going offline. She doesn't.

> **How's the dad thing going?**

If I told u, I'd have to linger on the beach longer

> **Good point. Mine sent me £1000 when I was at uni**

£1000???

> **Yup**

I look down at the Jordans and decide that I will never feel guilty about them ever again.

He'd got a new girlfriend and I didn't hear much from him for a few years. It didn't really bother me. We'd run out of things to say to each other. Then he'd seen that newspaper article about my grades. He wanted me to know how proud he was and sent me the dosh

And then?

I sent him a thank you. It would have been rude not to

And?

And that was it. Though I've always kept his address handy, just in case. You never know when the attentions of a guilty father comes in useful, right, Spey?

I imagine her standing there in a convenience shop in Tokyo trying to message me and eat her ice cream at the same time.

Get off the beach, Spey. Go and see the aunty. That's the mission you chose to accept

Then another picture. A close up of a melty bit of green ice cream.

Got to go, little bruv. Got my own important business to take care of

OK

I recentre my map. I hope Benni finished talking to Mum before he noticed I was gone or that was going to make their conversation even more awkward. I suppose this could be normal family life, where parents end up having massive rows about their kid.

I turn away from the sea and cut under a subway, back

on to a shopping street. This isn't far from where I left Benni. I send him a message.

Meet you back at the station

As I swipe back on to map his reply pings up. He tells me to wait for him. I ignore it and check the map again. I need to go up a hill and through a park. I can see the castle ruins from here. They look ready to tumble into the sea. I wonder if Dee ever went up there looking for flowers. Queen Dee looking down on us all.

Dee

Chez's arrived. He's angry because he couldn't get a ride from London and had to take the train. He's says he's gonna take the money for the ticket from me. He pulled out the panel beneath the bath and checked the drugs. Then he checked the money. He said that there wasn't enough drugs or enough money. He said it's my fault. I should have kept the key safe and made sure Ingram couldn't get to the drugs. I should have gone to get electricity myself or called Chez as soon as I knew Ingram wasn't coming back. He shouted so hard I could see his spit.

He says I'm as useless as my mother.

He says we're street scum and I'm lucky he'll have anything to do with me.

His phone rang and he says that when he comes back, he'll take care of me.

He won't take care of me like Nan took care of me.

Or Aunty Janet tried to take care of me.

Or Mum wanted to take care of me.

He means he's gonna take care of me in a bad way. He means he's gonna hurt me.

The kids on our block always came to Nan if they hurt themselves. When it was sunny, she'd sit outside so she could see what was going on. She had plasters and antiseptic cream and tweezers for splinters in a box behind the front door.

But sometimes things can't get fixed.

What Spencer did couldn't be fixed.

Dee

Ripped open, torn up, pages screwed up like they're gonna make a fire.

Spencer smashed my book. Spencer smashed open my drawer and smashed my book.

I couldn't even find Nan's message. I ain't got nothing

left of her. Not even the way she writes my name.

I try and remember how she says 'Dee-Dee' but it's like I'm making her up. My brain takes pictures but can't record no voice.

Dee

Galium aparine

GOOSEGRASS

CATCHWEED

STICKYWEED

CATCHTONGUE

ROBIN-RUN-THE-HEDGE

CLEAVERS

Cleavers stick to you. They used to grow in our vegetable bed. Me and Nan used to dig them out together. I saw them in the woods near Chalkleighs too.

Spencer left a phone under my pillow in a plastic bag. I turned it on and checked the messages. There was a picture of my broken book and dead pages. Spencer had sent the picture to Chez and he'd sent it back to me. He said I had to remember that he could break things, even if he wasn't there. He could break people I loved, even if he wasn't there.

He didn't want me to be broken. He wanted to help me.

Wherever I go, he'll be there. He's stuck to me.

224

Spey

I follow the line on my map. My mash-up brain turns the moving blue spot into my footsteps, one in front of the other, hurrying along the path like there's treasure at the end of it. I miss the entrance to the park first time and have to double back. And here's my first load of treasure, a heap of after-Christmas crap – squashed tissue paper, party hats, even a cracker that's collapsed in a dirty puddle. The joke's torn and muddy.

I go into the park. It's like the Lidl booze section got tipped into the rose bushes. I stop. Rose bushes? It's December, but some of them have still got blooms, pink ones hanging around like they've missed their last tube home. Scraps of dirty plastic are stuck to the thorns. I pick a few off, even though they feel damp and gritty. I shove the rubbish in my pocket until I find a bin. I touch a rose petal. Yes, it's pink, but Dee always made me look harder, so I bend closer. Some petals are the same bright pink all the way through. Others look like the pink got bored before it was finished doing its work.

I think about Dee at her birthday tea, holding up a flower catalogue and telling me which ones to cut out. *This one's called Hot Shot and this one's Blueberry, though it's not really blue.*

God, now I remember something else. Dee said she'd

never tasted blueberries so I asked Mum to buy some and bring them to nursery. Dee put one in her mouth, bit down and spat it out again. Her nan had shrugged.

'Tell you what, Spey. You're bloody lucky that she gave it a go at all. My Dee's not one for trying new stuff.'

A pink rose sticks out by itself. The other roses are in a clump of three or four. I look at the stems around the solo one. Four of them have been snapped off. Maybe someone was desperate for a last-minute present.

I carry on along the path, past the war memorial and its circle of poppy wreaths, around the playground and then the outdoor gym. The playground is buzzing with kids. I reckon there's at least three new scooters with matching helmets and an older kid on a unicycle. A bald guy's working the gym. He finishes his sit-ups, checks his watch and grins.

The path heads uphill past tennis courts, then between two fences and I'm out on the street again. It's like *everyone's* out on the streets, scratching to get free from their house even if it means shivering outside a cafe drinking coffee. My map takes me up some steps next to a pub and I'm looking at a row of terraced houses. They're different colours, like the ones in the cheesy films Mum watched after she split up from Pete. I used to ask her why those films didn't make her feel worse. She said that she was fully aware that it was a fantasy for men and women to fall in love the way they do in those films, but the bit that made her furious was the impossible assumption that single women in London could really afford houses like that.

Dee's Aunty Janet lives in a house like that. She's gone from a flat on our tatty old estate to a pale blue house with window boxes and a dark grey door. There's no path nor doorstep. You just go straight up to the door and knock. I don't. Not yet. I just stand there with my arms hanging by my side. My phone starts ringing. It's Benni. I reject the call, close down the map and stick my phone in my pocket.

I've come all this way. I've left Benni in a shop doorway getting yelled at by Mum. Whatever I do, I'm going to get yelled at by Mum too. So I might as well do it. I walk up to the door, lift the knocker and let it drop. I step back. The door opens straight away.

I say, 'Um, Miss, Ms . . . Janet?' I realise I don't even know her surname. I feel myself blushing.

She frowns. 'Do I know you?' But she says it in a way that sounds like she thinks she does.

We look at each other. I only saw her a couple of times at Dee's, but I would have recognised her straight away. Her hair's purpley-red, short and spiky, not long and black like it used to be. She suddenly smiles.

'I'm Spey,' I say. 'From—'

'Dee's little friend! Of course, it's you! Though not so little now!' She shakes her head, still smiling. 'It's been how long?' She counts her fingers. 'Eight, nine years? But still . . . What a lovely surprise!' She frowns again. 'A very *unexpected* surprise, as I had no idea you knew where I lived.' She steps aside. 'But anyway, come in.'

I stay where I am. 'It's okay. I just . . .'

'You found out my address, got on a train down from London and knocked on my door.' She smiles. 'I'm not gonna leave you on the doorstep, sweetheart.'

Got on a train straight from London, by myself, no hassles. I wish. I step in. There's no hallway. I'm straight into her sitting room. I look around. I don't know what for. It's not that I'm going to find Dee hiding behind the sofa. There's a shoe rack right next to the front door. My eyes land on that.

Janet says, 'If you can take your shoes off, that would be great, love. The world outside's pretty scuzzy. I don't want to bring it in.'

I slip off my Jordans with the laces still done up.

Janet sighs. 'Mum was always going on at Dee for doing that. I hope she didn't get it from you.'

'Sorry.' I pick up each trainer and unknot them.

'I was just joking,' she says. 'I'm making some tea. Have you got time?'

'It's okay. I just want to know—'

'Hold on.' She goes through a door opposite. I don't want tea. My stomach sounds like a bin lorry and it feels like the inside of one too, turning and churning. I don't even know why I'm so nervous. I stand by the sofa. It's covered in cushions. Am I supposed to move them or plonk down on them? I move one and sit on the other. There's a proper fire burning, though, real logs in a fireplace and a basket full of wood and a pile of newspaper next to it. I always wanted to have a proper fire when I was kid, even though Mum kept pointing out that our block didn't have any chimneys, or fireplaces. Then we moved. There are definitely chimneys on the roof of our house, but Mum reckons they've been filled in so we can't use them. There's a stack of books in our fireplace instead.

Janet's mantelpiece is loaded with pictures. I spot a school photo – a class one, where the teacher sits on a chair in the front with rows of kids around them. In my class, there was always a bundle to see who'd get to stand on the bench behind the teacher, because it was the only time you'd get to be taller than them. And you'd all be daring each other to make a 'you stink' face just as the photo was taken.

'Tea and cake.' Janet's holding a tray with mugs, a teapot, milk and sugar, plus two wedges of chocolate cake. My bin-truck stomach churns again. She settles the tray on a coffee table next to the Christmas *Radio Times*. I almost blurt out that my grandma always buys that, but somehow I don't think that's information Janet wants to know right now.

'So,' she says. 'What does bring you here?'

She's looking at me and her face is like … it's like in those police programmes, where the detective knocks on a door and the camera pans to the family's faces as they wait for the bad news. She starts to pour the tea. It's the same colour as Mum's Christmas gravy.

'I'll leave you to add your own milk,' she says. 'I know people can be fussy like that.'

My tea turns from gravy to puddle as I pour too much.

'Well,' Janet says. 'I'm assuming the reason you *are* here is because of the person we have in common.'

I nod.

'My lovely Dee,' she says.

'Yes.'

'And . . . is there something . . . ?'

'I just wondered if you knew where she was.'

'Oh.'

The fire crackles and I can smell burning paper.

'I thought you might know,' she says.

'I'm sorry. I thought you did.'

She shakes her head. 'I suppose I'm always waiting for someone to knock on my door. It was the same way with my sister. Always waiting for that knock, until it happened. Two months ago. Gloria passed away in hospital from pneumonia.' She takes a deep breath. 'Why are you looking for Dee?'

'I'm sorry about Gloria,' I say.

She nods. As I tell her about the collage, she looks like she wants to cry.

'Dee came with me when we had to clear out Mum's flat. I thought it might help us with our grieving, though sometimes it's hard to work out what Dee feels about things. She keeps it inside her until it bursts out. I found the collage under her bed.' She looks embarrassed. 'I actually thought it was rubbish and chucked it in the bin. Dee really went off on one, saying something about it being yours too. So it came to

230

my flat and then, I suppose, to Chalkleighs, the home here.'

Janet stares at the mantelpiece.

'Do you recognise her?' she asks quietly.

I look at the rows of pictures and feel bad. Maybe Dee should jump out at me without me even thinking about it, the same way I knew 'I Was Born to Love You', even though I couldn't remember how I'd even heard it before.

Janet laughs. 'Sorry. That's unfair.'

She takes the school photo off the mantelpiece and hands it to me. I'm surprised I didn't see Dee straight away. She's right there, standing on the bench with Janet next to her.

'I became a teaching assistant,' Janet said. 'Especially so I could keep an eye on her.'

Janet's hand is on Dee's back. I'm not sure if it's to stop Dee falling off the bench or to make Dee feel okay. Dee's not looking at the camera. Of course she's not. Maybe if the photographer had ordered the kids not to look at the camera, Dee would have given him a full-on stare. Instead, her attention's on the head of the kid sitting in front of her. And *that's* why Janet's touching Dee's back. It's a warning. *Don't you dare!*

'There's something called oppositional defiant disorder,' Janet says. 'It's like a posh name for the kids that don't behave the way everyone wants them to. An excuse. That's what I told the psychologist when he mentioned it . . .'

Janet stirs her tea so hard the mug rattles.

'It's easy to give something a long name and look satisfied.

It means that they can throw some medicine at her rather than get to know her better. It's an excuse to put her in a box. They wouldn't understand. Dee saw the world differently. Rules just . . .'

'Weren't there,' I say.

Janet nods. 'Yes, weren't there. It's like she wasn't really breaking the rules because she didn't know they existed. You understand, don't you, Spey?'

'Yeah.'

'But you try telling that to a furious headteacher. And me and Mum ended talking to so many furious teachers. And then social workers and counsellors. It's like everyone was looking for a diagnosis, then when they got one, didn't know what to do next.' Janet takes a sip of her tea. 'Though there were times, I'm sure, when she was just being naughty. And why not?'

I think of Chez's face when it was hit by the paint water at nursery.

I sip my tea as well. Mum once told me about mirroring other people's actions in interviews. Is that what I'm doing now? Except the tea's still boiling hot. I put the mug down so quickly some of the tea sloshes on to the tray. Janet doesn't seem to notice.

I say, 'Where do you think she is now?'

Janet picks up her plate of cake. 'I could always see what was going to happen to Dee,' she says. 'It sounds terrible, and, god, I didn't want to be right. It's not Dee's fault, but it's the way things work, isn't it? If you don't fit in . . . if you don't *want* to fit in, no one knows what the hell to do with you.'

I nod. I kind of understand. Maybe that's why me and Dee got on so well.

'I still try and find reasons for what happened,' Janet says. 'The poor soul was premature, completely unexpected. Gloria had no idea she was pregnant. Thankfully she was at Mum's when her waters broke or god knows what could have happened. Dee needed oxygen at first, even when she came out of hospital. Social services agreed that Mum would be Dee's main carer as Gloria was nowhere near dropping the drugs yet. We still told Gloria she could see her daughter whenever she wanted, as long as one of us was with her. I suppose we hoped that this tiny baby would be the thing that pushed Gloria into sorting herself out. And now Dee doesn't know that her own mother's . . .' She takes another loud breath. 'Did you ever meet my sister?'

I think about Dee's birthday and the smell and Dee colouring in so hard she tore the paper. Then Gloria's voice, *It's my girl's birthday. And I remembered.*

'Yes. When I went around for Dee's birthday party.'

'Oh. Yes. *That* birthday. Mum said you were so good about it, staying with Dee and making your collage while there was chaos all around. Do you know that's the only time Dee ever had a birthday tea with a friend? We always asked and she always said no.'

I feel my face burn. I want to yell, 'I might have been a decent kid, but I'm not Saint Spey! I've let Dee down!' Instead, I shrug and smile.

'Gloria was lovely,' Janet says, 'when she was her real self. But we saw less and less of that. She used to shoot up in Mum's bathroom.'

My mouth moves, but it's ahead of my brain. What can I say?

'It was Mum's idea. She wanted her to be safe. Mum found out about needle exchanges, safe gear, everything.'

She's crying and I don't know what to do. I want to go. *That's* how saintly I am now.

My phone's probably loading up with messages – Benni and Mum, tapping away, message after stressed-out message. But I pick up my plate of cake. Mirroring again. Janet uses the side of her fork to slice off a bit of cake. I wait, then do the same.

'I could say it all started going wrong for Dee when Mum died.' Janet's voice is croaky from crying. 'But it was long before that. No school could keep Dee, and I include pupil referral units in that. She'd just walk out. A girl like Dee, she was always going to be an easy target. Gloria was well known, and some of those bastards, they must have thought – like mother, like daughter. And . . . they made it turn out like that.'

My fork lands on my plate. 'Dee took drugs?'

'No!' Janet rests her fork down too. 'I didn't mean that! Dee was never on drugs when they brought her home! She

234

didn't really drink, neither. I suppose I should thank her oppositional defiant disorder for something! All the things she was told she should do, she didn't. And that included the booze and the drugs. But if you're wandering the streets for long enough, you're going to go bleep on the wrong folks' radar, aren't you, Spey?'

I wonder if Janet had her own version of The Talk that she gave to Dee.

'She came to live with me after Mum died, but it was a disaster. Like I ever thought I could take Mum's place. Dee wouldn't go to school. She wouldn't tell me where she was going or who she was with. She'd never let me know if she wasn't coming back in the evenings. It was too much.' She touches her heart and replaces her plate on the table. Down goes mine.

'Social services stepped in. They had to, because I couldn't keep her safe. They shipped her down here to Chalkleighs, a special home for girls who are in danger of being exploited. Bastards!'

Her head jerks as she spits out the words. For a moment, I think she means social services.

'Can you believe it, Spey? This crap happens to so many girls they have to set up a special home to help them!' She breathes out slowly. 'But still. It felt so wrong that my Dee was down here by herself, so I came too.' She gives a little laugh. 'And I thought that I'd have a rest from Gloria knocking on my door and asking for money. But in the end, I never got to see Gloria again and I only saw Dee once.'

'Couldn't you visit her at the home?'

'I tried. But every time I called to speak to her, she wasn't there. They said I shouldn't worry. She was getting on all right. She even had a quiet place she'd go to in the woods. And I did feel relieved. Mum gave her this flower book and I imagined her walking through the woods trying to find all the flowers she'd never see in London. But I forgot something, Spey. Anyone can do what you did and get a train down from London.'

I remember what Astrid said. *Some of them places are like Argos for gangstas.*

'They came for her,' Janet says. 'They came for her. And they found her.'

'How do you know?'

The fire crackles. I bite the inside of my mouth. Did *he* find her? I want to tell her how I'd been there in the market. I'd heard what he said he was going to do to her.

'I saw her, Spey. I was actually coming back from putting flowers on Mum's grave. I was at the back of the train and Dee was right there, on the concourse. I called her! I'm sure I did! I don't think she heard me. Then I saw this boy. He must have been on the same bloody train as me. Jesus! If I'd known.' She shakes her head. 'He goes through the barriers, goes up to her and kisses her like she's his girlfriend. I felt sick, Spey, because it was all wrong. I'm trying to run along the platform and you can see I'm not built for running. Then I drop my handbag

and everything falls out and I have to stop and pick it all up.'
She sighs. 'Then by the time I come out, they've disappeared.'

'What did you do?'

She makes a face. 'I called the police. I didn't care. I hoped they'd catch that boy with whatever it was he had on him.'

'How do you know he had drugs?'

'He was carrying a bag.'

I don't say anything.

'She'd got in with a bad lot in London. He was one of them. I knew it.'

'Did the police come?'

'They told me to call Chalkleighs and let them know. She hadn't looked like she was in danger. No one was hurting her and she'd actually been waiting, so maybe he was just a friend. I wanted to scream! They know about the county lines stuff, of course they do. But I suppose they can't arrest any Black boy carrying a bag.'

She sounds like she really wished they could.

'I came out of the station and looked up and down the road, but I couldn't see her. She'd slipped through my hands. I walked home the long way, looking and looking . . .' She shrugs.

'Did she go back to Chalkleighs?'

'Yes. They called me to let me know. But I couldn't rest, Spey. I knew that wasn't the end of the story. *I knew.* So, yes, she went back. Then a couple of days later, she disappeared. Nobody knew where she went. She hadn't packed all her stuff, so it looked like she was going to go back. But now she's officially a missing person. I'm pretty sure she's not in Hastings any more, but I still walk around looking out for her. Just in case.'

Janet stands up. I do too.

'I'll wrap up that cake for you,' she says. 'You can take it back with you.'

For the first time, I notice the vase of roses on a chest of drawers next to the door to the kitchen. There are no decorations up anywhere in the room, except for a few Christmas cards and a small twist of tinsel around the vase. There are four pink roses. I think of the rose bushes earlier and the snapped stems.

'Aren't they lovely?' Janet says. 'I was a bit naughty, though. I stole them from the park. Roses always remind me of Dee. I lost them, Spey – Mum, Gloria, Dee. I think about them all the time. It's stupid, but those roses are like the four of us are back together again.'

She goes into the kitchen while I slide back into my Jordans. She brings back plastic containers full of cake.

'I bought way too much food,' she says. 'I forget it's just me.'

She opens the front door.

'Please let me know if you find her, Spey.'

'Yes,' I say. 'I will.'

Janet closes the door and I'm back on the street. As I walk towards the station, the sea stays behind me. I take a deep breath and check my phone. Ten missed calls. Five each from Benni and Mum, like they're playing Stress Spey ping-pong. My phone starts ringing. Astrid's number flashes up.

She says, 'You need to go to Brighton.'

'Why?'

'Because Uncle reckons that's where your girl is.'

'How come?'

'The line she's working is down that way now.'

'Right. Thank you.'

'And if you're heading that way with your dad, tell him to be careful. Richie's got that info too.'

Dee

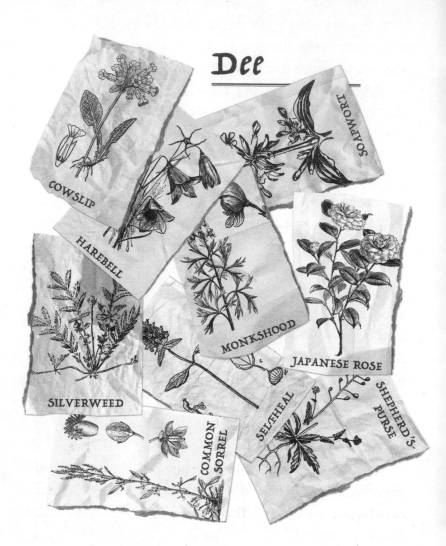

Spencer broke my book and I lay on my bed awake all night. My flowers were still on the floor. When I walked across the room to go to the bathroom, they slid underneath my feet

and I almost fell over. I turned off my light and opened the
window. When I first came to Chalkleighs, I thought I could
hear the sea, but really it's too far away. It's just trees in the
wind. I still liked the sound, but I couldn't imagine floating
away on it and being somewhere else.

A day happened.

And then another day.

Samira bought me another flower book. It was big with a
shiny cover and the flowers were photographs, not drawings.

Abi said there was space on the shed wall for a mural.
I could choose some flowers and help design it.

Spencer was moved out of Chalkleighs, not because
she broke my book but because they said she was at risk
and put me and Anissa at risk too. Anissa laughed out
loud in the meeting. She said that a dumbass like Spencer
couldn't hurt her because Spencer thought she was a queen
bitch gangsta girl, but really didn't know shit. Then Anissa
spat at me. She said, no matter what, you don't grass. The
spit missed me and got Abi instead. Chalkleighs was full
of shouting again.

The night after Spencer left, the phone she left me started
vibrating. I answered and it was Chez. I hung up and he
called again. Then again. Then he messaged me and told me
I need to answer.

He said he wasn't gonna go away.

Cleavers.

He sent the picture of my broken flower book again. He

told me he knew where Aunty Janet lived and that he could hurt her too. Then he said loads of nasty things about my mum and I wanted to throw my phone against the wall. Then I sat down on my bed and I thought about it. If he could find me, he could find Aunty Janet. He might know she lived in Hastings too.

I sat there and thought about how my behaviour affects other people. If I didn't do what Chez wanted, I could stay at Chalkleighs. But it was never for keeps. I didn't know how long I'd be there before I was moved somewhere else. It didn't matter if I left now because I'd have to go one day anyway.

It *did* matter if Chez hurt Aunty Janet.

Chez rang again and I answered.

Next morning, I had to go to the railway station. I was supposed to see Samira after breakfast, but it didn't matter no more. I waited for the train from London and then I saw this boy get out. I didn't know him, but I knew his look. He walked like he was happy, but his hands were fists. He came through the barrier, kissed me and told me he'd brought the present. He took my hand into his fist then we walked away together. He was holding my hand, but I didn't know his name.

When we were outside the station, he said he was gonna show me where I needed to deliver the gear. Suddenly, he pulled me around the side of a Subway. He said there was a white woman following him. She'd been on the same train as him and was still on his tail. Chez had told him to watch out because the police were trying to disrupt operations down this way and he didn't want to take no chances.

'That's her,' he said.

I must have breathed in too loud, because the boy grabbed my wrist so tight I thought he wanted to snap it.

'What?' he said.

I told him it was my aunty.

'Your aunty's out looking for you?'

Aunty Janet walked past Subway. She didn't see me. He didn't let go of my wrist.

'She know what you're doing?'

I'd pulled my hand free. 'No!'

'Because that's some major coincidence. Woman's walking out the station the same time as you.'

He'd seen me waiting on my own. I told him that. And I told him that she'd been on *his* train. He said he had to tell Chez. Now he'd know for sure where my aunty was.

I wish I'd called out to Aunty Janet.

I wish she'd stopped and turned around and seen me.

When I left Chalkeighs, I didn't even run. I just walked out the gate and up to the crossroads, through the car park to the woods. I walked down the path to the bottom of the hill. The sun was shining on the sea. It made it look hard and white, like it was made of ice. Chez was waiting. He smiled, like I was the best thing he'd seen in the whole world.

Spey

'What the hell kind of stunt was that?'

Benni's standing outside the station, his hands shoved in his pockets like he's scared what they'll do to me if they're let out into the light.

'It wasn't a stunt,' I say. 'I came here for a reason.'

'You should have waited for me.'

'You were too busy agreeing with Mum!'

'She's right, Spey! You shouldn't be chasing after this girl. Your mum says you haven't seen her since you were six or seven. You didn't tell me that!'

'I saw her last year,' I say.

His eyebrows shoot up. 'Really? Your mum doesn't know.'

'No.'

His mouth's forming a 'why'. I really haven't got time for this.

I say, 'I suppose you told your mother everything, right?'

He looks at me. I'm getting better at reading his expressions. This one's 'hurt' plus 'sad'. I realise why. I'd forgotten. I'd honestly forgotten.

He says, 'My mother left me in a baby basket in a doctor's surgery, Spey. So, no. I didn't.'

I blink. He stares back then his eyes drop away from me.

He says, 'Sorry. I shouldn't have dumped that on you.'

No! He shouldn't have! What is it? Punishment for going off without him?

I glance up at the train information board. I can't see any direct trains to Brighton. I look back at Benni. He's staring at the floor. Mum once said, *He's a good guy who's done stupid things, Spey.* When he asked me if I ever was ashamed of him, I didn't tell him everything. I was actually proud of him. Before I knew about Nelson Mandela, I'd told myself stories about how my father ended up in prison. I'd decided that he was in a bank when some robbers tried to steal the money but they ran away and the police thought it was him. Then when Mum explained he was actually one of the robbers – *though, he never hurt anyone, Spey* – I reckoned he must have had a friend who was really poor and because my father didn't have any money himself, he stole stuff to help her so her children didn't starve. Mum had looked really sad when she had to tell me that wasn't the case, neither.

And here he was, a bit short and tired-looking and grumpy, ready to fill in the gaps.

'I'm sorry,' I say. 'I really didn't mean to say that thing about your mum.'

'I know.'

'How old were you when your mum left you?'

'Coming up to three months, according to my files. So at least I don't remember that glorious moment.'

'Did you ever look for your mother?'

He shakes his head. 'I know your grandma can be a bit of a terror, but my mother top-trumps her all the way. It wasn't a spur of the moment thing when she dumped me. She didn't suddenly crack and decide she couldn't cope. I suppose that's what I'd assumed all those years until I read the notes and joined up the dots in my head. She and my father planned it.'

'I don't understand.'

'She dumped me at Wednesday teething clinic,' he says. 'So no one noticed another crying baby until she'd gone. She'd left a note with my name on it, but it was before everything was on computers so they had to go through all the birth registers to find me. But she must have had some twinge of conscience, because she phoned in after there was something in the local news. She made it very clear that she didn't want me back.'

'And your father agreed?'

'They were married, remember.'

I still can't get my head around that. I think of the four pink roses in Janet's vase.

'Dee's mum was a drug addict,' I say. 'I don't think she ever managed to look after Dee properly, but she wanted to try. I suppose it goes both ways. People who can't, want to, and people who . . . maybe . . .' I don't know how to finish. Should everything have been all right because they were married? Mum's done all right, even though she's never had a husband.

'I know it's complicated,' he says.

I nod.

'So what happened when you saw Dee last year? Why didn't you tell your mum?'

I can feel my face going red. Yet another time when I could do with a bucket more melanin.

I say, 'I'm going to Brighton to find her.'

He carries on looking at me. 'You can tell me, Spey. I won't judge you.' He laughs. 'I'm not in any position to judge you.'

'I can get you a ticket back to London.'

'I'm not leaving you. Your mum wants me to bring you home.'

I shake my head. 'Not yet.'

'Why Brighton?'

'I heard from Astrid.'

'And?'

'She said Richie's on his way there too.'

He closes his eyes and takes a deep breath.

I say, 'I can still get you that ticket to London.'

'No, Spey. I can't keep running in the wrong direction.'

Dee

Chez brought me here. He gave me another phone and told me what I had to do. I didn't bring much with me. Chez said I should make it look like I'd just run away for a little bit but I'd be going back. He said he'd give me money for new clothes. He hasn't, though. I was going to bring the picture I made with Spey on my birthday. I'd taken it from Nan's to Aunty Janet's. She'd offered to look after it when I went to Chalkleighs but I wanted it with me. I liked it because it had Nan's writing on the back. After my book got torn up, I knew it wasn't safe any more. I asked Samira to send it to Spey at the address on the back. Now he's got both pieces.

Ingram didn't want me here. He thinks that girls like me shouldn't do this, but he won't tell Chez that. He's worried that Chez won't give him free drugs no more if he complains. Though I think Ingram's like me and he's got people he doesn't want Chez to hurt. Chez's always telling me about what he'll do to Aunty Janet if I take any of the money or drugs. Maybe *that's* where Ingram's gone. He took just enough of the money and wraps to keep him okay while he made sure his son was all right.

I checked in his room and he'd left some food. None of it had been opened. There were mince pies and pork pies and crisps and orange juice. He left the key to the box with the drugs and money. It was my key. I didn't know that Ingram had taken it.

I'm in the bathroom now. I've pulled the drugs box out from under the bath. I have to wiggle the key around before it unlocks. Chez showed me how but I couldn't always do it. Sometimes, Ingram would help me. The lock clicks. If I want to, I can open it. Nan said that drugs are poison and they can kill you. But Mum says they make her happy and keep her happy.

I don't know if drugs will make me happy.

Spey

This train's busy too, even more than the earlier one. Benni's been silent for most of the journey, hunched against the window. I don't mention Richie. He doesn't mention Richie. Neither of us mention Mum. She's been quiet too, so she must be driving back to London. As soon as she gets home, I know we're going to be hearing from her.

Benni straightens up as the train stops and everyone starts getting off. We pass through the barriers and out on to the main concourse.

'I came here too,' he says. 'When I was little. It was one of the taxi-driver trips.'

'You came to Brighton by taxi?'

'It was a charity thing. For poor kids. You been here before?'

'Yeah. With Mum a couple of times, but Southend was easier.' And cheaper.

'Brighton's bigger than Hastings. Did Astrid give you any clues?'

'No.' I check my phone. 'I had a look online to see where there's been recent drug arrests or just drug hotspots. Kemp Town comes up a bit. It's either that or up in the estates.'

'Which is closer?'

'Kemp Town.'

'Can we walk it?'

I check the map. 'It's about forty minutes.'

And then what? He doesn't say it. He must be holding it back, because that's all I can think now. What are we going to do? Walk from street to street, hoping we bump into Dee in a local corner shop?

We head out of the station into the full Brighton light. The hill tips towards the sea. A crowd of seagulls are hunched around a puddle like they're planning a riot. Benni does a full 360-turn like he's kicking off one of those flash-mob videos. I wait for the guy behind the pasty truck to start playing a violin. He doesn't. He carries on selling pasties.

'Are you okay?' I ask.

'Yeah. Just remembering this place. Can we head down to the sea?'

I check my map. It's not the quickest route. But Benni's already started off down the hill. The sea seems to make the sky thinner above it, like it's slowly being stretched apart.

I catch up with Benni. 'It would be quicker if—'

My words are drowned out by a car stereo. Brighton doesn't look like the type of place where there'd be a huge number of J Hus fans.

'Sol?' We say it together.

A car's stopped at the traffic lights. It's a sports car, roof back, even in December. Some old white bloke with dreads is at the wheel. Benni and I must have both breathed out together because we both laugh.

Benni says, 'We could really do with Sol right now. He knows how to run these things.'

And Astrid. If she isn't there, Dee's going to be surrounded by men.

'I reckon he'll still come,' Benni says. 'Once Sol's got a sniff of a lines operation, he doesn't give up.'

'And Richie?'

'Yeah. He'll be here.'

'Why?'

'Because I owe him. And he's right. I'm overdue.'

And suddenly, Benni looks old. I mean, he didn't look seventeen to start with. I think of Dorian Gray and his portrait. I wonder if Benni read that one too.

We can see the sea properly now, darker grey than the sky.

Benni says, 'How's your sister?'

I'd forgotten he knew Fi. Actually, it's weird to remember that he knew her before I did. Mum said she and Benni never really lived together. I wasn't exactly planned. Nor was Fi. So we're equal there.

'She's okay,' I say.

'Still angry with the world?'

'You mean angry with me?'

'I don't think she was ever angry with you.'

We keep walking down towards the sea.

'She was,' I say. 'Because I made Mum find out that she was seeing her dad in secret.'

'It wasn't fair to make you keep that a secret from your mum. You were only little.'

I shrug. Even Fi says that now, but . . . it wasn't just that. I'd been happy with our family. Me, Fi and Mum. No dads. We didn't need them. I thought we were strong and special because of it. Fi and me had even made a pact a couple of years before. If Mum ever tried to have a boyfriend, we'd behave so badly we'd put him off. But then her dad turns up and everything else is forgotten.

'What was he like?' Benni asks. Even to me his voice sounds a bit too casual.

'He seemed all right.'

Fi would drag me along to her football practice every Wednesday when Mum was working late. One time, her dad turned up. He was a white guy, proper white, not like me who looks white from certain angles. (Actually, most angles.) His hair was a mixture of dark brown and grey. The grey was in a thick line above his forehead. He'd reminded me of Kaneki in *Tokyo Ghoul* and how Kaneki's hair had turned white after he'd been tortured. But it was his eyebrow shape that did it, like jet skis, just when they're rising out of the water.

I knew those eyebrows. I saw them on my sister's face every day. Fi looked just like him. She knew what both her parents looked like, the way they mixed up to make her.

'I hated lying to Mum,' I say. 'She always asked Fi how practice went and Fi would go on about how fit she was getting and how she could dodge past the hardcore midfielder, but leave out the fact that her dad came along every week.'

Fi would sometimes flick a grin at me. I wouldn't even nod to back up her stories, but Mum never noticed.

'This doesn't end well, does it?' Benni says.

'How do you know?' Did Mum tell him all this already?

Benni laughs. 'I'm looking at your face, Spey. The message is clear.'

Maybe I should go to prison to learn how to hide myself more.

I say, 'I just got really fed up with it. So one practice, I smuggled Fi's phone out of her bag when she was warming up. When her dad came, I asked him if I could borrow money for an ice cream. I think he was so shocked that I spoke to him that he gave it to me. I went over to the ice cream van and when I knew he couldn't see me, I called Mum.'

'You told her about Fi's dad?'

I shake my head. I hadn't even been that brave.

'I suppose you could have done that any time at home, couldn't you?'

I feel a blush crawling its way up from my neck. 'I told her I had a really bad stomach ache and that I needed her to come and get me straight away.'

I'd cried so hard and bent myself over in such convincing pain, I think I put half the queue off their future ice creams.

'And she came,' Benni says.

Mum's car had screeched into the car park fifteen minutes later. Not that I was in the car park then, but I can pretty much imagine Mum doing a handbrake turn by the recycling bins and storming down the path to find me.

'Yeah. And, well, Mum . . .'

'Doesn't hold back when she's angry,' Benni says.

'No.' I suppose that's where Fi gets it from.

Mum had come striding across the grass and stopped dead when she saw Fi's dad. I really had wanted to throw up on the spot. Mum had spat out a few swear words. Mum never swore, not in front of me, anyway. Fi's dad had gazed up at her, his hand guarding his face from the sun, or maybe the swear words. Mum's shadow next to him looked like the Iron Giant.

'Robert?' she'd said. 'What the hell are you doing here?'

'I've come to see my daughter play football.'

'Your daughter?'

Then Mum did a whole lot more swearing. I'd glanced towards the pitch. Fi was speeding towards the goal. She hadn't noticed Mum yet.

'You have no right to call her your daughter,' Mum had shouted. 'I've done everything.'

'Hardly my fault, Gild.'

Mum's shadow had trembled and I clutched my stomach. I felt like I'd swallowed an ice cube whole and it was trying to find its way out.

'Really?' Mum had said. 'Did you ask your wife's permission

to have a baby with me? Because when she came to find me, she was far from pleased.'

And that's when I'd got really confused. Not only was there a dad, but there was another wife?

Mum had stomped right on to the pitch. The coach whistled and a player swerved round Mum towards the ball. The whistle blew again, hard, and play stopped. Everyone watched Mum as she walked towards Fi, grabbed her arm and dragged her away.

That was the moment I realised that Fi swore even better than Mum.

Both Benni's and my phone make their message sounds at the same time. We look at each other, then at our phones.

'Mum's on her way down,' I say.

Benni doesn't say anything. He just carries on looking at his phone.

Dee

Atropa belladonna

DEADLY NIGHTSHADE

DEVIL'S CHERRIES

BEAUTIFUL DEATH

BELLADONNA

I stay in the bathroom. The box that was full of drugs is lying on its side. I'd emptied it out. I can see the rubbish left under the bath. It's rolled-up newspaper and rags and pieces of plastic. There's even a hammer and bent up nails.

I count the wraps again. There are twenty-one. I pick up the first wrap and untwist the plastic.

Spey

My phone rings. I answer. Mum's so surprised she doesn't speak for a moment. Then she does. A. Lot. Finally, she stops for breath.

'So, where are you now, Spey?'

'I'm by the sea.'

'Don't play me for stupid.'

'I'm not. I could take a picture and . . .'

She hangs up.

Benni's phone starts ringing. He raises his eyebrows at me and I nod.

He answers. 'Yes, Gilda. I'm still with him. We'll be home soon . . . No need to come down.'

While Benni's going back and forward with Mum again, I send Astrid another text then search for more info about county lines in Brighton. I wade through what Google thinks I should see. It's just what Astrid was saying. Some of the gangs rent places on a short-term let and they're gone by the time the neighbours start to complain. Or they find someone who's vulnerable, maybe a drug user or someone with learning disabilities, and take over their place. It's nasty. I read an article by someone who used to be a housing officer but was so depressed by it all they had to give up their job or

258

lose their faith in humanity. Kemp Town's definitely a hot spot. At least some of the shops and market traders are up in arms. A while back, the council set up a new team to try and deal with it. There are pictures of big men in helmets like Robocop, smashing down doors. There's nothing about how they're helping girls like Dee. I send the links to Astrid so she's knows I'm not completely helpless.

'So it's off to Kemp Town, then?' Benni asks.

'Yes.' I check my map again. 'How's Mum?'

'Furious.'

'Is she coming down?'

'Not yet. There's been some sort of lorry spillage on the M23, so she's less than eager. But you know your mum. If she wants to come down, she'll find a way, even if she has to drive through fields.'

'We better hurry up, then,' I say. 'If we head east . . .'

'The Palace Pier,' he says. 'This brings back memories.'

I can see it. It's one of Brighton's biggest landmarks, but I'm a Londoner. I know a tourist trap when I see one.

'There used to be two piers,' Benni says. 'The other one burned down. You can still see the leftovers.' He points in the opposite direction.

I don't want to see leftover pier. I want to see Dee. Benni crosses the road. I follow him.

'I had a good time here,' he says quietly. 'I was staying with some foster carers in Crawley. The old man was a cab driver. That's how I ended up on the taxi-run down to

Brighton. Man, now I think about it, that's how I first met Richie. He came down on that trip too. I don't know about your friend Dee, but not all my time in care was bad. Some of it was good fun. It was just the not-knowing that was so damn stressful. Who I was. Who I was even gonna be living with. And, as I got older, what was gonna happen at the end of it all.'

I look east along the sealine. Wind turbines spin out in the distance.

'They never used to be here,' he says. 'Things are always changing.'

And suddenly, it feels that he's letting me read him. It's like all those stories where someone ends up disguised as something else – the beast in *Beauty and the Beast*, the wolf in *Little Red Riding Hood*, even the scarecrow in the film *Howl's Moving Castle*. He's stepped out from all the things he's pretending to be.

My dad's a scarecrow-wolf-beast? No, I don't mean that. I mean that there's all this stuff he must keep inside him and now he wants me to see it.

I say, 'I don't really know who I am. I mean, I know Mum's side, but not yours.'

He's looking at me like he wants to read me properly too.

'What do you want to know Spey?'

'My grandparents. Your parents. Did you ever meet them again?'

'No. I don't even know if they're still alive. I'd wasted too much energy on them, Spey, trying to work out why they couldn't keep me.' He takes a deep breath. 'Do you want to know why?'

All the reasons go through my mind. Drugs, drink, violence, not enough money. But that would be easier to explain.

He taps the back of his hand. 'I wasn't what they were expecting, Spey.'

'What were they expecting? An alien?'

I clap my hand to my mouth. An alien? This was not the moment for the kind of comments that made teachers chuck kids out of class.

He taps his hand again. 'I *was* the alien, Spey.'

Then, shit! I get it! I should have before, what with me and my family.

'Your parents were white, but your mum . . . Your real dad wasn't.'

He laughs. 'Half right. My mum *was* white. Her husband, who really was my father, wasn't. He was mixed race. I just didn't look enough like him.'

'Babies don't look like anyone,' I say.

'You looked a bit like Buster Bloodvessel.'

'Thanks.'

'You know who he is?'

'Mum says Bad Manners are her guilty pleasure.'

'God,' he says. 'I miss your mother.'

He's walking on to the pier and I'm following. This isn't east to Kemp Town. It's south, out to sea.

He says, 'I'm sure there used to be turnstiles. You had to pay a few pennies to enter.'

He stops by a sweet stall. The vendor looks hopeful then bored again. Benni takes my hand. I'm not expecting that. I start to pull my hand away. It's a reflex thing. He holds tight.

'When people see us,' he says, 'do they reckon I'm your father?'

I glance at the sweet-stall vendor. He's started to rearrange the packets of flying saucers on display. His 'bored' has changed to 'a bit curious'. Other people are passing us, checking us out, then looking away. I'm pretty sure that men holding hands isn't a big deal in Brighton, unless one's a teenager and the other one looks old enough to be his father.

'I don't think they're bothered,' I say.

'You reckon?' He lets go of my hand. 'Anyone ever asked about you and your mum?'

I'm about to shake my head. I'd always assumed I've got at least three white grandparents and it shows in my skin colour. But my nose and my mouth? My Black side's there for anyone looking, and some folk really were looking, especially when we came back from holidays. I'd go brown. Well, medium beige. It was enough for complete strangers to tap Mum on the back in supermarkets to ask her where my dad was from.

'I was born fair and got darker,' Benni says. 'That's why I got three months' probation in the family home before my parents passed me on. The brown genes set in.' He waves his hand. 'My father didn't like the questions, so my mother had a choice between me and him. She chose him.'

I'm glad he's not looking at me. I've turned into an open-mouthed clown on a fairground stall. Throw the ball down my throat and win a prize! I think about Mum and her pale skin and grey eyes and straight, light-brown hair and thin nose and how everybody in our family looks like that apart from me. Did she ever look at me as I grew out of my Buster Bloodvessel stage and think about the questions she'd get asked? Knowing Mum, almost definitely. And she would have opened a whole load of tabs to help her make her argument. But there would never have been any questions about her choosing to keep me. Or Fi, over *her* dad.

We walk further out to sea.

I say, 'Do you know if you've got any brothers or sisters?' *My aunties or uncles.*

'Yup. A sister and a brother. Both younger.'

'Have you met them?'

He shakes his head. Some of the rioting seagulls have arrived. It's like they're following us around Brighton just to shout at us. The sea's noisy too, like it's got to slap every pebble on its way in and back out again.

'Parents kept them.'

His phone buzzes. He takes it out his pocket, glances at it and replaces it. And suddenly, he's changed. His face and the way he stands. He's back to being the bloke just out of prison, the bloke who can't be a proper dad, the bloke who turns up at his ex's house with a pair of bougie trainers to win over his long-lost son and then not having any idea what that's going to mean for that son.

He says, 'Stay here.'

'Why?'

'I just need you to stay here for a minute, Spey.'

'Where are you going?'

'In here.'

'Here' is the arcade.

'No! We're going to Kemp Town!'

He strides into the arcade.

'Benni!'

I run after him. It's real portal stuff. The wind and the waves and the mad pigeons outside are a different world. In here, it's flashing lights and robot machine voices and the same grey carpet they've got in the staff corridor at school.

If a sign could shout, that one would have lost its voice.

The ceiling is domed, glass and metal, like this place should be full of palm trees instead of kids feeding coins into slots with Minions and Star Trek and Marvel all yelling out for their money.

Benni taps a coin-sweeping machine. It's loaded with 2p coins and badges and earbuds and a whole lot of other stuff that it would be cheaper to buy than try and win. I still want to do it, though – roll my coins down the chutes to see if they'll nudge the others along the shelves.

'I really used to love these,' Benni says. 'After I came here that first time, I saved all my 2ps and 5ps in a plastic bag, hoping I'd come back.'

He fishes in his pocket and finds a handful of 5p coins. He looks around and sees another coin-sweeper. There's a glint of silver inside. He drops a couple of coins in the slot.

'Benni,' I say. 'We haven't got time for this.'

'I know,' he says quietly.

He's staring. It's not at me. It's behind me. I have to turn around to see why. I don't want to.

'Hey, Benni! You enjoying the sea air, my man?'

I make myself turn and look. The guy's about Benni's age, maybe mixed race and somewhere between me and Benni on the colour scale. He's pulled a furry hat low down on his head so the earflaps droop over his cheeks. He's got a face like the fox that pulls rubbish out of our bins in Hackney. He's wearing a long coat and woolly gloves, like he's trying to avoid any skin contact with the air. Though looking at his thin smile, I think the air's avoiding contact with him.

'Benni,' I say. 'Let's go.'

I touch his sleeve but he flicks my hand away. There's a swirl of something between these two men and I'm standing in the middle of it, though I'm outside of it too. I feel frightened but I take a silent breath, lifting up my chest, straightening my spine, fixing my face so it says nothing. Me and Benni seem to move closer to each other, then he steps sideways so he's in front of me.

'I see you're catching up on daddy time,' the man says.

'You know why we're here, Richie. Why don't you let us find the girl, then we'll sort out our problems afterwards?'

So this is Richie. If him and Astrid were standing next to each other, I wouldn't put them as related, but that's probably because I don't want to. She's wrapped hardness around herself, but there's spaces where it doesn't quite join, like she's offering you a tiny chance to see her for real. Richie's hardness reminds me of the stuff they make plane windows from. Everything's sealed inside. Nothing's getting out. Not even light.

Richie shrugs and looks around. 'You don't seem to be doing much looking, unless the girl's doing her drop-offs on the helter-skelter.' He slaps the coin-sweeper. 'And you got money for this now?' He looks me up and down. 'Your dad's easily distracted. But I've heard you're a clever boy. You must have worked that out for yourself.'

Straight spine. Keep my face saying nothing.

'Where's Sol?' Benni says.

'He's not my business, Benni.'

'I went to him for help,' Benni says. 'You know what it's like to have your girl caught up in that crap. Let me and Spey go and find his friend, then you and me can talk.'

'You and me can talk now. Isn't that what this meet-up's about?'

Meet-up? I frown.

Richie's mean mouth stretches into a smile but his face is too narrow for it to get very far. 'You think I'm here by accident, Spey? Your man here chose the time and place.'

'You were already on your way!' Benni's voice has risen. 'I don't want you tailing us round Brighton! I just want to ask you for more time. Until the end of today.'

'And then you're gonna shake your money maker and pay the debt in full?'

'You know what it's like on the out, Richie. I haven't got no work yet. I'm getting minimum benefits . . .'

'I understand.' Richie takes another step forward. I take one back. Benni stays where he is. 'I've been down that path myself, remember? That's why I have to trust the folks I help out. I trusted you. Though god knows why.' He looks at me again. 'He's always been a slippery one. Cadging a fiver here and a tenner there and never paying nothing back. It's a bit of a habit, right, Benni?'

The arcade has emptied out. It wasn't busy before, but

now there's just us. I see a face peeping out from one of the change kiosks. And, yeah, there's a security guard coming towards us. He's short but he's walking like he knows he's got Hulk on back-up. I feel my chest starting to sag. I push my shoulders back so hard the left one cracks.

'Trusted me?' Now Benni steps forward. 'With what? Keeping your pockets topped up, Richie?'

'I don't force my money on you, Benni-boy. Every time you get out the cage, you come and see me and tell me your sob story and I put my hand in my pocket for you. Then, *whoosh*!' He flaps his hand. 'You're back inside with not a penny paid back. Is that your plan this time? A flying visit to your little boy. Buy his love with some new trainers, then off again?'

'Lads!' The security guard has stopped walking towards us. He's nowhere near as close as he can be. 'No trouble, please.'

Richie and Benni ignore him. I don't, but he's not interested in me. He takes his walkie-talkie out of his pocket.

Richie points at my trainers. 'Nice, aren't they, Spey? They look like a good fit. I'm impressed he got the size right. Or did he have to ask your mum, because he had no idea?'

I swallow and glance at Benni.

He says, 'Richie, please don't . . .'

Richie's still looking at me. 'But you know what surprises me more? That your good old daddy brought you here with him. What did you think, Benni-boy? If I saw your boy flashing those new trainers I'd be so overwhelmed with joy, I'd let you off the grand?'

'Grand?' Benni's voice is low and hard. 'You still charging prison rates, Richie?'

I want to step out of this portal. Now.

'You think you're some big baron out here? Man, Richie, you're standing there all righteous about your money but you wouldn't lift a finger to help your girl when she needed you most.'

I've never seen someone punched up close. When I was little, I used to watch the fight scenes in films on TV, my nose virtually pressed against the screen. It was because Mum had said it was all pretend, but I wanted to see the pretend. I wanted to be sure the punch missed and the thumping sounds had been added in afterwards. But I couldn't. It was always the wrong angle.

I see Richie's arm swing round. I hear the dull crack as his knuckles connect with Benni's face. I feel the air in my lungs shift, but it won't turn into a shout. Then it's like I'm dividing in two. One Spey wishes he'd never come, wishes Dee could just have done what she was told, wishes he'd stayed in London. And that Spey wants to turn around and walk away. The other Spey has to make himself stay still, completely still, because if he moves just a tiny bit, he's going to throw up.

Benni stumbles back against the coin-sweeper and then the other sounds explode back around me. The security guard shouts. The Minion calls for customers. Benni groans. And Richie's shoes make no noise at all as he walks away. Benni rubs his face, spreading blood across his cheek. He braces himself like he's trying to get up, but slumps back down again.

'I think the bastard broke my nose,' he says.

I stare at his nose. It should look broken. It should be a bit wonky. It should . . . Why am I thinking this? I should go to him. I should help him. My body's not working, because a third Spey's arrived at the scene. He's yelling at me hard. He's telling me to face the truth. Benni knew Richie was coming. He still brought you here. Richie was right. You were supposed to be the distraction.

Dee

Taraxacum
CLOCKFLOWER
LION'S TOOTH
MONK'S HEAD
TELLTIME / IRISH DAISY
MILK WITCH / DANDELION

When I was at Chalkleighs, Samira asked me about my happiest memory. It was when Nan gave me my flower book.

When Spencer tore up my flower book, it was my saddest memory. I still have the pages, though. Samira said I could hold on to the memories. It was in pieces, but it wasn't destroyed. She said that wildflowers are strong. The bluebells cover the woods and then they disappear, until the next year. I remember the bindweed in the carpark. They cut it down but Nan was right. It all came back again.

When Chez first brought me to Ingram's flat, I couldn't see no flowers at all. Then I saw dandelions growing through a crack in the concrete outside. The flowers were big and bright yellow. I watched them every day. Dandelions close at night and open again in the morning, like they're holding in the sunshine. Some dandelions have two hundred petals. The most I ever counted was a hundred and eighty. It's like the sun broke into thousands of pieces so everyone can have some shine.

At night, when the street light was on, I'd see them hugging themselves. I was gonna pick one and bring it inside with me. I found a dirty jam jar that Ingram threw in the rubbish. I washed it and filled it with water. But the dandelions looked like they were shining together. I didn't want to take one away. Then I forgot to watch them for a few days and when I remembered, most of them were gone. They must have turned into puffballs and blown away. When I was little, there was a story about a tiny giraffe that ate dandelion clocks. I think it was Spey who told it to me. I used to think they were real. If I looked hard enough, I'd see tiny giraffes running through the park.

There's still one dandelion left. It's like it doesn't want to change. It wants to stay there and shine for me. But I know the rest of the plant is there under the concrete. In spring, there will be more flowers. So when you look down from the street, all you'll see is suns.

Spey

The security guard crouches down next to Benni. Still not that close, though. He says, 'Can you stand up?'

Benni nods, then swears and closes his eyes. His nose bleeds harder. A second security guard joins us. He's tall, Black and looking at Benni with a ffs face. It could be: *ffs, why are you messing up the arcade so early on in the day?* Or: *ffs, couldn't you be white?*

I want to yell, 'It's not Benni's fault! He got punched!' And, 'You know what? It's not his fault if stupid folks are going to make links between the two of you.'

Spey number three whispers, 'It is his fault. What else did he expect would happen?'

The white security guard tells us that the police are on the way.

'Good,' the Black one says. 'We should have it all sorted before it gets busy.' He looks up at the ceiling. 'We've probably got everything on camera. Recognise them?'

'Not locals. I know all the usual troublemakers.'

'The police are coming?' It comes out of Benni as a groan. He looks old again.

'Yeah,' the white one says. 'And an ambulance. Do you know the guy who hit you?'

'I don't need an ambulance.' Benni's voice sounds like it's draining down a plughole.

'I saw what happened.' A blonde woman joins our group. She's wearing a Palace Pier T-shirt and carrying a bunch of keys. 'The other one attacked him.'

The white security guard shakes his head. 'I'm pretty sure I saw this one punch the other bloke first.'

'We'll check the CCTV.' The Black security guard looks over at me. 'You know the other guy?'

'Richie,' I say.

Benni prods my leg. He manages quite a hard poke for someone who looks like they're bleeding to death through their nose. He gives a tiny shake of his head.

'Ritchie?' the guard asks. 'As in "Guy"?'

I look at him. 'I don't know.'

He sighs and turns back to Benni. 'We have to move you out of here.' He turns to the woman in the T-shirt. 'Can you check who's on the cleaning shift this morning? We need to clear this mess up as soon as possible.'

'I'm all right,' Benni whispers.

I step back and my head's hurting badly. It feels like the Christmas recycling bin, with so much crammed in there that it's starting to burst out. Too much noise. Clangs and whooshes and robot voices and the guards talking about what they're going to do next. Benni going on about being all right, but he's not. There's blood across his face and down his neck. I see drops of it across the carpet. The tissue he's holding to

274

his nose is heavy with it.

I head towards the door. The Black security guard stands in my way. 'Where are you off to?' Then he looks at me closely. 'Sorry,' he says. 'Are you okay?'

'Just feeling a bit . . .' I make a face and rub my stomach.

'Yes. That's must have been a shock to witness.'

He opens the door for me. I step out of the portal and stare into a face hole.

Stick your face through the hole and—
Point! Shoot! Post! You're a rock-star!

The cut-out looks old enough to have been around when Benni and Richie were kids. I wonder if they poked their faces through the same holes so they could be stars.

I move away and lean against the railings and close my eyes. I think my ears have their own memory loop. The sound of Benni's breaking bones is going to shape everything I hear from now on. The screaming gulls sound like arcade games yelling out for attention as Richie swings his arm back. The approaching sirens are an alarm, warning me that the punch is about to land. Even the waves washing over the pebbles on the beach could be the rattle of broken bones.

Then my anger swoops back and nearly knocks me sideways. *That* was the real Benni. Not the one who was looking all sad as he told me about his bad parents. It was the one who'd use me as a human shield so he doesn't catch grief from the prison buddy he owes money to. I don't care if his mum and dad didn't want him. That was long ago. He hasn't got an excuse – for prison, for leaving Mum, for leaving all of us.

I don't care what happens to him any more than he really cares about Dee.

I look down at the Jordans. And what were these? An investment to help him get back in Mum's good books? God, didn't she give him money on Christmas Day? He's probably scammed a whole load off her already. He admitted it himself. My mother is a soft touch. I crouch down and undo one set of laces and then the other. I take off the trainers and I stand there holding them, feeling the damp, clammy planks beneath my socks. I can see through the gaps to the waves below. Do Jordans float or sink? I hope the tides take them all the way to France, so some lucky kid can fish them out and wear them without the backstory.

But . . . I still need to find Dee. I can't walk to Kemp Town in just my socks. Richie was right. All this was just a distraction. I should have been over there right now, searching. I do need the trainers. I just don't need Benni. I quickly put the Jordans back on and look around. No one witnessed the weirdness. I walk, quick but steady, back towards the main road.

I pass two police cars and the ambulance. Then I run.

I can't run for long. My body doesn't like it. Well, it probably would if I ever gave it more chances to find out. Fi's always been our house athlete. I jog past a zip-wire tower. That would have been a pretty quick route if it was open, though it sums up my whole world right now – heading in the right direction, then – *slam!* – along comes Benni! I hope the bounceback at the end takes me somewhere I want to go.

I try and speed up again, even though my legs are yelling, 'Why?' I'm trotting parallel to the mini railway. On the other side, the sea looks almost silver now. A couple of paddle boarders are heading west, like me. They're going against the tide, but still overtaking me.

Where the hell *am* I going? And what will I find when I get there?

I cross the road, looking for the way up from the promenade. I passed a slope earlier; I should have taken that. I carry on, and finally, there's steps back on to the main road. Any of those streets heading upwards and away from the sea will take me to Kemp Town. And, I'm going to hope, to Dee.

My plan is … I still don't know. Even though I'm on my way, I haven't got a clue. That didn't seem so much of a problem when Benni was with me. I wanted to believe that he had my back. I message Astrid.

I'm in Kemp Town. Is that right?

How big even is Kemp Town? I take out my phone.

277

According to Wikipedia, it's a small community. Small compared to what . . . ? London? New York? Beijing? I check the articles I'd bookmarked for more clues. There were drug busts on neighbouring streets last year and I go back over the meeting between the council and shopkeepers about dealing with all the mess from the drug-using off St Monica's Street. It was two years ago, but maybe . . .

I finally turn away from the sea. It even feels like it's nudging me away. I can't see the pier now. I suppose Benni's getting his nose sorted, or talking to the police. Maybe both. And then it's in my head again. *Crunch!* Benni falling backwards. And blood.

I stop walking. I'm sweating but I'm not even hot any more. I need to do two things. One, try and get Benni out of my head, so I can just concentrate on finding Dee. And, two, actually find Dee and use any non-Benni help I can.

Another message to Astrid:

Richie found us on the pier and thumped Benni

This time she replies straight away.

I kno. Sol tried to talk him down

but he was riled. Where r they now?

Which one? Don't kno where Richie is. Benni's on the pier

U with him?

No

Man's got a criminal record as

long as my arm and u jus left him?

Before I can reply, another message pops up from her.

> **Uncle Sol says I need to let you and ur dad sort out ur own business. He's got more info on Dee. Yeah, prob in kemp town.**

> **Quentin line opened for business in October. Most drop offs round St Monica's. She could be staying round there. Let me kno what u find. Heading over once Uncle's found dad**

OK

I think she's finished, but the phone buzzes again.

You didn't see what way my dad was heading, did u?

Sorry. He moved pretty quickly

I check out the best way to St Monica's Street. It seems like all roads head there, so I follow the slope up past a small public garden and on to a main road. The streets round here look like London, a kind of Shoreditch-Soho hybrid, but with no black cabs. I pass cafés all bigging up their vegan options, a couple of closed bars, and a post office. A girl's begging outside the Morrisons. She's wearing a stripy scarf and trainers with no laces. A shopping trolley leans against the wall with a rolled-up sleeping bag strapped to the handles. I fumble in my pockets, but I left my last coin in the arcade. She's watching me and I give her a 'sorry' smile. She looks round me at someone else.

There's a Black girl around our way who always wants money. She's got quite a posh accent and she tries to shake your hand before asking you to go to the cashpoint for her. There's another woman who looks like she's the same age as Mum. She barges into shops, begging customers for money to get a cab to the doctors. Sometimes I see both of them chilling together on the bench outside the town hall. The older crack addicts and gambling guys hang out in the alley next to the Best Home furniture place. All the people on the edges know each other.

The girl outside Morrisons. She might know Dee. I could ask her.

Ask her what, though, Spey? Seen a girl who's a bit shorter than me? She's white with brown hair and brown eyes and probably got a pocket full of crack or heroin? I can't even give this girl 10p. She's hardly going to open her heart to me. So what do I do? Just stand here? I'm literally at a crossroads. It's south towards the sea, or if I head north, I'll pass the hospital. St Monica's Street goes from east to west. It's a long road. Dee could be fucking anywhere! This is stupid and pointless and . . .

For a second, I think one of the cafés has ratcheted up the music. It's The Chemical Brothers. I have to thank one of Fi's boyfriends for knowing that. The music gets louder, the bass so hard it's like it's trying to push back the sea to France. It pushes the fog out of my brain too.

I turn right, into a street of Victorian terraces. I scan the buildings on both side of the road, though I still don't know what I'm looking for. Some doors are decorated with wreaths, some aren't. Some windows are full of Christmas tree, like the neighbours opposite us in London. Others have drawn curtains like Christmas is being shut in – or out. Most places have three or four doorbells, so I suppose they've been converted into flats. I pass a door that's got splintered wood in the middle like someone's given it a good kick. Another place has dog-poo bags dangling from every other railing like Halloween goodie bags. The next place has lost the glass in the door panel and it's been patched up with cardboard. A basement window's covered up by a mattress and the front is piled with rubbish.

I have to knock on one of these doors. I have to start asking. But which door? It's like I'm looking for clues, but unless someone handed me a bag and said, 'These are clues, Spey,' I have no idea what to look for. What the hell do I expect to see? A fidgety queue outside her door, waiting to collect? Dee standing in the window looking out for me? My feet keep walking. I'm by another church now. Three guys are having a loud drunk conversation in the garden outside it. The young mixed race one's in a wheelchair with his leg in a splint stretched out in front. He takes a swig from a massive plastic bottle of cider then offers it to one of the older white guys sitting on a bench.

Ask them!

Ask them what, exactly? Where the local crack house is?

I wish Benni was here.

No, I don't. I don't need him.

I make myself walk along the path towards them. They don't notice me.

The old guy's still holding the bottle. 'Des, you piss in here or what? That's what it tastes like. Proper bad piss.'

Des reaches so far out his wheelchair to snatch his booze back, I think he's going to land on the grass. 'Two quid ain't gonna buy you fresh-pressed French apples, Redman. You want better quality, hand over the dosh.'

Redman shakes his head and passes the bottle to the man next to him. He looks like he could be Redman's brother – same white hair, bitty beard and even the same unbuttoned black coat. Though he's wearing a blue jumper and Redman's sporting a Pogues T-shirt. He lifts the cider to his lips and takes a long hard swig, then wipes his mouth. It returns to Des.

Des cleans the neck with his sleeve. 'That's half the damn bottle, man! You got the channel tunnel down your neck?'

I stop in front of them. They all look at me.

'Still tastes like piss,' Redman says.

I say, 'Sorry to bother you,' then realise that I sound like a doorstep charity collector. 'I was wondering if I can ask you something.'

'Vicar says we're okay as long as we don't leave mess,' Des says.

'Or blaspheme,' Redman adds.

'It's . . . I need to find my friend. I think she may live round here. I was wondering if you might have seen her.'

They all carry on looking at me, though I'm not sure if Redman's holding his focus.

I plough on, 'She's white, sixteen years old, but looks younger. She got caught up in some drug-dealing stuff. But it's not her fault.'

Redman snatches the bottle from Des. Des doesn't seem too bothered.

'What do you think it's got to do with us?' he says.

'Nothing. I'm just worried about her. I thought you might know what's happening round here.'

Des shakes his head. 'Me, I know nothing.'

Redman laughs. 'I could have told the boy that from the start.'

The other man leans forward. 'What about that lass who moved in with Ingram? Granddaughter, my arse! It's not the first *granddaughter* he's had there. Been some grandsons too. I said to Ingram, "Why you letting kids sell drugs out of your place? Tell 'em to go to school!" But he said he couldn't. Some boy was going to beat him if he stopped. It must be a stupid boy, leaving a load of drugs in Ingram's place. Though I reckon he gave Ingram a share instead of rent.' He takes the bottle from Redman. 'Even so, it's like locking us lot up in a brewery overnight and expecting us to drink water.'

All the articles I read said there were thousands of kids dealing drugs in county lines. There must be a fair few down here. Can this guy really be talking about the one person that I know?

'It could be my friend,' I say. 'Do you know where Ingram lives?'

The third man is mid-swig. He lowers the bottle. 'Got no idea. You know, Redman?'

Redman shrugs. 'He's not one for visitors. Not unless they're bearing gifts and none of us have got anything he wants. Though, Des, didn't you used to . . .'

Des laughs and nods towards the church. 'I saw the light. I don't do that stuff no more. It's mad. And the people you gotta deal with, they're mad too. I stay well away now.' He makes a grab for the bottle. 'This will do me. The only stress is the security guard at Tesco. But Ingram? Last thing I heard, he was living on Roper Street.' He points further along the road. 'Just off there.'

'Thank you.'

'No problem,' Des says. 'Though he's not gonna be there now.'

'Sorry?'

Des looks at Redman then back at me. 'Wasn't it one of you lot who told me? They found Ingram flat out in the station on Christmas Eve. Still alive but not feeling too pretty.'

'Yeah,' Redman says. 'Lucky bastard. I bet he did it deliberately so he could get a proper Christmas dinner in the hospital.'

'Right,' I say. 'But he lives on Roper Street?'

'Yep,' Redman says. 'And feel free to buy us a drink as a token of your appreciation.'

My phone rings. It's Benni. My fingers and brain have an argument about how I should deal with it. My fingers win.

I stop the call. Then I block him. I need to focus. I block Mum too, for now. I check where Roper Street is. It's just off St Monica's, on the right. It's a dead end for cars with a small alley between back gardens that, according to my map, leads into Wheelwright Street. Hang on! I've already looked along here. It's the street with the kicked-in door and mattress window.

I trot back towards it and stand on the corner waiting for my heart to stop beating. Dee could be right here. There's a life-size Father Christmas hanging off a chimney. I hadn't even noticed that before. I almost want to climb up and see if he's got Dee hidden in his sack. I'll walk down one side of the street then up the other. There's only thirty buildings, but maybe over a hundred flats. I pass wheelie bins with cardboard boxes and wrapping paper bursting out. Recycling bags that can't even close round the empty bottles inside. A roughed-up old *Frozen* scooter left on the street for someone to take. I check out all the scrappy places, the ones with paint flaking off their door and window frames and rubbish down the stairs and mattresses left outside . . .

. . . and mattresses blocking the window instead of glass . . .

. . . and fuck . . .

I've found her.

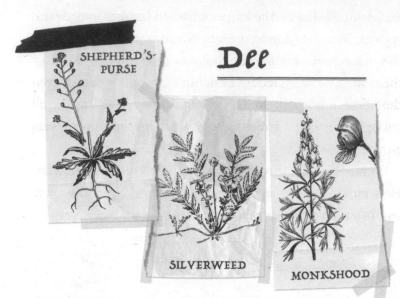

SHEPHERD'S-PURSE

SILVERWEED

MONKSHOOD

Dee

He's here.

Not Chez. Spey. He's here.

We were friends. He was my only friend. And then he stopped coming round to see me. Nan said it was his snobby mother that stopped it. She said that it was good to have friends, but we couldn't always rely on people. At least we had each other.

We only had each other until she died.

I sent him the birthday picture because I knew he'd keep it safe.

Now he's here, standing outside.

When I first came here, the radiator in my room was leaking. Ingram gave me some black tape to stick over the hole. It didn't work. The water came out round the edges and dripped down. The carpet's turned bright orange with the rust. But then I used the tape for something else. I stuck the pages from my flower book on the window. Some of them were so wrinkled up I couldn't flatten them out, even though I left them under my mattress. There was still enough. When the street light was on, it made my flowers glow.

I can see Spey through the cracks between my flowers. He's looking down at my flowers. I'm waving and waving and I think he can see me too.

Spey

A mattress blocks a window. I saw it before and I walked on. I didn't look properly. I barely looked at all. I should have seen the window next to it. Or I should have seen the dandelion sticking out between the concrete and rubbish, like a signal.

The window next to the mattress is spotted with dirt. There's almost no light, as if it was absorbed by the black bin liners heaped up under the window.

But the flowers! How did I miss them? Some of the names come creeping back.

SCARLET PIMPERNEL.

WOOD ANEMONE.

RAGGED ROBIN.

Dee

SHEPHERD'S-PURSE

SILVERWEED

MONKSHOOD

Spey!

ALEXANDERS

BIRD CHERRY

MUSK MALLOW

Spey

I need to move, to go down there. I can't see behind the window. It's too dark. *Princess Scarlet Anemone and the Ragged Pimpernel*. That was the story I couldn't tell Mum because I thought 'pimpernel' was rude.

That doesn't matter now.

I need to move.

I need to walk past that rubbish and find Dee.

What am I going to do? Knock on the door? Push away the mattress and climb through the broken glass?

Astrid was right. I don't have a plan.

'You need something?'

It isn't Sol's voice. It isn't Richie, neither. I know who it is and all the feelings sweep back, my words escaping, the twisting nausea. Chez's face is all hard lines. I've changed a bit since nursery, though. Does he know who I am?

'You hear me?'

Chez's voice is loud, his expression meant to intimidate. He must practise it in his mirror, holding the stare, his mouth set tight. And, man, it works. I try and keep my face friendly, like I'm here by accident, just a bit lost and not sure where to go. I'm not here to rescue a girl with no damn plan how to do it. I stop myself glancing down at the window; Chez would guess why I'm here. Maybe he already has.

I look down at Chez's big leather satchel instead. It's slung across his body like he's been delivering pizza flyers. My look slides down to his hands. I think of them sweeping through the air and his fist landing. *Crunch*. How can one person make everything inside you feel sick? I should be brave. I've come all this way, but the nausea isn't just in my stomach, it's spread through my whole body.

'Got an answer, then?' Chez steps towards me. 'You're hanging round here like you're looking for something.'

I'm not looking for something, Chez. I'm looking for someone. She's my friend and you hurt her.

He jabs my shoulder. 'You deaf, bro?'

I shake my head.

'Gonna be on your way, then?'

I take a deep breath and say, 'Yeah.'

He prods me again. I step back.

'Off you go.'

And I do. I go off. I want to take my phone out, call the police, unblock Benni, shout for someone, anyone. I want to look back, but my stomach hurts, as if Chez's stare's so rough it makes me heave. As I turn a corner, I do glance round, and, yeah, he's still there, staring after me. I keep walking and don't stop until I feel like I can reach out and touch the edge of the sea.

Spey

I've found Dee. I've done what I've come here to do. I don't need to be the one who goes in and brings her out. Sol can deal with Chez, no problem. Astrid's there for Dee. I'll get the train back to London before Mum comes down in person.

Grandma gave me an anthology of fairy tales when I was four. There's an illustration in *Sleeping Beauty* of a wall of thorny bushes protecting the castle. Mum used to say that it was protecting the princess with good reason; the last thing she needed was some strange bloke breaking into her palace and smooching her when she was asleep.

'Spey,' she'd said, with her serious face on. 'That prince is not a good role model.'

Does that make me a good role model for not even trying?

I unblock Benni and send him a message.

Dee's in Roper Street. Basement flat with a mattress against one of the windows.

I send Astrid the same thing. Her phone must be in her hand because I've only just pressed 'send' and she replies.

Yeh, sounds right. We're with dad at the police station. Be there soon as. U with her?

I don't answer.

U with her, Spey? She ok?

I don't know. Because I'm *not* with her. I left her again. That first time by the canal, I let Chez's brother grab her arm and take her away. Later, I'd told myself a lie. If anything like that happened again, I would do something. But I didn't. The second time, it was worse.

Last year, I'd had a girlfriend called Danaii. She went to the private girls' school near the Barbican. I met her when she was skateboarding with her mates in Hackney Wick. I never mentioned her to Mum, even though Mum would have loved her for so many reasons. She was Black, she went to a posh school and wanted to set up a microbusiness charity in Zimbabwe. (I had to google 'microbusiness'.) Danaii would have been Mum's proof that she was doing everything right with me and, I know this sounds like real ungrateful-son stuff, I don't think I could have handled that.

And I suppose I knew from the beginning that Danaii wasn't that serious about us because she was into her grades. She said her parents weren't paying good money for her to come out with mere 7s and 8s. (Mum wasn't paying anything for my grades, but she'd be spitting blood without a good showing of 9s too.)

I usually hung out with her at the skate park or we'd go into central and wander around Soho or the Southbank. One time, though, we stayed local because Danaii wanted to get some Ankara fabric to make a birthday cushion for her little sister. She reckoned her best bet was one of the stores off Ridley Road market. We looked in a few – well, Danaii did while I stood around – then we went back to the one we started with. I waited outside while Danaii went in.

The market was on. I was standing behind a fish stall watching the fishmonger gutting a big ugly fish. I'm not sure why I was watching with so much interest. I think it was so I could avoid meeting the eyes of a guy on the hustle with a tray of cheap lighters. He was about two stalls away, hassling a woman by the toy store. She must have had a special superpower, a reverse Superman, so she could see or hear nothing that wasn't right next to her. She just carried on browsing through a box of plastic tiaras while he kept trying to get in her way, offering a special deal. Me? I wish Mum hadn't brought me up to be so polite. I can't ignore anyone.

The market's always noisy. You've got a mobile phone stall blasting deep dub at one end and the curtain stall wrapping itself up in old-school crooning in the middle. Walk up and down and you hear Femi Kuti, Toots and the Maytals, Pussycat Dolls and that song from the beginning of *Guardians of the Galaxy*. (Danaii hadn't seen the film. Maybe that's when I really knew our relationship was doomed.)

There's always a fair bit of shouting. The veg- and fruit-sellers are calling out 'a pound a bowl' bargains. That day, there was a Socialist Worker stall with a megaphone and a boy preacher praising Jesus outside the party shop. He was accompanied by a girl who looked like his sister with a guitar and a portable amplifier and a big book of hymns. That's why I didn't hear the argument at first.

Though it wasn't really an argument. It was one person shouting and when I saw him, I knew him. I recognised Chez straight away, though I hadn't seen him since nursery. Some little kids have chubby faces, but Chez's was never like that. More than ten years later, he still had the same long, stretched-out face, but on a bigger boy's body. And it was a big body. Man didn't get guns like that lying on his sofa playing *Lego Batman*. Chez was wearing a white vest for everyone to see how many bench presses he'd been working. It was like he'd watched every prison scene in every American crime series, sussed out who had the smallest brain and biggest chest and thought, *Yeah, that's who I want to be.*

I thought he was with the girl he was shouting at, but then I realised that he was following behind her. I've seen ugly boys out with their mates, chirpsing girls. They know they've got to prepare in advance to style off the knockbacks. They've got this look on their face, words all planned out to make the girl sound stupid for rejecting them. A couple of times, though, I've seen a boy flash up a couple of seconds of shame. I bet they've got mums or sisters like mine who are going to tell them about themselves if they find out they're disrespecting women.

Chez wasn't chirpsing. He didn't care about bounceback. He was fuelled. If the International Space Station was powered with madness, Chez would have kept that thing orbiting for a century. He called the girl all the names, the ones that Mum says punch women in their heart. And he was shouting that when his dad came out of prison, he'd find Dee's aunty and make her pay for snitching to the police. But Dee was going to pay first. Hard.

People just parted for him. My chest hurt and my legs felt like they were forgetting what they're supposed to do for my body. I thought I was going to topple into the fish stall because I saw the girl clearly. It was Dee. I remember her nan had kept threatening to cut her hair because she kept getting nits. And every time, to Mum's fury, she passed them on to me. So Mum got my hair cut short instead. Now Dee's hair was shorter than mine was at nursery. She stopped and turned to him. I saw two red hair-clips, shaped like flowers, just above her ear, holding two tufts together.

'Shit!' Danaii was back by my side. 'It looks like it's going to kick off here. I really don't want to hang around. I've got the fabric. Let's go.'

The guy selling kitchen stuff came out from behind his stall. He was a big white guy who looked like he'd built the shopping centre next door by himself. He strode right up to Chez, yelling at him to leave the girl alone.

'It's probably druggy stuff,' Danaii said.

'Why do you say that?'

Danaii had given me a sharp look. 'The boy – god, you don't kick off like that unless you're on something. And the girl doesn't look like she's eaten for a month.'

Dee had stopped walking, like she had no strength left to take her any further.

'I'm going to call the police.' Danaii took out her phone. 'I can't call myself a feminist and ignore crap like this.' She leaned towards the fabric store, away from the noise.

Yeah, I was supposed to be a feminist too. And Dee's friend.

Stoke Newington police station was just up the road. In spite of the posh SPAR shop and the Marks and Spencer food hall and the Costa, stuff still kicked off round here. The police would come. But I didn't have to wait for them. I'd made a promise. If there was a next time, I would help Dee.

'Okay.' Danaii looped her arm through mine, pulling me like I'd been looking in a shop window for too long. 'Police should be on their way. I don't want to stand here and watch. Macho bullies like that get off on having an audience.'

Chez and the stall holder faced off to each other, waving their arms and yelling. Some idiot onlookers thought it was a joke – two muscle men, different ages, getting ready to crash into each other like stone giants. I didn't care about them. I was watching Dee. I couldn't see her face, but her hands were opening and closing like crab pincers.

'Go!'

I'd said it out loud. Danaii yanked her arm out from mine. 'What?'

'She needs to go,' I said. 'While he's looking the other way.'

'Maybe she doesn't know how to.' Danaii relooped herself. 'She probably needs him.'

I looked at Danaii. 'What?'

'Because she's still standing there. Maybe she doesn't know how to go.'

'She just needs help.'

Danaii's voice was very quiet. 'Go and help her, then, Spey. Do something and do it now, or you're just a bystander like everyone else.'

Danaii took a step forward and it was like she was synchronised with Chez. He'd dodged round the stallholder and taken a step towards Dee. Then he punched her.

And my heart – my fucking heart – was punching its way out of my chest. I opened my mouth and called Dee's name but it was just speech bubbles with no words in them. Chez's fist had thudded into her stomach. No crunch. No blood fountain. She bent over, tipping towards the dirty floor, and people rushed towards her, holding her up. A security guard ran past me and I could hear sirens.

And I was still standing in the same place.

'Show's over, Spey.' Danaii sounded angry. 'Or are you waiting for the sequel? Because from here it looks like that poor girl's got enough going on, without the whole world enjoying her humiliation.'

I shook my head. 'Sorry. I'm coming.'

'Let's go this way.' Danaii pulled me towards Dalston Lane. 'We can get a 56, if you still want to come round my place.'

Dee was surrounded by people now. A woman came

out of the fabric shop with a cup of water. Someone else had found a chair. For a second, the crowd cleared and I saw her. The side of her face looked bruised and swollen and there was a cut beneath her eye. I could swear he hadn't hit her in the head.

No, not this time.

Other times. He must have hit her other times.

Everything about me was knots. My stomach, my brain, even my hands felt like I was hanging from a cliff.

I looked around. 'Where's Chez?'

'The bastard who hit her? He made a dash for it. No one was going to stop him. Do you know him?'

'We went to the same nursery.'

'Was he always such a charmer?'

'He was just a normal kid then.'

'Serious? Well, something went wrong. What about the girl?'

I turned back to Dee. She was looking at me. Her mouth was open and she was crying. The knots tightened. My hands squeezed together and I realised I was holding Danaii's hand. She squeezed back.

'Do you know her too?' Danaii asked.

Dee was hidden again. If she was still looking at me, I couldn't see. She probably hadn't even recognised me. Her hair was shorter, but mine was as long as school would let it. Danaii had said I looked like an ethnically ambiguous Frodo. I told myself that Dee had been hit hard. She probably couldn't focus. She couldn't know it was me. I was just a face in a crowd and there were enough strangers around her. What was I supposed to do? Fight my way through them to give help that was too late?

YES! That's what I should have done. And why didn't I?

Because I was so damn scared that he'd come after me too.

It's not even third time lucky, because I'm walking away again.

Spey

And then I'm running.

Because I'm not leaving her.

Not this time.

SHEPHERD'S-PURSE

HAREBELL

SILVERWEED

MONKSHOOD

JAPANESE ROSE

SOAPWORT

COMMON SORREL

SELFHEAL

Spey didn't look down. Spey didn't see me. Spey talked to Chez then he walked away.

Chez slams the door as he comes inside. I run away from the window and I sit on the bed. I won't let him know that I saw Spey. I've learned to keep my feelings inside all the time.

He shouts, 'I couldn't find that Ingram bastard anywhere!'

He drops his bag on to the floor. He usually says that everything's so nasty in here, he doesn't even want his trainers to touch the carpet.

'But I'm gonna make sure no one's gonna serve him up nothing. He's gonna be shaking so hard he's gonna have to come right back to me.' He's grinning now, staring at me. 'Crawling, man. Not even walking.'

He picks up his bag. He walks out. He's going to the bathroom. He'll see what I've done.

He's found out because—

He's screaming my name.

He runs into my room and he doesn't stop. He knocks me into the wall and I can't breathe.

He says he's gonna kill me. I'm scum. I'm a drug whore like my rancid mother and her mother too. He's pushing me hard against the wall, like he's trying to make sure there's no room for my breath to come back. He's shouting and his spit's all over my face. I still can't breathe properly.

He's shaking me, forward and back. My head thumps against the plaster. My heart thumps under my skin. And it's like something's coming loose inside me. He drops me and I fall to the floor.

I won't cry.

I reach out for my jar, the one I'd saved for the dandelions. I close my eyes and imagine it's full of sunshine. I see petals opening one by one. I feel its warmth on my hands and on my face.

Chez snatches it out of my hand. My eyes snap open and I duck as it smashes against the wall behind me.

Chez says he told me I'd pay. He'd told me I was nothing. He'd told me he'd take care of me. He hits me once and my head jerks back. He lifts his hand again. I watch it turn into a fist.

Spey

I'm banging on the window, but no one can hear me. I'm screaming Dee's name. The jar hits the wall behind and I see her looking at him. Chez hits her. It's silent. His fist flies back. She's so close. His punch will—

Not again. This can't happen again.

Dee's looking straight through the window at me. I look back.

Dee

Impatiens glandulifera
HIMALAYAN BALSAM
KISS-ME-ON-THE-MOUNTAIN
POLICEMAN'S HELMET

It takes over and it grows taller than your head.

Touch its pod.

Seeds explode out.

Spey

His fist flies towards her stomach. That's where he hurt her before, that time in the market. That's where he's going to hurt her again.

And I'm just what Danaii said I am. A bystander.

Dee's hands fly across her stomach. She knows what's coming. But she's holding something. I squint but can't see. Her mouth moves. I think it's a scream, but it's a word.

She's saying my name.

I hammer against the window as hard as I can. Chez turns. His arm keeps moving, towards her, towards her—

And everything stops.

Then Dee is on the bed and Chez is clutching his fist. Blood seeps through his fingers. He holds up his hand and looks at it. Blood dribbles down his arm.

Dee just stares at him.

I crouch down behind the bags of rubbish and I throw up.

Dee

Red.

Superhero roses. Red Double Knockout roses. Eternal Secret roses. Danse de Feu. Common poppies. Scarlet pimpernel.

Red like the nail polish on Nan's toes.

My body doesn't work properly. It wants to lie on the bed. It doesn't want to get up. I make my eyes stay open and make myself breathe properly like Samira showed me. My hand opens and the piece of glass falls out. I was holding it so tight there's blood spots on my skin. But there was more blood on Chez.

He was wrong. I am not 'nothing'.

Spey's banging on the other side of the window. I have to let him in. I know he wants to help me.

I have to get off the bed.

I can hear water running in the bathroom. There are new stains on the rug. Not Ribena.

I have to get off the bed.

I can feel more glass underneath me. I have to be careful. Get off the bed. Go past the bathroom. Open the door. Let Spey in.

I move and the glass moves on the bed too. I make sure I don't touch it as I stand up. I make sure I don't walk on the rug. I have to hold on to the door as my body doesn't want to go near Chez. But Spey's here. He'll help me.

I pass the bathroom. I see Chez in there trying to wash blood off his hands. The sink is full of red water. He calls me names and tells me that he's gonna hurt me, but I know he can't.

Chez never locks the front door when he's here. He said I knew what would happen if I tried to run away. If he didn't find me, he'd find Aunty Janet. I go to the door and stand there. Then I look back to see if Chez's coming for me, but he's still in the bathroom. I keep looking even though I'm pushing the handle, pulling open the door.

Spey's waiting there for me. He tells me his name although I already know it. He says he's sorry and should have been there for me before.

He's here now. I need him now.

Spey

When I walk into the flat, I want to throw up again. I swallow hard. I want to laugh too, though it's one of those wrong laughs that bubble out of you when something is anything but funny.

I've never seen *Carrie*. I've read the book, though, and Dee would have been that girl who the bullies try and destroy. She's standing in front of me now with blood smeared across her top. It must be Chez's. I hope it's Chez's. Then suddenly, it's like everything in her crumbles and I just manage to catch her before she falls over.

I say, 'It's okay. The police are on their way.'

She doesn't say anything, but I can feel her shivering. I don't know what to do. I don't want to go inside that flat. I saw the rip across the back of Chez's hand. The blood trickling around to his palm. He couldn't do anything to us now.

But – I don't want to go in there.

I have an arm around Dee's waist and she's leaning on me with all her weight. It's like her shivering is catching, because I'm shivering too.

I say, 'Where's Chez?'

'Inside.' I can only hear her because we're hunched into each other.

'Is he hurt?'

She nods.

'I'm not "nothing".'

'I know.'

'Hello?'

That's Astrid's voice, calling from street level.

'We're down here!' I call back.

'Sweetheart!' Astrid rushes down and gathers Dee in her arms. It's stupid, but I'm not ready to let go.

Spey

Five months ago, I found Dee. That makes it sound like I did something clever. It was Dee who was clever. She made herself found.

It was only five months ago, but we're both a year older. I went bowling with Shauna and the others for my sixteenth then had a posh brunch in The Shard with Mum. Today's Dee's birthday and I'm back by the sea. She's going to be seventeen. Chalkleighs isn't what I expected. It looks old on the outside, like something from the beginning of last century. According to the website, it's been a kids' home for nearly a hundred years but it's been renovated on the inside to 'meet all modern needs'. Me and Mum only got to see the reception. Dee was allowed to show her Aunty Janet her room and when they came back down, Janet was smiling. It must have been tough for them. One of the first things Janet had to do when she saw Dee after all this time was to tell her that Gloria had died. Then she had to fight hard for Dee to come back here. There was a waiting list and her room had been given to someone else. There were loads of meetings and Dee was given an advocate to help her say what she wanted. She was bounced around different places and even stayed at Aunty Janet's for a few nights.

But finally, she could come back. It's her old room too.

I thought about buying Dee a new flower book for her birthday, but Mum said it wouldn't be the same. The one that got torn up wasn't just a book of flowers, it was a book of memories and stories. It would be like her nan was on every page. I suppose what happened to the book is also part of the story. It's what brought us all together here.

I wish, though, there'd been an easier way.

And it hasn't brought *all* of us together. Benni isn't here, and no matter what Astrid says, I still won't call him 'Dad'. Of course, I'd rather have Benni over Richie, but, man, there's got to be better choices out there. Though, like I've said before, I don't need anyone else. Mum tries to talk to me about Benni, but I won't say anything. In the end, she'll have to give up. I hope.

It doesn't look like *he's* ready to give up. Mum tried to hand me a letter he's written but I wouldn't take it. She pushed it under my bedroom door and it's still there on the floor, next to what Mum calls 'the smelly shirt basket'.

But today isn't his day. I don't want to talk about him.

'Am I late?' Astrid rushes into reception and me and Mum stand up like she's the Queen. She gives me a hug, which is a bit of a shock. The first time we met, she didn't even want to look at me. But maybe in that stinking basement in Brighton, I passed some secret test.

Astrid had managed to persuade Dee back into the flat and wrapped a blanket around her. Sol was trying to park up his car so it didn't block the road for the police and ambulance, so I was sent to check on Chez. He could have been bleeding to death, but being really honest, I don't think that bothered me at the time. I was more worried that he'd kind of resurrected and that he was waiting for me in the bathroom.

I'd yanked the door to the bathroom open like I was in an American cop series with Chez crouched on the other side, holding a knife or a piece of piping, ready for me. He wasn't. He was slumped by the bath, running his hand under a tap. The plug wasn't in, but all this rust-coloured water was pooling in the bottom. The sink was already full. His eyes went wide when he saw me, then he managed what Mum calls a thug look. He held his hand out in front of him. More blood, a dark jagged line of it, even though it had just been underwater. I could see a spike of glass buried in his skin.

I stepped back, ready for Chez to come at me. I'd slam the door shut and lean on it as hard as I could until Sol or the police arrived. But he just stayed on that dirty floor. He kept trying with the screwface, but I saw it then. Chez wasn't some big monster drug-lord. He was mean and nasty, but also, the same age as me.

It was hard to find my voice. 'There's an ambulance coming.'

'I don't need a fucking ambulance!'

He jumped up. He was quick. I didn't have time to bang the door shut. He pushed past me, dripping water and blood across the bathroom floor, across my trainers. Out into the hallway. Out of the front door. Up the steps outside.

He didn't get far. Sol was waiting.

Astrid brought Dee into the bathroom. Some of the bathwater had seeped away but there was a still a dirty puddle. I hadn't wanted Dee to see any of it. She was walking, but it still seemed like Astrid was carrying her. Astrid tried to help Dee wash her hands, but there was no soap and no towels. They used toilet paper to dry off, but little bits got stuck to their skin. It made me think of the cherry blossom petals in Fi's photos.

'I did it to him,' Dee had said.

Astrid had frowned then squinted into the bath. I looked harder too. The plughole was blocked with plastic – thin stuff like clingfilm. Astrid made a face as she peered into the toilet.

She said, 'Hun, did you flush all his gear away?'

Dee had nodded. Astrid had hugged her. 'You brave, brave girl.'

Then the police had arrived and an ambulance.

Astrid's impressed by Chalkleighs too.

'It's a pretty nice place, this one,' she says. 'I saw that new mural on the shed. Is that the one Dee's helping with?'

It's a dandelion and a red rose. I nod.

We all gather together and set off for our walk – Dee, her Aunty Janet, Astrid, Mum and me. There's also a woman

315

called Samira who works in the home. I thought that the other girls would be there. One's called Anissa and when she walked through reception she looked like she wanted to kill us all. The other one's new and apparently she's really shy and doesn't talk to anyone. They may live together, but it doesn't mean they have to be friends. It doesn't seem to bother Dee. Why should it? She's not into following rules.

No one warned me that this was a proper walk, though. Benni had told me that Hastings is full of hills, but I need to get him out of my head and keep him out. We walk up a narrow road that must be a mountain in its spare time, then turn off to follow the path by the castle. It's not really a castle now, but I can imagine it as it used to be, balanced on the cliffs looking down across the sea. And Dee *is* the birthday queen strutting past it. She's arm-in-arm with Astrid and Mum's chatting to Samira and Janet, who've gone right ahead with the food and blankets.

We come out on to the top of the cliffs. I sink down. I'm not even going to wait for the blankets to appear. The grass is warm and dry. And my legs hurt like hell. As Mum unpacks the food, I shift so I'm slightly closer to Dee.

Astrid raises her eyebrows. I'd forgotten about her trampoline brows.

'Got your breath back yet, Spey?' She grins. 'I heard you puffing like an old man.'

Dee smiles. It's like her old smile, where she took her

face swimming in the water bowl at nursery and almost made Laura faint. I hand Dee the bag with the birthday present just in case she isn't into a public pressie-opening moment. I thought she could check it out in her own time. But she tips the bag upside down on the blanket straight away. I realise that all the talking's stopped and everyone's watching.

I wrapped the present in yellow tissue paper. (More environmentally friendly, according to Mum. The tissue paper. Not the colour. But in the sunshine it looks like it's glowing.)

'Go for it, honey,' Astrid says.

Dee tears the paper apart and my present's on the blanket for everyone to see. I feel myself blushing. (Scarlet pimpernel. Poppy. Nosebleed)

It was a stupid present! Dee isn't a small kid! Why would I think she'd want anything like this? She opens the box and eases it out.

'A flower press?' Astrid asks.

Dee nods and smiles that smile again. I breathe out so hard my stomach touches my back.

'It's so I can make my own book,' Dee says.

'Yes,' I say. 'It is.'

Mum's bought her a hardback sketch book, glue sticks, pencils, and gold and silver gel pens.

'Well.' Astrid stands up. 'Let's go and see what we can find.'

She stretches out a hand to both of us.

'Don't pick anything endangered,' Mum calls to us. Dee laughs. 'It's okay. I'll follow the rules.'

Spey

Dear Spey,

I hope you're okay. I know all letters start like that so it's stopped meaning anything, but I do hope you're okay. Of course, I hope you're more than okay. I hope you still shine.

I understand if you still won't talk to me. I will wait for you, Spey. As long as it takes. Gilda says you won't even talk about me. I don't want you to sing my praises, Spey. Honest. It's the opposite. You're keeping your hurt and anger behind the barriers, like I did. It doesn't do no good.

I've heard that Dee and Astrid are mates now. That's a good thing that grew out of all this sh crap. Astrid will be there to help Dee when it comes to court. They're not always the easiest places. That's one thing I am an expert on. And like I told you, prison isn't the easiest of places, neither. I'm sure that boy Chez will try and style it off good and proper. From what I hear, his dad and brother have already done time. He'll be a real cell warrior, I'm sure. I know that Oscar Wilde says the truth is rarely pure and never simple. Well, there is a pure and simple truth about prison. The first time you've banged up, you're scared as hell.

And the thing is, Spey, you'll probably hate me even more

319

when I say this. I wish Chez well. I don't condone nothing he did to Dee. All of us are standing on our families' shoulders, for good or bad. You don't want to step off because when you fall, you don't know where you'll land. But that's what I'm trying to do now, step away from all the early chaos. Maybe in time, he will do too and find he can be someone else.

I've still got that hope for Richie, but he's too caught up in all his side-hustles to think straight. Of course I was never going to press any charges against him for thumping me. I suppose I knew that one day I had it coming. Blokes like that can't lose face. Like Chez, I suppose. But, Spey, I am so damn sorry you had to witness that. Richie knows how much you mean to me. I thought that if he saw us together, he'd hold back. I was wrong. Very wrong. Sol's stepped in to try and sort things out. The man's so good, he could talk Nelson off his column. Though I reckon it's going to take more than Sol to bring you and me together, isn't it?

So I'm heading up to Glasgow next week to see Ernesto, your little brother. I'll send Gilda a picture of him, in case you want to see what he looks like. Becks, my oldest girl, just sent me one of her and her girlfriend, China. Gilda's getting that too. I still don't think Becks looks nothing like you, though. Tell me what you think, Spey.

I know you and me have still got so much to understand about each other. I've heard that even Fi's trying to convince you to give me a chance. She's coming back for Christmas this year, isn't she? Good luck!

320

So what's there left for me to say? I'm sorry again that I hurt you. I didn't expect Richie to act that way. Truly, I didn't. But I do want you to know that I love you. I did before, but so much more now we've spent that time together.

My door is always open for you. Always.

Love Benni, your dad

Acknowledgements

Massive thanks to:

The Hachette team who helped put this book together and nudge it into the world. Naz Abdillahi, Namishka Doshi, Joelyn Esdelle, Flic Highet, Polly Lyall Grant. And to Jenny Glencross and Maurice Lyon.

Michelle Brackenborough, cover designer extraordinaire and, oh, those chapter headings ... May your clover always have four leaves.

Dapo Adeola for that splendid cover reveal and doing such justice to Michelle's cover design and Flic's animation.

Emma Roberts for your work with me on the early stages of this book, curbing my pop culture excesses and even more importantly, flagging that all-important link between Bilbo's bottom and suburban zombies. Nerd sisters forever.

Caroline Sheldon, my agent who encourages me, nurtures me and protects me from the toughness of the publishing world.

My Free Lunch writing group – Nathalie Abi-Ezzi, Katherine Davey, Jenny Downham, Anna Owen, Elly Shepherd. This book wouldn't be here without you.

My many glorious friends who have lifted me in difficult times including Az D, Fen and Kerry of Letterbox Library, Lucy D, Jane E, Jo H (a week to reconnect with London – thank you!),

Melanie RB, Miranda M, Nat B, Sarah B, Sheryl B, Savita K, Teri T. Special shout-out to Odina N – I got that mattress in!

Laura Janes – probably the most inspiring human being I know.

Eve Ainsworth, Maisie Chan, Catherine Coe, Natasha Farrant, Leila Rasheed, Sunny Singh, Fabia Turner and many others who are working so hard to support emerging children's writers from under-represented backgrounds get a foot in the publishing door. We need new stories. We always need new stories.

The book bloggers and readers who give their free time and passion to support writers like me. You are invaluable.

J - we've both agreed that it's a good idea that you don't read my books, but I wouldn't be me without you.

SUPPORT

If any of the issues raised in this book are directly relatable, here are some organisations that may be able to help:

Childline A private and confidential service for young people up to age 19. **Available 24 hours**.
Call free on **0800 1111** *or talk online at* **www.childline.org.uk**

Howard Reform League for Penal Reform Confidential legal service for young people under 21, including those in prison. *Call free* **0808 801 0308 / 0808 802 0153**

Missing People A UK charity lifeline for anyone affected by someone going missing. *Free and confidential:*
Call **116 000** *Text* **116 000** *Email* **116000@missingpeople.org.uk**
www.missingpeople.org.uk

The Care Leavers' Association *Young Person's Project* has been set up to give younger care leavers the necessary advice and skills to get on in life. **www.careleavers.com**
Call on **0161 826 0214**

Abianda A London-based social enterprise working with young women affected by gangs and county lines.
www.abianda.com
Email **hello@abianda.com** *Call on* **020 7686 0520**

Family Rights Group Confidential advice for parents and family members when social workers or courts make decisions about their children's welfare. **www.frg.org.uk**
Call free **0808 801 0366**

Kinship Support for family and friends looking after a child whose parents are unable to care for them.
www.kinship.org.uk
Call on **0300 123 7015**

Prison Advice and Care Trust (PACT) Provides support for prisoners, people with convictions, and their families. www.prisonadvice.org.uk
Call free **0800 808 2003** *(National Helpline, England & Wales)*

Families Outside Support families in Scotland affected by imprisonment. **www.familiesoutside.org**
Call free **0800 254 0088**

NIACRO Supports children, young people and families who are affected by imprisonment, who have offended, or who are perceived to be vulnerable to offending. **www.niacro.co.uk**
Call free **0800 169 2207** *(Ireland)*

Spurgeons Support to help improve the lives of children and their families who are affected by a parent being in prison.
Email **info@spurgeons.org** **www.spurgeons.org**

Unlock Provide a voice and support for people who are facing stigma and obstacles because of their criminal record. www.unlock.org.uk
Call on **01634 247350** *Text or WhatsApp on* **07824 113848**

User Voice Created for and by people who have been in prison and on probation, giving a voice to the most marginalised people. **www.uservoice.org**
Call on **020 3137 7471**

Women in Prison Provide holistic, women-centred support in prisons and the community. **www.womeninprison.org.uk**
Call free on **0800 953 0125**

National Criminal Justice Arts Alliance Their vision is to ensure the arts are used within the criminal justice system as a springboard for positive change.
www.artsincriminaljustice.org.uk

PATRICE LAWRENCE

Patrice was born in Brighton and brought up in an Italian-Trinidadian household in Mid Sussex. This meant great holidays and even better food. Her first novel, *Orangeboy,* won the Waterstones Book Prize for Older Readers and the Bookseller YA Book Prize. Her second novel, *Indigo Donut,* and her fourth novel, *Eight Pieces of Silva* won the Crimefest Award for young adults. *Eight Pieces of Silva* was also awarded the inaugural Jhalak Prize for children and young people and the Woman & Home Book Club Teen Drama of the Year.

Patrice's ideal mixtape includes drum 'n' bass, Bruce Springsteen and Studio Ghibli soundtracks. Music can't help creeping into her books.

@LawrencePatrice

 facebook.com/patriceLawrence.author

patricelawrence.wordpress.com